Film Strip

Also by Nancy Bartholomew

Film Strip

—Nancy Bartholomew—

Nancy Bartholomew (signature)

ST. MARTIN'S MINOTAUR 🅜 New York

www.minotaurbooks.com

Library of Congress Cataloging-in-Publication Data

Bartholomew, Nancy.
    Film strip / Nancy Bartholomew. — 1st ed.
        p. cm.
    ISBN 0-312-26161-6
    1. Lavotini, Sierra (Fictitious character) — Fiction.   2. Women detectives — Florida — Panama City — Fiction.   3. Stripteasers — Fiction.   4. Panama City (Fla.) — Fiction.   I. Title.

    PS3552.A7645 F5 2000
    813'.54 — dc21

                                                                00-031736

First Edition: October 2000

10 9 8 7 6 5 4 3 2 1

For Adam and Ben—

I love you with all of my heart.

Acknowledgments

This book would never have happened without the support and love of my family and friends. Their constant encouragement carried me through many harried moments. They are my first line editors and my coaches. I am also eternally grateful to my critique group. I am extremely fortunate to have them in my corner.

Sierra Lavotini and I would also like to thank Kelley Ragland for always being in our corner and for pushing us to be the best we can be. The world of exotic dancing and murder is better for Kelley's guiding hand.

Lynn Salsi and Maria Johnson also get a big note of thanks from this author. Thank you for all your help.

All my love and appreciation go to my husband, John, and my two sons. They make it all worthwhile.

Film Strip

One

When Venus Lovemotion died it was a giant pain in my ass. Literally. I was bending over to unlock the door of my '88 Camaro when I heard the shot and felt a stinging sensation in my left cheek. Venus's agent started screaming; Bruno the bouncer started shooting; and I started to feel something warm and wet run down my leg.

I would like to tell you that my life flashed before my eyes as I sank slowly to the ground, but it didn't. Instead I thought about Panama City Homicide Detective John Nailor—not because he would wind up catching my killer, but because I had never seen him naked. Now, *that* was a regret. In fact, that one thought probably kept me alive. That, and the fact that a wound to the left posterior is in no way life-threatening.

I am told that the bullet tore through Venus's carotid artery on its way to my ass. But I don't like thinking about that. I prefer to think about what a lovely evening it had been, at least up until the moment that gunplay broke out. Venus and I had teamed up, the visiting porn star and the house headliner, together in a rousing number designed to stiffen the resolve of the most passive customer and loosen his already-thinning wallet. We had danced to "When You Wish Upon a Star."

Venus was lowered carefully from the ceiling, perched on the tip of a quarter moon. I swung in slowly from the diametrically opposed corner of the stage, clinging to a huge sequined star. It was poetry in motion. We were wearing complementing G-strings; hers was gold, mine was silver. Our pasties were gold and silver stars, the very tiniest things imaginable.

Venus's agent, Barry "The Snake" Sanduski, made Vincent Gambuzzo, the Tiffany Gentleman's Club owner and my boss, take out extra insurance on account of how he didn't want to suffer the consequences of our risky routine. See, according to Tonya the Barbarian, one of Venus's former roommates and a Tiffany girl, Venus was the eighth wonder of the world, carefully constructed by the finest medical care money can buy.

Tonya said that Venus had more silicone in her body than a sucker-lot special has Bondo. She said Venus used to be flat-chested and pudgy with mousy brown hair and an astigmatism that made her squint.

The Venus I met had 48 triple D's and a waist like a Barbie doll's. Her eyes were large and contact-lens purple. Her lips were pressed into a permanent kissy pout and her hair was something between spun gold and cotton candy. Her brain, however, left something to be desired. Venus was a fluffball, but that ain't at all why men paid to watch her strut across the stage.

So when the first few strains of "When You Wish Upon a Star" rang out, and Venus and I were lowered slowly from the ceiling, the men in the house were not thinking of Jiminy Cricket and Walt Disney. They were watching the finest talent on the northwest coast of Florida. I mean, you pair a girl like Venus up with a girl like me, and you've got serious lust action. While Venus is definitely artificial, I'm the genuine article: five feet ten inches in my stilettos, long blond come-hither hair, legs that won't quit, and a pair of 38 double D's that have never known a surgeon's scalpel. Furthermore, I got the know-how to crawl inside a man's head and drive him wild.

Barry "The Snake" Sanduski and Vincent Gambuzzo couldn't have been happier with our number. Probably because the house take, according to Gordon, the doorman, had never been higher. I know I'd never seen the house so crowded, even during spring break or Bikers' Week. It is a given that the Tiffany is a class joint, and that is why we attract such high-caliber clientele, but when you import traveling talent and appeal to your locals, you've got a moneymaker. I can say these things, because it was my idea to call in Venus Lovemotion.

Of course, I let Vincent take the credit, and I don't spread it around, but lately I feel as if I'm the brains behind the Tiffany. I mean, business was a little slack, it was off-season. I figured, why not call in the southeastern traveling circuit out of Atlanta. People from Atlanta always head to Panama City for vacation; why not call in some of that city's biggest talent to make the tourists feel more at home?

I didn't expect Vincent to come up with such a brilliant marketing ploy. See, Vincent comes from a used-car-lot background. He talks a good game, and he intimates that he's connected, in your Italian "family" sort of way, but it's all smoke and mirrors. When it comes to business savvy, I'm your go-to girl. So you can understand how I came to feel that it was all my fault that this horrible tragedy had befallen Venus. It was, after all, my idea.

When Venus arrived I made sure we came to an understanding. She was the visitor and I was the host. We worked the room my way and we didn't pull any of that work-the-pole stripper stuff that your B-grade porn artists fall back on when they can't do much more than walk and chew gum. I taught Venus the routine. I insisted that she learn how to put her heart into it and not just her anatomy. And in the end, we were of one mind: mine.

Two

We closed out the night with an encore of our star act and were in the process of heading out to the Waffle House for breakfast when all hell broke loose. Venus and Barry were heading for his car, which was a beat-to-death Grand Am that only reinforced my guess that Barry wasn't exactly raking in the business. Bruno, the steroid-impaired, all-neck and no-brains bouncer, was watching from the back stoop. The parking lot was fairly empty, being as how last call had gone out over an hour ago. Vincent was standing by his fire-engine-red Porsche, trying to decide whether to lower himself and eat breakfast with us or go home to his empty high-rise condo. Most of the other staff was leaving, shooed out by the cleaning crew. As I mentioned before, I was unlocking my car door.

All of a sudden, I hear a pop like a cap pistol and screams echoing throughout the parking lot. The other sound I heard was people racking the slides of their guns. See, in your customer-service-type professions like ours, it is not uncommon for people to carry personal protection. I settle for Mace and a lovely little Spyderco knife that my big brother Francis gave me.

As I slid to the ground, people were taking cover and looking for a target. Only Bruno seemed to have a bead on the location of the shooter. The rest of them seemed about to shoot anything and everything. I swear, I never saw so many guns in my life. And when the cops arrived, I never saw so many guns mysteriously disappear.

I tried to roll under my car, but for some reason I couldn't get my left leg to move. I figured I was about to be riddled with bullets, and maybe from friends of mine looking to plug a killer and settling for a blonde. I brought my hand up to pull myself along and saw that it was covered in blood. That's when I started thinking about John Nailor and what a shame it was that we would never consummate our undying physical attraction to each other.

Sirens wailed in the distance, but Barry Sanduski's voice rose above them.

"Oh God, she's dead! Venus, don't leave me, baby!"

Bruno sent a couple of rounds from his .45 winging over our heads and into a group of pine trees that separated our club from the adjoining strip mall. Then he came running down the stairs, leaving the shelter of the steel-lined back door to jump behind a trash bin. He waited a cautious moment, then rolled out to Barry's car.

Gordon, the doorman, materialized by my side, having run at a crouch from the darkened lot. He was out of breath, and from the look on his face, new to violence and bloodshed.

"Oh Lord," he gasped. "You're hit!"

I peered up at Gordon. He couldn't have been more than twenty-two or -three, reedy thin with a tiny black goatee. I did not want to die in his arms. He was no John Nailor.

"Gordon," I said, trying to sound like I knew what was going on and less like I was taking my final breath. "Where am I hit? Is it squirting blood or just seeping?"

He turned even paler. "Oh God, oh God."

"Gordon, look. Keep your head low and check my ass; it hurts something terrible."

He gently rolled me onto my side. "It's a gusher, all right."

The sirens were coming closer, screaming out into the early Panama City morning, disturbing the retirees who'd come to Florida for peace and quiet and instead found Party City, USA.

"Gordon," I said, shuddering as I did so, "apply pressure."

"Where? To you?"

Gordon was neither a ladies' man nor a paramedic.

"Do it, Gordon!"

Tires crunched into the parking lot, squealing to a stop. Panama City's finest had arrived—well, finest minus the very finest. Nailor was home in bed, I knew that much; whether he was alone or not was another matter.

"Over here," Gordon cried. "She's hit!" He jumped up, forgetting all about his first-aid ministrations, and ran off.

Great, I thought, while he's fetching help, I'm bleeding out. And I did feel faint. Things did go dark, but only because at that moment, the parking lot light nearest my car went dead. I actually passed out, briefly, when the EMTs picked me up and put me on the stretcher. The rest of the time I was conscious. Waiting. Eventually some eager-beaver cop was gonna piece it together that I was *the* Sierra Lavotini. Then he'd call my buddy Nailor, just to give him a heads-up that his favorite dancer was lying on her stomach in the emergency room, her derriere exposed to any and all who cared to walk by.

I'd been lying there only an hour, doped up on some kind of painkiller, when he made his appearance. He stood there in the doorway, knowing I'd sense his arrival before I even saw him. He was leaning there with the nurses all passing by and admiring his dark-haired good looks and the way his trademark white oxford-cloth shirt complemented his tanned skin. He didn't mean to be pretty; it just came with the territory.

The son of a bitch didn't even have the courtesy to act all torn up about my well-being. No, he was smirking. Of course,

7

that's his job. He has to act unconcerned, to laugh in the face of danger. He was probably trying to make me feel safe, as if some crazed maniac hadn't just killed my new buddy and taken a bite out of me.

"Well, if you'd wanted to see me, Sierra, you coulda just called. You didn't have to generate a homicide and assault with intent to maim your own person."

I lifted my head groggily from the gurney and favored him with the Lavotini raised eyebrow. "Hey, Nailor. Kiss my exposed ass."

"Sure, honey, if you think that'll help."

"Nailor! How about a little sympathy and concern here? I am wounded."

"Superficially."

How is it that the man could smell so good?

"I could've been killed, you know. That maniac could've been aiming for me."

He pulled up a stool and sat close to my head, reaching over and taking my hand. "I know, honey," he said. He leaned a little closer and stroked the side of my face, gently pulling a strand of hair out of the way. "Does it hurt bad?"

I moaned, but it was not on account of the pain. I loved the feel of his work-roughened fingers paired with the gentleness of his touch. I could get used to those fingers. "Ummmm," I moaned again, louder.

"Sierra, are you in pain?" Now I had his concern.

"Oh, yes," I sighed. "Big, big pain. Oh, baby, I might not make it."

This would've been fine had I not giggled.

"Sierra!" He pushed back and sat up, taking his lovely fingers with him. "We're in the ER, for Pete's sake!" He looked at me again, his eyebrows knit together like a stern father. "Well then, I think you're up to answering a few questions." And with that, he whipped out a little notepad and settled down to work. Damn, I'd lost him again.

"You heard the shot that hit you and Venus, did you not?"

I moaned, this time because the medication was wearing off. It felt like my little chihuahua, Fluffy, had sunk her teeth into my left cheek and forgotten to remove them.

"I heard it, but I was facing my car, so I didn't see a thing."

Nailor took great care to write this all down.

"Did you see anything suspicious right before she got shot or maybe earlier in the evening?"

Outside the tiny examining room I could hear the banter of nurses and cops, the sounds of carts wheeling past and equipment being prepared for other patients. I wanted nothing more than to go home to my trailer and crawl into bed.

"Sierra? Did you see anything suspicious?"

"Nailor, put two and two together here. I work in a strip club. It would be better to ask if there was anything unsuspicious going on."

Nailor sighed. "You know what I mean," he said.

I thought back over the immediate few moments before the shooting. Anything suspicious? No. I let my mind drift back over the events of the evening. The regulars had all been there, a few newcomers, out-of-towners. I started to shake my head and then stopped.

"Well, there was one new guy who seemed to be paying a lot of attention to Venus." Meaning he had overlooked the real talent. After all, I was the headliner.

Nailor looked up. "What do you mean?"

I thought for a moment. "He sat at a table down front, didn't watch any of the other acts, didn't talk to the girls that were circulating, and only seemed to pay attention when Venus walked out."

Nailor stretched. "What's unusual about that?"

It was all I could do to answer him now. The pain was spreading throughout my body, making it hard to concentrate.

"He didn't watch her like a customer. He wasn't inspecting the merchandise. In fact, he didn't look too happy with her."

"Description?"

"Tall, a little husky, but like it was muscle, not fat. One of them gotta-shave-four-times-a-day guys. He put me in mind of Salvatore Minuchin, a wiseguy from the old neighborhood. Salvatore was the muscle for Lucky Pagnozzi, back before Lucky took the whack outside of the Sons of Italy Social Club. I don't know what Salvatore's doing now. I sorta lost track of him after he went to prison." I was drifting, my eyes weighted down by the late hour and the pain.

"Was he wearing a suit or leisure clothes?" Nailor asked.

"Salvatore? No, I think it was a blue prison jumpsuit if I recall correctly."

Nailor sighed and flipped his notebook shut. "Not Salvatore, Sierra, the guy from the club, the one watching Venus."

"Yeah," I said. A nurse entered the room with a syringe on a tray. World peace was at hand. "He was wearing a charcoal-gray Brooks Brothers suit."

Nailor sighed again. "Sierra, focus."

"No kidding. I know my suits and this was a Brooks Brothers. I make my living off of knowing my customers. He wasn't stargazing and he wasn't looking to shop the talent. He was suspicious, just the man you want to talk with."

"If you don't mind?" The nurse glared at Nailor. He was holding her up, endangering her patient's welfare.

"He don't mind," I muttered. "He don't mind at all."

Three

$\mathcal{J}$ohn Nailor drove me home in his unmarked brown Taurus police car. He stretched me out on the backseat, covering me with his coat and treating me as if I were a bubble about to burst at any second. I felt nothing. I floated on a cloud of Demerol-induced nirvana, not really caring that a bullet could've permanently scarred one of my main sources of income. Life was good.

Fluffy, my hairless chihuahua, waited on the stoop of my trailer. She did not share my euphoria. She was hungry and I was late.

Nailor pulled me out of the backseat and was holding me up, his arm around my waist, and my head on his shoulder. Fluffy approved of this, at least. Her little tail started to wag and she yipped.

"Hey, Fluff," Nailor called softly. "Hungry, girl?"

"Starved," I answered.

"Hold it right there, buddy," a voice called out. Nailor and I froze, for two different reasons. I stopped because I recognized the sound of my crazy neighbor, Raydean, the woman voted most likely to be unpredictable and violent by the members of the Lively Oaks Trailer Park. Nailor froze because he had heard the unmistakable sound of someone chambering a round into a shotgun. Nailor knew Raydean, so he knew what he was up against.

"To my way of thinking," Raydean called softly, "it is not at all gentlemanly to get a young woman drunk and then try to have your way with her. We don't do things like that on *this* planet."

Raydean was late for her Prolixin shot, that much I could tell. Raydean on a good day is insane. On a bad day, when she hasn't had her anti-psychotic medication, Raydean is your worst nightmare: an alien hunter who sees little green men crawling about everywhere. This was a very bad day.

"Raydean," I said, instantly sober, "it's me and Detective Nailor, honey. He's not trying to have his way with me."

Ba-boom! The gun erupted into the early-morning air, echoing in the narrow alleyway between our trailers. John threw me to the ground and dove on top of me. Fluffy ran back through the doggie door, into the trailer. Raydean laughed.

"Lookit them suckers run!" she cried, and fired the shotgun again, this time shooting toward a pine tree behind my trailer.

"Go home to the Mothership!" she yelled.

"Raydean!" I yelled. "Knock it off! You'll alert the starship troopers."

That stopped her in her tracks.

"Summonabitch," she muttered. "That's all we need."

I raised my head just a few inches and looked around. There was no sign of life in the street, but curtains twitched at all the windows of the surrounding trailers. Folks were used to Raydean's antics.

Five trailers down a door opened. Raydean lifted her gray-haired head from its resting place on the barrel of the gun and looked. Pat, the charter boat captain and my landlady, was about to face Raydean down.

"Aw, Sierra," Raydean whined, "now look what you've gone and done!"

"Me?" Nailor was lying on me like a heavy carpet.

"Yes, you. Now *she's* coming. She'll be carting me off to the mental health center for a shot, and the next thing you know, I'll be sitting in group therapy with some young chick social worker named Mavis, talking about what day it is and who's the damn president. Shee-it!"

Nailor snorted, stifling a laugh.

"Don't move," I whispered. "It isn't safe just yet." Nailor's body went limp against mine; well, sort of limp. "Raydean," I said, "put the gun down, honey. You know how Pat is about weapons."

Raydean slowly lowered the shotgun. She stood there on her stoop, her stockings sagging down around her ankles, the pockets of her faded pink housedress stuffed with balled-up tissues and gun magazines.

"First I got to contend with a Flemish invasion, and now I got to put up with *her*. It just ain't fair."

Raydean was firmly convinced that the Flemish were alien beings. It was a delusion that, thus far, not even medication could remove. But Raydean is my friend, and a useful ally upon occasion, and if believing in a Flemish invasion is one of her minor quirks, well then, let he who is without neurosis cast the first stone.

Pat walked the length of the street, right out in the middle, like a gunslinger at high noon. She walked slow, probably because her arthritis was bothering her. At seventy, Pat was the only woman I knew who was still physically able to do the hard manual labor that comes with running a charter fishing boat. She is tenacious.

Pat was taking in the scene, her snow-white hair gleaming in the early-morning sunlight, her work jeans on, yellow rubber gloves hanging off a tool belt that stretched around her ample waist. Pat wasn't about to take any shit off Raydean.

She strolled up, stopped, and looked over at Raydean, who had dropped the gun and was standing like a sullen schoolgirl at the top of her stoop.

"Let's go on now," Pat said, her eyes never leaving Raydean's face.

"Tomorrow," Raydean said.

"You said that yesterday and where did it get us?" Then Pat looked over at Nailor lying on top of me, a long sigh escaping her lips. "If you two are going to monkey around, the least you could do would be to take it out of the gutter and into the bedroom. Why do you think trailer parks have such a poor reputation? Really, Sierra!"

Nailor, sensing that the dangerous moment had passed, slowly rose up and helped me to my feet. My leg gave way again and I staggered against him, drawing the attention of both women.

"Sierra, are you injured?" Pat asked quietly.

"Naw, that'un's taking advantage of her good nature and easy ways," Raydean interjected.

"I got shot," I said.

"In the line of duty?" Raydean's antenna was aquiver at the possibility of further alien activity.

"Yes, Raydean, in the line of duty. I was leaving work when someone shot another dancer and hit me, too."

Pat's face grew worried. She sees herself as my surrogate mother and doesn't particularly fancy my line of work.

Nailor broke in. "I'm working on getting her inside and into bed," he said.

"Oh, I can see that!" Raydean crowed.

Pat shook her head and motioned to Raydean. "Come on, honey. Let's go. We'll deal with Sierra's situation later." She meant afterward, after Raydean was back on the planet and calmer heads could prevail.

I sighed and leaned heavily against Nailor. "You know," I whispered, "in my condition, I really shouldn't be left alone."

Nailor chuckled and I felt his arm tighten around my waist. Oh yes, I thought, I most definitely don't need to be left alone.

Four

I thought he would stay. And even though I wasn't in fighting trim, I was prepared. I limped off down the hallway to my bedroom, stripped off my clothes, and pulled on my sexiest nightgown. It was a white cotton number with lace bows and plenty of buttons. It was virginal, and perfectly appropriate for our first golden moment. Nailor had seen it before, but at that point in time he'd been in no shape to remember it. He'd remember it now, I thought.

I ran a brush through my hair and walked slowly down the hallway. He was in the kitchen, the phone in one hand and a can of dog food in the other.

"The witness heard her make the threat?" he asked, stooping to put the food in Fluffy's dish. Fluff licked his hand and the spoon in her rush to get to the food.

"Pick her up." He straightened. "Yeah, now. I'll be right there."

Shit. I looked down at my gown and back over at him. He hadn't even noticed. Well, there went the best-laid plans of one Sierra Lavotini.

He clicked off the phone and set it back on its base.

"Pick up who?" I asked.

He turned, his eyes taking in the Lavotini package. A half

moan escaped his lips. For a moment he was distracted, then back on task.

"Marla," he said.

"Marla! You're picking up Marla in connection with the murder? You think Marla shot me?"

Marla was my arch-rival at the Tiffany Gentleman's Club. She liked to think that her fifty-two-inch chest size made her the better dancer. Her main act was to dress up in a silver sequined outfit with wings that fit over her arms to make her look like a plane. She'd swoop out over the runway attached to an elaborate set of wires and pulleys, grab her tits, and yell, "Bombs away, boys!" The local airmen from Tyndall loved it. I thought it was trite and overworked. But I digress. Marla hated me, but why would she kill Venus Lovemotion?

"I'm not saying she shot Venus Lovemotion or you, either. We're just interested in speaking to her. There are a few discrepancies in her statement, that's all. I'm sure we can get it all cleared up."

Fluffy yipped again. I looked down at her. She was smiling. I was not the only one who could picture Marla squirming on the hot seat down at police headquarters. In fact, if Nailor needed help with the interrogation, any help at all, well, I was at the ready.

"I've gotta go," he said. "Get some rest. I'll be back later to check on you." The way he said that last part made me know he hadn't completely missed out on my intentions.

He walked toward me and my heart started hammering. It was always this way. It was his eyes, the way he smelled, the raw, untamed part of his being that reached in and connected with my own wildness. Somehow, there was always something that came between us, stopping us from going full steam ahead. But one day . . . one day. I sighed and stood perfectly still. He reached me, pulling me into his arms and pressing his lips firmly against mine. His hands pressed the small of my back and began roving. For a few minutes we stayed that way, Venus Lovemotion's killer a million miles from our thoughts.

I was feeling warm and floaty. His hands were doing things to my body that I had only imagined possible. And when he moaned, I knew I had been equally effective.

"I'll be back," he said, breaking away from me.

"I'll be waiting," I whispered, my voice stuck somewhere inside my body.

Fluffy picked this moment to throw up her hastily consumed meal. Maybe she felt threatened by the new presence in my life. I am sensitive to her feelings. Dogs are like children. Whatever her inner issue, it broke the spell. Nailor was out the door and I was swiping up doggie retch with a paper towel.

"Girl," I said, reaching out to scratch Fluffy behind her ears, "it will happen to you someday. That special someone will come along, and you'll be out of your mind, acting like a crazy fool." Fluffy let out a long belch. Clearly she didn't expect herself to ever lose control.

"Well, mark my words," I said. I shook out another pain pill and swallowed it with a large swig of my pa's homemade Chianti. Ma says Pa's Chianti thickens the blood. She gives it to us whenever something's wrong, emotional or physical. I figured the way my blood was raging and my derriere was aching, Chianti was my only hope.

It must've done the trick. Within moments my head was heavy on the pillow, Fluffy curled by my side. I fell asleep thinking of all the lovely little surprises I had in store for a certain Panama City homicide detective. I woke up to a living nightmare.

Someone was banging loudly on my door and calling my name. Fluffy was barking her tiny head off, and I seemed to be moving in slow motion, drifting down the hallway toward the back door. Why wouldn't they leave me alone?

I snuck a peek through the curtains in the living room. Vincent Gambuzzo's Porsche sat on my parking pad, dripping black oil onto the clean cement. Behind it was another car that I didn't recognize, a Chevy something or other.

"Sierra!" Vincent called. "Open up!"

"Keep your pants on," I muttered, fumbling with the lock and trying to peer through my peephole. All I could see was Vincent's black eye staring back at me.

"This is pointless," a pouty female voice said. "She knows it's me."

Damn. The door swung open, and before I could slam it shut, Vincent had his foot in the door, a stubborn, determined look on his face. Marla. He'd brought the slut to the trailer, with me suffering; the very woman who might've killed me, given better aim.

"I'm not in the mood," I said. "Go away."

Vincent stood there, three hundred pounds of resistance, packaged in a black suit, black shirt, and black tie, wearing his wraparound black sunglasses and scowling with his jaw twitching nervously.

"Sierra, this ain't no freakin' social call."

"Then bye." I moved to slam the door, but he muscled his way into my kitchen. Behind him, shielded by his girth, stood Marla and her scuzzball boyfriend, Little Ricky. His name was Rick, but I called him Little Ricky on account of the rumors floating around about his steroid use shrinking up a certain part of his anatomy. Little Ricky aspired to a career as a pro wrestler, the kind you see on TV. A fake. He was a mass of muscles with very little brainpower to support it.

Ricky smiled at me, the flirt, and reached his hand up to smooth his thick brown hair. He figured to be God's gift to underprivileged women. I figured him to be garbage looking for a dump site.

"Sierra, listen to me. This is Tiffany business. We got trouble and that means we all gotta pull together. Our livelihoods are on the line here, Sierra. Now quit fooling around."

Why me? Why do they always pick on me? Do I look like a troublemaker? Do I have "Will Give You a Hard Time" stamped on my forehead? Did someone tape "Kick Me" to my ass?

"Make coffee," I said, looking only at Vincent. "You got five minutes and then I'm heading back to bed." Little Ricky looked interested. Marla caught him and stamped on his foot. Usually this would've provoked some smart-assed comment from her, but not now. She was strangely silent.

Vincent rummaged around my cabinets, grabbing a filter and the coffee, then making his way to the sink to fill the coffeepot with water.

"Sierra," Vincent said, "sit down. Take a load off." His tone had changed dangerously. He was acting nice, a sure sign of big trouble.

"I'll lean," I said, taking a position against the counter. Little Ricky and Marla pulled up barstools and perched at my kitchen table, a round, rejected hightop from a failed nightclub.

Vincent measured the coffee, poured the water, and hit the switch on the coffeemaker. He turned his attention back to me.

"As you know," he began, "Venus Lovemotion got herself whacked in our parking lot. We invited her, so we are responsible." He stressed the word "we" like he was really meaning "you, Sierra."

"Now, in the interest of justice, and because we cannot let this savage attack go unpunished, I feel we must supplement the efforts of our loyal but upon occasion unprepared police department."

That got my back up. "Hey, them guys are doing the best

they can, given the situation. John Nailor is working the case personally. He'll get to the bottom of it."

Vincent Gambuzzo hated John Nailor. He hated the way Nailor gave him no respect. He hated the effect Nailor had on the club. And he particularly hated the effect Nailor had on me. But to my amazement, he said nothing about Nailor.

"Be that as it may," he continued, "the police department has obviously received some erroneous information and is proceeding in a fruitless direction with their investigation."

The coffeepot hissed loudly. Marla and Little Ricky were avoiding making eye contact with me, preferring instead to focus only on Vincent, as if he were some kind of a prophet.

Even in my dazed state of consciousness, I could tell I was being had.

"Vincent," I said, "leave us cut to the chase." My backside was beginning to favor me with a dull, unrelenting ache. I wanted to drink another glass of Pa's Chianti and go back to bed.

Vincent busied himself pouring me a cup of coffee. He was figuring the best approach and coming up short. Finally he sighed, handed me a steaming mug, and looked over at Marla.

"Sierra, I know you and Marla ain't on the best of terms."

Best of terms? I thought back over the countless times Marla had tried to sabotage one of my acts, or to flat out manipulate me into giving up my status as club headliner, or talked trash about me to the other girls. "Not on the best of terms" didn't begin to describe my feelings for Marla.

"You could say that," I answered.

"I did say that," Vincent puffed. "But blood is thicker than water, Sierra. And here at the Tiffany, we're all one big family."

"Bottom-line it, Vincent."

He looked at me, his jaw twitching double-time. "The cops are trying to frame Marla for Venus's murder. It ain't right. It's up to us to catch the bastard what done Venus and you, and get the heat out of our house."

Vincent straightened up so maybe he looked taller than his natural five feet seven inches. He wore lifts, but I didn't feel the need to let the rest of the world know.

"So," I said, letting my gaze run over Marla and Little Ricky, "how is that a problem for me? Guilty or innocent, we get rid of the prima donna and life is golden for me. I say, let her fry!"

Marla squeaked but otherwise stayed silent. She was chaffing. On a normal day, we'd have taken this little dispute outside, but not now. Marla was scared stiff. She was grasping at straws. She needed me.

When this realization hit, I stopped and savored it. Marla needed me. Well, well, well. The worm was turning.

"Sierra!" Vincent's voice cut into my pleasant reverie. "Put your personal feelings aside and think of the higher good."

"I am," I answered.

"Sierra, let me see you in the living room." Vincent brushed past me and I didn't move. "Please?"

Vincent had to be just as desperate as Marla, a fact I found amusing. Nonetheless, I followed him.

He walked a few feet away from the kitchen, into my living room, and began pacing across the bare wooden floor, his reflection echoed in the mirrors that lined the back wall. It made me angry. He was invading my practice space.

"Sierra," he said, his voice lowered in an attempt to keep Marla from overhearing him, "we can't all be you. Marla's not the brightest light on the Christmas tree, but you gotta admit she brings in her share of the business." I was obviously unimpressed. "Sierra, she ain't got nobody but us."

He stopped and stared at me. He knew that would do the trick. Inside, I felt a small twinge knock on the door of my conscience. Nobody? That figured. But still, a girl alone in the world.

"She's got Little Ricky," I sputtered.

"Oh, Sierra, come on. That half-wit? He's about as loyal to her as a snake. Little Ricky runs through women like butter through hot pasta. He can't keep his zipper up long enough to have a relationship."

I glanced back toward the kitchen. Little Ricky caught my eye and smiled. Marla pinched him. I looked back at Vincent.

"Sierra, the club would take a major hit if we lost her right now." Vincent was actually sweating. "We can't afford to lose the business."

An eerie feeling started squeezing my gut. There was more to it than Marla and the club's not-so-sterling reputation.

"Ante up, Vincent. What's really going on?"

Vincent's face paled around his dark glasses. "I'm into some guys for twenty big ones, Sierra. If I don't pay up by the fifteenth, I'm toast."

"You're into the mob? Vincent, how could you! You know what they'll do to you!"

"Sierra, calm yourself. It's worse than that, actually. I, um, underestimated the club profits. The IRS wants the money by the fifteenth. I'm pretty sure I can pull it off, but you gotta help us. If I lose Marla, I won't make it. Please, Sierra."

What a pretty picture this was. Vincent into legit organized crime and Marla about to do twenty-five to life. All my troubles could be effectively wiped out, but unfortunately my livelihood would go with it.

While I might make noise like I didn't care, and on occasion actually quit my job publicly, there was no other club where I'd work. The Tiffany was a class joint. Furthermore, we were family. Good or bad, we dancers had to stick together. After all, people tended to view us with little respect. If we didn't cling together, we'd sink like rats. I knew what was coming. I could feel it rise up inside myself like bile.

"All right, Vincent," I said, "but let me have my fun first."

Before he could answer, I whirled around and walked back into the kitchen.

"So," I said, standing right in front of Marla and staring her down, "you got a problem, and you need my help."

Marla tossed her long black hair like maybe she was looking to debate the point, but fear won out. "Yes," she said, and swallowed hard. "I really need help."

Seeing the pitiful way she knuckled under took all the fun out of toying with her. Shit. She was family.

"All right," I said. "Suppose you tell me all about it."

Marla looked at me then, her eyes filling with tears. This was pathetic. If we weren't careful, she was going to end up saying stuff we both would regret later when we were back on a level playing field.

"Marla, try and rub two brain cells together and come up with a statement, all right?"

The angry flash was back in her eyes, replacing the sappy gratitude that had threatened to overwhelm her.

"That bully detective of yours thinks I killed Venus Lovemotion," she said.

"Why?"

Marla looked away from me, glancing nervously at Little Ricky. "Sierra, can we do this in private?"

Little Ricky didn't pick up on her tone, that it was somehow about him. No, he was trying to peak through the gaps between the ribbons of my gown, looking for an unobstructed view. Considering he spent every night of his sorry little rodent life sitting in the club, viewing all of us naked, I failed to see why he felt compelled to ogle now, in this time of crisis.

"Sure, Marla," I said, grabbing my coffee mug. "Let's go sit outside on the steps."

The sunlight was blinding. Somehow early morning had

slipped away and become mid-afternoon. I grabbed my sunglasses on my way out the door and gingerly lowered my aching body down onto the top stoop. It was almost tolerable if I leaned to the right.

"Okay," Marla sighed. "It's like this: Rick, he's basically a good guy and all, but he can't help himself; he likes women." That was one way of looking at it, I supposed. "Most of the time, I can handle it. I mean, the other girls all know he's kidding. They wouldn't take him seriously." No, Marla, I thought, the other girls know he's a lowlife snake in the grass. "But Venus, I don't think she knew."

Marla looked sideways at me, to see if I was going to defend Venus. I kept my face neutral.

"Anyway, I caught her and Ricky out on the back stairs. She was all over him! I had to set her straight. I sent Ricky inside so she and I could have a little heart-to-heart." Marla's face fell. "I guess someone overheard us and took it wrong."

"Took what wrong, Marla?"

If she squirmed any harder, her black spandex short shorts would snag a splinter from the stoop.

"Well," she said, sighing, "if you took what I said out of context . . ."

"Marla, what did you say?"

Her face darkened, and her eyes were hard, flat black disks. "I told her that if I saw her so much as look at Rick, I would kill her."

I took a silent deep breath. "Anything else?"

"Well, I said I had a gun and I'd used it before, so she should be certain that I meant what I said." Marla sighed at the memory.

"Did you?"

"Did I what?"

"Did you mean what you said? Did you have a gun?"

Marla sighed again. "Well, at the time I meant it. And yeah, I have guns."

The sun beat down on my head and it started to pound in time with my pulse. This was not what I wanted to hear.

"Guns, plural?"

Marla looked over at me, her eyes wide, no longer hard and threatening. "Doesn't everyone?" she asked.

"Marla, no. Not everyone has a gun, and certainly not everyone has more than one. How many guns do you own?"

Marla shrugged. "I don't know. Four? Five? I'm not a collector or anything. I just have 'em around. You know, I grew up in Alabama." She said this as if I should understand that in Alabama they do things like this. Now, if she'd said Northeast Philly, I could understand, but Alabama?

"Marla, you said something else." Marla raised her eyebrows. The talk of Alabama had pulled her back into her little Southern-belle attitude. I hated that most about her. "You said you'd used your gun before."

"Oh, that!" Marla tossed her head and laughed. She sounded as if at any moment she could teeter off the edge of rationality and become hysterical. "I shot my high school boyfriend."

"What!" This was a side to Marla that I hadn't known, otherwise I might not've pushed her so hard.

"Well, Sierra, it was an accident and he wasn't hurt bad. We were duck hunting and I sort of mistook him for a teal."

"Marla, you didn't!" As I said, Marla isn't exactly the sharpest knife on the rack.

"Did." Marla calmly picked a piece of lint off her spandex sports bra. She sighed wistfully. "He made a full recovery, and of course they didn't bring charges—around Eufaula that kind of stuff happens now and again. Of course, we were never the same." Her eyes welled up. "I just loved him to pieces!"

I'd hate to see what she did to men she didn't love. Still, this was a pretty flimsy basis for a murder motive, but maybe not in Nailor's eyes. After all, he didn't know her like I did.

"Marla, where were you when the shot was fired?"

Marla screwed up her face, as if the effort to remember was taxing her very deepest inner being.

"Oh, I was walking out to my car, out over by the edge of the parking lot, right where I always park."

Yes, right by the stand of pine trees, right where the shooter had been if Bruno was any judge of shots, and he certainly knew his gunplay. Marla was in trouble, all right.

"So, you can clear this up, can't you?" she said.

I grabbed the railing and pulled myself up slowly, looking down on her. A queasy feeling that could've been painkillers but probably was doubt filled my gut.

"Sure thing, Marla," I said. "We'll have this licked in no time flat."

Marla sighed and smiled. "Thank you, sweetie," she said. "I was just praying you'd know what to do."

Well, if that's what she'd been praying for, God was playing a serious joke. I had no more idea of how to pull her out of this mess than I did of how to find the real killer. But I knew where to start, and judging from the brown Taurus that was rounding the corner onto my street, so did John Nailor.

Five

*M*arla, Little Ricky, and Vincent scattered when they saw Nailor's car come to a slow stop in front of my trailer. Nailor unfolded himself from the driver's seat of the Taurus and started to walk up the driveway, staring after my departing guests with a puzzled expression on his face.

"What was that all about?" he asked.

"Professional courtesy."

He frowned, not understanding, then stopped to look up at me. This time he noticed straight off. He looked up and down the street, then back to me.

"You think you should be standing there like that?" he said.

"Like what?" I was still in my white gown, my hair down around my shoulders, barefoot and holding an empty coffee cup.

"You look . . . well, you're . . ." Nailor couldn't find the words, but he found the steps and mounted them quickly, moving with me inside the door, closing it behind us with only one brief cautious look toward Raydean's trailer.

"She's probably still at the mental health center," I said. "Probably won't be home till Pat goes to pick her up. That could be hours," I added softly.

"Hours," he murmured, pulling me toward him and folding me into his arms.

I would've let it go. I would've drifted away with him had I not remembered that things were different now. I had a responsibility. Ma didn't teach me to fool around when the chores still needed to be done. No. Work, then play.

I pushed back and looked Nailor in the eyes. He saw the change right off.

"Am I hurting you?" he asked.

"Not a chance. I just need to ask you a few questions first, that's all."

"First?" He grinned and went right back to running his fingers down my body, trailing them across the fabric of my gown, lingering in all the right places.

"Yeah," I said, pushing him away, "first. You want coffee? You should have coffee 'cause this could take a little time, and you should keep up your energy."

He gave up. "Yeah, coffee would be nice."

He'd gone home and changed since I'd seen him. He was wearing a dark brown suit and another crisp white shirt. His tie was silk. Expensive. He smelled like aftershave, not cologne. Nailor didn't wear cologne. He always smelled faintly of leather and some spice I couldn't identify. He was clean-cut, a little more clean-cut than I liked, but then, I'd always had a penchant for bad guys. Nailor was one of those men who straddled the fence, just over the line on the good side, but willing to do whatever it took to get what he wanted.

I thought about that as I poured his coffee, shivering as he walked up behind me. We were entering a new frontier, him and me. We were closing in on a relationship. I didn't think either one of us was gonna go down easy on that issue.

"You're thinking about something, Sierra," he said softly. "You scared?"

Mind reader. "Hell no," I said, turning to hand him his coffee and sloshing it over the rim of the cup as I did so. "I've got something on my mind, all right, but it don't involve fear."

He let it go and allowed me to lead him over to the futon that sat along one wall of my almost empty living room. I sat down, pulling him with me. It was fine, as long as I leaned toward him and tried not to think about my injury. How was I ever gonna dance? I couldn't afford to take time off. I guessed I'd do it slowly, leaning against the pole and working it to my advantage. But that was tomorrow, today I had business to attend to.

"What was up with Marla?" I asked.

Nailor's face went professional on me, tight and closed. "That's an ongoing investigation," he said, his voice deepening as he spoke.

"Nailor, I'm not a damned reporter. Lighten up and tell me what happened."

Nailor wasn't budging.

"All right," I said, "I'll tell you. Marla threatened Venus. She was in the right place at the right time and she owns a gun. She's your only suspect."

As I ticked off the evidence, I looked at him, trying to tell by his eyes if I was scoring a hit with the truth. He only went flat when I said Marla was the only suspect. Hmm, what could that mean?

"Sierra," he said, "are you asking because you hate Marla, or is there something going on?"

I straightened a little, placed my coffee cup on the floor beside me, and turned back to him.

"I'm taking a personal interest in this," I said. "I think with my expertise I might be able to lend a little help to the investigation."

Nailor didn't laugh me off. He knew I could help, but that I would offer to help the police, well, that was new.

"I don't want to tread on any toes here," I continued. "But I think you may be off on the wrong investigatory path. Marla couldn't plan and execute a murder, no matter how worked up she was."

Nailor put his coffee cup down. "There's things you don't know, Sierra. Marla may look harmless, but I assure you, she's not."

"Oh, you're not telling me anything new there. Marla's capable of all kinds of things, but killing off a rival isn't one of them. If that were so, I'd have been dead long ago." I thought of the one or two times Marla and I had engaged in fisticuffs. The look in her eyes had not been blood lust; it was more a look of fear.

"A killer needs the conviction to do the deed," I said, quoting him from prior occasions. "Marla ain't got conviction. Deep in her heart, Marla knows Ricky's pond scum."

Nailor softened. "Sierra, I'll work it out. If she's innocent, I'll soon see that, but it doesn't look that way now. Let me do my job. You don't need to go stepping into something that really doesn't concern you."

I was starting to bristle. He was talking to me as if I was Joan Q. Citizen, and I assure you that I am not.

"I'm in it, Nailor. I'm going to help Vincent and Marla, and there won't be a thing you can do about it." There, the glove was down, the challenge made.

His face reddened and he struggled, torn between his anger and his desire to get into my pants. I felt for him, I really did.

"Sierra, you'll only . . ." He broke off, not wanting to go there.

"What, Nailor, be in the way? Is that what you think? Well, I can handle myself, you know."

He eased up, working hard to control his temper. "I know you can handle yourself," he said slowly. He reached over and untied the top ribbon of my gown. "But can you handle me?"

I felt my resolve weakening. I leaned a little closer toward him, my head resting on his shoulder.

"Have you recovered the gun?" I asked softly, my hands wandering down the length of his body. "What size was the, um, bullet?" My fingers slipped below his belt, teasing him and distracting him, looking for the information I wanted.

Nailor said nothing, his breathing quickening. He untied the second ribbon, and my gown fell open, exposing my breasts. Oh God, I wanted this man. I'd waited too long for this.

"Have you found any fingerprints that would link Marla to the murder?" I asked softly, my breath caressing his ear. He moaned.

"You're hopeless," he said softly. "Come here." He pulled me down until we were lying side by side on the wide futon. He kissed me then, letting his lips form a trail of fire across my neck and down to the tips of my breasts. I moved against him, every bit of my self-resolve disappearing as I gave into the sensations. Now, I breathed silently, now.

"See," he whispered, "you don't need to go spending your time on a boring police investigation. You need this." His fingers slipped below the waistband of my panties. "You don't see me dancing at the Tiffany, do you?"

The haze cleared and I pushed away to look at him. "No, Nailor, that's not the point."

He tried to pull me back, to continue, but I had a point to make.

"Vincent asked me to help Marla, as a favor to him. Furthermore, she is all alone and you guys will run right over her. She's not the sharpest tack in the box, Nailor. You manipulate her and she'll confess out of confusion."

Nailor groaned. "No, Sierra, don't do this. Just do your job and let me do mine. What do you know about investigating a murder, anyway?"

"Well, maybe in this particular case, I know more than you."

He straightened up, pushed away, and glared at me.

31

"Impeding a police investigation is a crime, Sierra. You get in our way and we'll deal with you accordingly."

"And what's that supposed to mean, Nailor? What? I'm fine to roll around with but shouldn't go thinking I'm an equal?"

"It means only what I said, Sierra. My job and this investigation come first. I play it by the book and that means I don't take on amateur partners."

Now I was mad and, truth be told, hurt, very hurt.

Fluffy picked this moment to make an appearance, tapping her way across the wood floor, her sharp nails clicking like tap shoes. She was happy, why weren't we?

I tied my gown together and looked right back at him. His pager went off, the sharp tone shattering what was left of our romantic inclinations.

"Maybe this was a mistake," I said, my heart sinking like a rock.

"Yeah, maybe it was. I've gotta go," he said, looking up from the pager, his eyes masked by anger.

Damn. I knew better. I knew better than to try and have a relationship. This always happened. Sooner or later the guy couldn't deal with having a woman who was every bit as strong and opinionated as he was. I had honestly thought Nailor was different, but no, he was just like the rest of them.

From the expression on his face I could tell he was thinking the same thing.

"I'll get back to you later," he said, heading for the kitchen.

"Don't let the door hit you in the ass," I called after him.

The slamming door answered me. Damn! What was it with us?

I went to the window and watched him. He sat there for a minute, running his hand through his hair, obviously pissed. Then, with a jerk, the car started off down the road, narrowly missing Pat's old pickup truck as it passed. Raydean's hand fluttered out of the passenger side window, waving at the departing detective.

"Well, girl," I said, turning to Fluffy, "there goes my love life."

Fluffy sighed.

"Yep, some days you get the bear, and some days the bear bites you in the ass."

Fluffy moaned and walked off toward the kitchen. It was going to be one of those days.

Six

*N*o one expected me to work my regular shift, but I had to get out of the trailer. The longer I lay around watching the backs of my eyelids, the more I knew I needed a distraction. What better one than a murder investigation, and where better to start than the scene of the crime?

I took my time getting ready, just like I do on any work night, even though I couldn't dance. See, in my business, it's all image. I am not the illusion men see onstage and dream about at night. *That* Sierra is a carefully crafted creation. I never let the customer know the real me. They don't want to know me anyway. Men come to the Tiffany looking for a passionate promise that their fantasy is out there, just beyond their grasp. That's what Sierra gives them, a promise. Then I get in my car and drive home, wishing for the same thing.

Again, I digress. I drove over the Hathaway Bridge that separates Panama City proper from Panama City Beach. Panama City Beach is the illusion, while Panama City proper is the real thing. Panama City Beach is lights and action while the town hangs back on the fringes, hiding its beauty from the strangers who fly past, eager to get to their dream vacation. The tourists never get it. They never stroll along the Art Deco storefronts, sip coffee on the sidewalks, or eat at Ernie's. They miss the gentle

Victorian homes that line St. Andrews Bay and the parks that edge the waterfront.

The tourists rush to the putt-putt courses or the mega-bars and dance clubs. They honk their horns and ogle the frenzied teenaged flesh that comes to town seeking the illusive best-ever vacation love affair. The older crowd, the men in their thirties to fifties, come to see me. I reassure them. They're not getting older; they're getting better. They are powerful. I am their love slave.

Hey, for twenty bucks in my garter, if you want to think you're Zorro, well buddy, I'll give it to you. It's a human service, costs less than therapy, and probably works better.

I pulled into the parking lot of the Tiffany and backed my Camaro into its space. I stepped out of the car and looked down. There was a pool of dried blood where I'd lain the night before. I shivered and looked diagonally across the lot at the spot where Venus Lovemotion had fallen. Suddenly the familiar seemed sinister. The shadows grew and moved. The customers pulling into the front lot seemed a million miles away.

The back door flew open, slamming against the brick wall, and I jumped. Bruno the bouncer stepped onto the back dock and peered out into the darkness. His hand rested on the butt of the .45 he carried strapped to his waist.

"Don't shoot," I yelled, half kidding.

"Don't give me a reason to," he growled. "Who's that?"

"Who do you think, idiot?"

Bruno's face broke into a smile. "Sierra? That you, baby?"

I let the "baby" remark slide. "Yeah, of course it's me."

He started down the stairs, looking both ways, as if making sure there were no shooters in the bushes this time.

"You shouldn't be here. You're injured. Go home. You know the boss'll pay you."

I walked up to him, wrapping my arm around his thick

muscle-bound waist and squeezing. "Yeah, but you don't see him comping me no tips, do you?"

Bruno laughed. "Son of a bitch wouldn't comp a crumb to a cockroach," he said. "Hey, you're limping! How you gonna dance with a gimp leg?"

"Slowly and not tonight."

Bruno shrugged. I had exceeded his maximum brain capacity for thought and memory.

"Who all's out front tonight?" I asked.

Bruno thought hard. The fuzz he called hair bristled as he rubbed his hand over it.

"The regulars. About the same as last night, only more on account of curiosity. And there's that Italian-Stallion-looking guy, been here the past couple of nights."

"With the good suit?"

"Yeah, him. I noticed that asshole on account of Charlotte telling me he stiffed her for a tip."

Charlotte was Bruno's current girlfriend, a situation that wouldn't last. Women always left Bruno, and I had no idea why. He was a nice enough guy. Maybe I didn't want to know why. There's generally two reasons why women leave nice guys, and only one involves money. I didn't want to think about Bruno and the other reason.

"Who else is here?"

Bruno growled. "That fuck, Little Ricky. Wiseass told me tonight he was gonna wrestle pro. I told him he couldn't pin his own salami. He actually said that wrestling was all fake and all you had to do was have a good act." Bruno shook his head, like Little Ricky had really lost his mind. "Fake. Don't that guy know anything? That ain't fake, Sierra. Wrestling is America's oldest sport. He's defaming our country if he thinks wrestlers are putting on a show. They wouldn't do that."

"Yeah," I said, "Little Ricky's got the brains of a fish."

"Yeah, and the dick to match." Apparently Bruno had heard the rumor, too.

"This something you know firsthand?" I asked.

"What, Sierra, you don't read? I used to use that shit myself, but I got educated in the nick of time. Carl Hiaasen, investigative reporter, in his book *Tourist Season*. Documented fact: use steroids, and your dick shrinks like a cotton sweater. Batta-bing, batta-boom, Buttafuoco."

I wasn't so sure Bruno had quit using steroids, and even if he had, I doubted it had been in the nick of time. There was too much cranial impairment. Still, there was no arguing with logic, not bouncer logic anyway. And it gave me an idea about Little Ricky and Venus Lovemotion. Maybe Venus had heard about Little Ricky. Maybe she had insulted him with her rejection.

When the girls caught sight of me limping into the club on Bruno's beefy arm, all hell broke loose, the good kind of hell. Half-naked women were running up and hugging me, some of them crying. Others were disappointed that I was back and spoiling their shot at greatness, but trying to hide it. None of them seemed more disingenuously happy to see me than Marla.

Marla was angling for the top slot. I could see this because she was sitting in my makeup chair when I walked in. She narrowly missed skinning her own ass jumping out of the seat when she saw me heading for her.

"Grabbing for all the gusto you can get, eh, Marla?"

Marla blushed an angry red and tossed her hair. "Why, Sierra, whatever do you mean? I was checking an eyelash in your magnifying mirror. I would never try to assume—"

"Can the crap. I bet you already got Vincent switching your name to the big letters on the marquee out front. Do I look like an idiot to you?"

I was right, of course. The room fell silent as the other dancers waited for the inevitable and predictable fight. But this time it didn't come. Marla, sensing herself jeopardizing her freedom from a life lived behind bars, stopped. With great effort she looked at me, and only me.

"Well, I must've been overcome. I wanted to do what was best for the Tiffany. We need leadership in this time of crisis. I was only trying to help. After all," she said, "I figured you'd be busy trying to catch Venus Lovemotion's real killer. With you working to save me, it was the least I could do to try and keep up morale around here."

"Oh, give me a break!"

Marla swallowed hard. "Forgive me, Sierra. We are so relieved to have you back. But surely you won't be performing?"

"Hide and watch, big girl, the show is about to go on."

I hadn't been planning to dance, but Marla had called my bluff and who was I to run from a challenge?

Seven

*J*ust before I went on I took a peek through the curtains, out into the house. I make a practice of eyeing the customers before I start into a routine, figuring who the big tippers are, who's a regular, and who's new and needs a little special attention to feel comfortable. Tonight I had an added edge to my curiosity. I was looking to get a bead on Little Ricky so I could warm him up for the interrogation that would come later, and I was looking for the Italian Stallion.

I found Little Ricky right away, in his usual spot two tables back, center. The Italian Stallion was harder to find. He didn't sit where the regulars congregated, back by the bar. He wasn't up front where the tourists and the businessmen sat. He was in a darkened corner booth, sitting so he could eye both the door and the stage.

A man who watches his back and the door is a particular breed. He is either a cop or a man used to fighting his way out of a situation. I fingered him for the latter. He was too immaculately groomed to be a cop. His hands were manicured. He had slicked-back black hair, a gold nugget pinkie ring, and a familiar bulge under his suit jacket. This surprised me, as Bruno usually caught that sort of thing and kept it out of the club.

I saw Marla crossing the floor to Little Ricky, accompanied

by her entourage. Marla, fresh off her encounter with me, would be putting the spin on things so she came out the winner. She'd be talking long and loud about how the cops were looking to frame her, but I was going to do the right thing and set them straight. She'd probably tell them that my cop boyfriend was too dumb to know the truth when he heard it. Well, I couldn't worry about that; I had a show to put on.

I looked over at Rusty, the young redheaded stage manager, and gave him the nod. He signaled the disc jockey to cue the music and dimmed the lights. This was going to be some act to pull off.

As the curtain began to rise, Rusty hit the button on the smoke machine. I limped out and took my place, waiting for the smoke to clear and the spot to hit me. I was dressed in a sheer white, gauze-layered gown, with my hair pinned up. I made sure that the pole was only a foot away, just in case my leg gave out at a crucial moment. True, my wound was superficial, with only a stitch or two required to close it, but it hurt like hell and I didn't want to take any more chances than necessary.

Sheryl Crow started singing "There Goes the Neighborhood" and I began to move with the music. It wasn't as hard as I'd figured. I scanned the audience. Little Ricky was drooling, so I winked at him. The tourists were slowly wandering toward the runway, drinks in hand and dazed looks on their faces, just the way I like 'em.

I ran my hands slowly down the length of my torso, licked my lips, and leaned back against the pole. I was the enchantress, the seductress of all their fantasies. I reached up and unhooked the front of my bikini top. It popped and I held it between my fingers. I controlled when it came off and it wasn't going to until the wallets opened.

When the first guy wandered to the edge of the runway and held out a twenty, I realized I had a problem: I couldn't stoop down for him to stuff the money into my garter. There was a frozen moment as I locked eyes with him and smiled very slowly. Then I bent over from the waist, my 38 double D's about to knock his eyes out, and said: "Go ahead, sweetie, reach up and stuff 'em where you think it'll do the most good."

His eyes widened like I'd opened the floodgates to heaven, and with trembling fingers he stuffed the bill right into my tight cleavage. Bruno, sensing a fine walk with the law on public indecency, moved up behind the dazzled patron and led him away. I straightened, quickly took the twenty and stuffed it in my garter. Then, as the next awestruck customer moved up to make his deposit, I slid slowly back against the pole, using it for support as I toyed with my bikini top.

"Slip it in my garter, sweetie, and I'll give you a big surprise."

The man, pudgy and sweating in anticipation, stuffed his bill into my garter. With that, my bra fell away, and the customer started stammering, "Oh God, oh God!"

I swung around the pole and moved off. Now the men couldn't work fast enough to help me. I shrugged out of the white gauze, leaving it to fall behind me on the stage. I was wearing a thin white G-string, carefully embroidered with translucent sequins. Men squirmed in their seats as I slid my thumbs under the thin strings that crossed my hips. They rushed forward, stuffing bills in my garter.

With one fast, painful move, I bent forward from the waist, pulling the pin from my hair and letting it fall down to brush the floor. There was a collective sigh as I straightened, pulled the tearaway on my G-string, and was enveloped in the thick smoke of the fog machine.

Rusty dashed out onstage, accompanied by Gordon the doorman, and helped me off as the curtains closed behind us. The crowd was wild and the music loud as the next girl got ready to strut on and do her thing.

"Tough act to follow, Sierra," Rusty said.

"Damn," Gordon said, and sighed. "You're the best. Can't nobody top you!"

"Well, you never know, Gordon," I said. "The competition's always breathing down my neck, wanting to topple me."

"Never!" he said.

"No way!" cried Rusty.

"Just let 'em try!" Gordon said. He was developing a crush. The new ones always did that with us dancers. I mean, after all, we create quite an aura. And unlike the strippers, we are not available for a quick tryout or bought for the price of a line of cocaine. No, we have mystique.

"All right, fellas," I said, shrugging into my purple silk kimono, "enough with the kind words. Thank you for helping me out."

"Well, I, for one, meant everything I said," Gordon murmured.

"Thank you, sweetie," I said, stroking his fuzzy chin with my fingertips. I limped off to the dressing room, counting my money as I went. As new acts go, this one had certainly brought in the cash. Just goes to show, it ain't always about how much you move, but more how simply you move. I was moving slow tonight, slow and savory.

By the time I'd slipped into my naughty French maid outfit and walked the distance out into the house, the Italian Stallion had left. Charlotte saw me eyeing his table and walked over.

"Didn't tip me tonight, either!" she huffed. "Just sat there, nursing a B&B, and making notes on little index cards. I'd think he was ATF, but they tip."

"When did he leave?"

Charlotte shifted her tray to one hip. "Right after you finished. He didn't look happy, but then, I have yet to see that guy crack a smile."

Vincent came up and stood right behind her, like he was applying pressure on account of her not doing her job. Charlotte saw him, sniffed, and walked away, her nose in the air and a definite attitude brewing. I felt sorry for Bruno.

"Sierra," Vincent groused, "I'm personally grateful that you took it into your head to show up and perform, but really, you shouldn't have worried. Barry Sanduski's sending in another girl tomorrow to help out, another one of the circuit girls. You know, that was a brilliant idea of yours, having them visiting artists. I got Gordon outside right now, sticking her name up on the marquee."

We wandered outside the front door and looked up. Sure enough, there was Gordon, a panicked look on his face, teetering on Vincent's old wooden ladder and sticking up big black letters: COMING TOMORROW NIGHT — FROSTY LICKS.

I looked from Gordon to Vincent and frowned. "Hey, I don't need no replacement. Venus was fine for a night. On occasion, a visiting artist has a place at the Tiffany, but don't go getting ideas that it should be a regular occurrence."

Gordon looked down at us, a huge letter K slipping from his grasp. "Yeah, Sierra's the queen of the Tiffany. One doesn't send in a scullery maid to be queen for a day." Gordon clearly missed his calling as a third-rate Shakespearean actor.

"Yeah, yeah, whatever," Vincent grumbled. Turning back to me, he started with his minor-league charm act. "Sierra, honey, sweetie, baby, it ain't nothin' to do with you. We need to pull them Atlanta tourists in here. They'll come when they see a name they recognize. And the locals will get to see the big-town movie-star talent. See, babe, it's pure financials."

"Vincent," I said, "bite me. I know financials and I know when I'm getting squeezed. You go pulling porn stars in here to do what trained dancers do, and the quality of your life here at the Tiffany will disintegrate. Your dancers are what make the Tiffany. Circuit girls are all right every now and then, but they got

45

no class and no talent. They're a novelty act, like looking at a two-headed chicken. Your dancers—now, they're your center-ring attraction."

Vincent's jaw was twitching. Behind us, out on the strip, cars drove by, slowing down when they saw me in my French maid outfit and honking their horns.

"See what I mean, Vincent? Quality. You mess with talent and it'll bite you in the ass every time."

I spun around and limped off, fuming. Venus Lovemotion was one thing, but a parade of B-grade bubble brains was quite another. Vincent was bucking for trouble, I could just feel it.

Eight

I can never seem to get enough sleep. I got home, fell into bed, slept for what felt like seconds, and look what happened. Someone was pounding on my door again. I woke up to Fluffy's shrill yapping. She was standing at the edge of the bed, doing her very best to ward off intruders. What was it with people? Did they not get it that I work nights? Why did all my visitors seem to invade my sanctuary in broad daylight? To further complicate matters, the phone started ringing.

I grabbed it and my robe, forgetting about my impairment as I jumped out of bed and felt a sharp stab run up my leg.

"Hello—ouch!"

"Sierra." Raydean's hushed voice rasped over the phone line. "You got company and it don't look like it appears."

"What?"

Usually the Prolixin shot kicked in as soon as they gave it to her, but it didn't sound like Raydean was too firmly grounded this morning.

"Approach cautiously. Examine for bugs or other alien subterfuge. It don't look right to me. Maybe it's a bomb!" The line went dead as the pounding continued at the kitchen door.

I peered out cautiously through the peephole and saw roses. I unlocked the door, swung it open, and came face-to-face with a delivery boy holding a mass of bloodred roses. Not my favorite color, but then, one mustn't look a gift horse in the proverbial mouth.

"Sierra Lavotini?" the pimple-faced teen squeaked.

"You don't know? I guess at your age, you don't know. Yeah, that's me."

"Okay." He shoved the vase of flowers into my arms and took off. Before I could do or say anything, he was driving off, the heavy thump of the bass line to his music vibrating through the neighborhood.

I peered over the roses to Raydean's trailer. The door slowly opened and she appeared, shotgun not quite hidden behind her back.

"See? What I tell you? Damn roses! Oldest trick in the book. Gain entry, subdue victim with charm, and take over the world."

"Raydean, these are harmless. Come on over here and see." Raydean was undecided for a moment, then started out of the trailer. "Leave the gun at your house, please."

She scowled but left it behind. She approached cautiously. "I'm telling you, there's something not right about receiving flowers from a stranger."

"Come on, I'll make coffee. Besides, Raydean, what makes you think they're from a stranger?" I knew who needed to be sending flowers. It was a lovely way to apologize, even if yellow or pink roses were the better choice.

Raydean walked behind me into the kitchen, still keeping her distance. "What does the card say?" she asked.

I reached into the bouquet and extracted the tiny florist's envelope, opened the flap, and pulled out the card. *"Hope you stay as lovely as you are. Stick with what you know. I'll take care of you."*

Well, if he'd wanted to apologize, John Nailor'd missed the mark. Raydean snatched the card from my fingers and read it, holding it out at arm's length because she'd forgotten her glasses.

"Aha!" she cried. "Alien death threats!"

I set the vase on the counter and started to make the coffee. My hands shook slightly and I watched them as if they belonged to someone else. No, it wasn't a threat. John just wasn't good with words. I poured water in the machine, measured the coffee carefully into the filter basket, and turned back to look at Raydean and Fluffy.

"I'll just call him and say thank you," I said softly, but I wasn't fooling anyone. It just wasn't Nailor's style to send flowers, to back down from an argument.

"Denial's a river in Egypt," Raydean said, her eyes soft with understanding.

I dialed the police department, holding the phone close to my ear, waiting for the call to go through.

"Criminal Investigations, Nailor." His voice was strong and familiar, and for a second that was enough.

"Hey," I said. "Thanks for the flowers and the card. They're lovely."

There was a long moment of silence, then the words I didn't want to hear.

"They weren't from me, but I guess that happens all the time." Now he was pissed.

"Not from you? But the card referred back to yesterday's misunderstanding."

"Yeah, well, maybe you got another guy misunderstanding you," he growled. "I figure that's right common, too."

I bit my tongue. "So you didn't send me a dozen roses with a card saying to stick with what I know and you'd take care of me?"

More silence. "I'll be right over," he said, and severed the connection.

"Called out the reinforcements, did you?" Raydean asked.

"No, but it seems they're coming anyway."

We were headed for disaster, that much I knew. Two steel-headed opponents, steering through a collision course. I knew what he'd want, what he'd say, and I wasn't coming down on the same side of the matter. The only thing a threat meant was that I was on the right track. Someone was afraid of what I'd uncover. To me, that meant I was the only person close enough to the murder to solve it. Nailor wasn't going to like it, but then, that was his problem, not mine.

Nine

Raydean and I stared at each other. Behind us the coffeemaker hissed to a stop, but neither of us moved to pour the coffee.

"Looks like we got us another kettle of fish to fry," she said. "Mayhaps the aliens want you, mayhaps the guy what done killed that pretty girl wants you 'cause you're on to him. Either way, you'd better CYA. In fact, your ass has already taken a good hit, I'd cover it extra special if I were you."

Raydean went and peered out the bay window. "Reckon that feller'll be screaming down the highway to save you." She and I snorted at the same time. "Way I recollect, you saved his bacon last time. I figure he'll be looking to repay the favor."

As if on cue, John Nailor's Taurus turned into the trailer park.

Raydean sighed. "Love, it's a turrible thing." She looked from the window back to me. "I think I'll clear a path and let you young kids have a shot at bliss. Nothing like the fear of mortality to bring two people closer."

Fluffy, sensing or perhaps hearing Nailor's car, flew into the room, skidded on the floor, and bounced off the window ledge. She yipped, shook her head, and kept right on going, out the doggie door and down the steps.

"See what I mean?" Raydean said, and opened the door.

Nailor looked up through his windshield, took in Raydean standing like a specter at the top of my stoop, and instinctively reached under his armpit for his holster. Just as quickly, he let his hand drop and moved swiftly out of the car, standing with the door as a buffer between him and Raydean.

"Don't worry," she said. "I ain't armed and you ain't man enough to take me anyway."

Nailor smiled. "No doubt, ma'am," he said softly.

Raydean sailed down the steps and out into the road, passing Nailor as if she were the queen and he a loyal subject. When she had crossed her yard and reached the top of her own steps, she turned to face us.

"You have my blessings," she said, and walked inside her trailer, the door slamming behind her.

Nailor shook his head and climbed the steps to stand beside me.

"You all right?"

"Never better," I answered. "You didn't need to come out here, you know."

"I know." His eyes melted into mine. He wasn't thinking about danger, and a moment later, neither was I.

"We got off on the wrong foot yesterday," he said. He reached out with one hand and touched my cheek.

"Hell, Nailor, we got off on the wrong foot just a few minutes ago."

He frowned. "Let me see the card."

I handed him the florist's card and he studied it and the tiny envelope, turning them over and over in his hands. Fluffy came back into the kitchen and stood next to him, panting.

"I'm with you, girl," I muttered.

"Which florist was it?" he asked.

"I don't know. What does the envelope say?"

Nailor held the envelope out for me to see. It was pure snow white, no florist's imprint. "Did you see the delivery van?"

"It was a kid in a car."

"Shit." We both spoke at the same time. I turned away and went to the coffeemaker, pouring us both mugs of steaming liquid, black, the way we both liked it, undiluted and strong.

"I figure someone thinks my nosing around might uncover something."

Nailor took a sip of his coffee and eyed me over the rim of the cup. "You aren't going away, are you?" he asked.

"Are you?"

We studied each other, the conversation hitting on two levels. "I have to be involved," he said.

"And so do I. I just don't get a badge and a gun to work with."

Nailor stepped closer to me. "This time you ought to know something about self-defense."

He smelled too good to resist.

"I think I can handle myself," I said softly. A moment later I felt my body falling, landing hard on the kitchen floor, pain shooting from the good side of my ass to the bad. He was on me, his hands pinning my shoulders to the ground, a determined look on his face.

"If you could handle yourself," he said, "I wouldn't be able to do this."

Fluffy went wild. She lunged at Nailor and bit him right in the meaty part of his forearm.

"Ouch!"

"Fluffy, no! It's all right, girl."

A thin trickle of blood ran down Nailor's arm. Fluffy stood back, snarling, ready to further defend me.

"Well," I said, Nailor still sitting on top of me, "guess I can handle myself. Guess if I really wanted you off of me, you'd be gone, or maimed by a killer chihuahua. Next time I might not call her off. I might let her chew a while longer."

Nailor shot Fluffy a nasty look. Fluffy smiled, but it wasn't her friendly smile. Her hero had suddenly gone south on her.

"Fluffy doesn't travel with you in a murder investigation, Sierra. You know what I'm saying. Now, let me show you a couple of things."

Pain was radiating through my backside. I wasn't in the mood. "Let me up."

"No," he said. "Make me."

I was getting angrier by the second, feeling the white-hot Lavotini temper well up inside me. Nailor didn't know what he was asking for.

He leaned forward and pressed his hands down on my shoulders. "I said, make me."

That was all it took. I tried bucking like a horse, tried to move my arms to gouge his eyes out, tried to kick, but he had me pinned.

"Want me to show you what to do?" He was grinning, enjoying himself.

"Fuck you, Nailor."

"That too, but not now. You want me to show you how to get out of this?"

I sighed. Men were such children. "Sure, show me. Knock yourself out."

"All right. Here, pull your leg up, outside mine, like that." He reached back and positioned my left leg. "Now, bring your arms up, inside mine, and hit here." He showed me a spot inside his forearm. "Hit hard, it's a pressure point. It hurts when you do that."

I whacked ineffectually and he stared down at me, his eyes meeting mine. "Oh, come on," he whispered. "Get your money's worth. Hit me."

I hit, hard, and he half fell onto my chest. "All right," he said, "use your leg, roll over and off."

I hurt. I was tired. And like I said, I wasn't in the mood.

Something inside me snapped and I heaved, using my leg to push him off balance. Over he went, but just as quickly he was back, lunging over top of me and positioning himself above me. This time his legs were outside. He was getting ready to teach me yet another of his little techniques, but I didn't wait. I brought both knees up, hitting him squarely in the most vulnerable area of his body.

He grunted. I hit his right arm, pushed him off balance with my left arm, and rolled away. Fluffy went ballistic, this time attacking Nailor's thick shoes.

I stood up and stared down at him. "Any questions?" I said. The adrenaline was surging through my body and I wanted to take him out. It took every effort not to kick him, but some last vestige of civilized behavior took over. He was, after all, only trying to help.

Nailor started to laugh, lying back on the kitchen floor, with my dog doing her best to kill his shoe.

"Hey, Fluff," I said, "you can knock it off now. He gives up." Fluffy looked at me, her teeth still gripping Nailor's shoe. "Want a doggie treat?" She dropped the shoe and came trotting over.

Nailor lay there for a moment, watching, then struggled to his feet and walked toward me, the smile fading slowly from his lips.

"Sierra, you know this is serious. It's not a game. Venus Lovemotion wasn't the victim of a drive-by or any other random act. Your friend Marla has never played on your team. She doesn't like you. For all I know, the bullet was intended for you and hit Venus only by accident."

"You think I don't know that?" I asked. "If somebody, and it wasn't Marla, wanted to hurt me, then I got all the more reason to find out what's going on."

Nailor shook his head. "I can't stop you, but it's suicide. I wish for once in your hardheaded lifetime you'd let someone take care of you."

"Yeah, well, I haven't had a great record with caretakers. And I find taking care of myself works out a whole lot better. I like a relationship built on a more solid foundation than one person needing another."

Nailor sighed. "It's not about that, Sierra. I'm in a position to help you out here. It's something I do for a living."

I walked over to him, slipped my arms around his waist, and kissed him gently on the lips.

"How about this, 'cause you know I'm not walking away: I nose around my way, you investigate your way, and we both watch each other's back."

He didn't like it. He thought I was playing with him, but what could he do? He pulled me closer and kissed me harder. His hands slipped up under my shirt, investigating. Things were starting to heat up when the phone rang. It was Little Ricky, his slick, weasel voice oozing through the receiver.

"Hey, Sierra, I want to see you. I think maybe I know something that can help Marla."

I choked off a thousand sarcastic responses and told him to meet me at the club. Nailor, sensing a change in the disposition of his afternoon, sighed and straightened his tie.

"You could meet me here later," I whispered, running my fingers across his shoulders and looking deep into his eyes. I had plans for this man, and they didn't include learning how to defend myself.

His pager answered for him, shrilling out into the quiet of my kitchen, instantly pulling his attention away. He looked at the little box, shook his head, and then looked back at me.

"Duty calls," he said.

Fluffy had had all the excitement she could take for one day.

Without warning, we both heard the unmistakable sound of water hitting the floor.

"Oh God, Sierra!"

I looked down at his shoes. Fluffy had finally claimed them as her own.

Ten

I reached the Tiffany Gentleman's Club by four o'clock in the afternoon. The parking lot was bright with reflected sunlight that bounced from the white stucco walls to the windshield of my car. In Florida, sunglasses are more than a fashion statement; they are a necessity.

I walked across the parking lot and stepped into the dark recesses of the Tiffany. It was that awkward time between the lunch crowd and the after-work crowd, when no one but losers sit on the barstools and only the lowest-ranking dancers vie for the customer's attention. It was naptime, and business was slow.

The bartender was grumpy from lunch and not looking forward to the after-work crush. The waitresses sat at the end of the bar talking among themselves, irritated if a customer tried to interrupt them with a drink order. After all, they'd done lunch with its hustle and bustle of impatient customers all trying to beat the clock and get back to the office.

Little Ricky sat with the losers. Wedged in between a fat telephone repairman and a bearded truck-driver type, he looked even seedier than usual. He spotted me instantly, almost before I could identify him. He was up and off the stool, making just enough commotion for his companions to notice that he was approaching me like an old friend.

"Sierra, honey!" he cried, and every head in the half-deserted bar turned to look at us.

"Don't touch the merchandise," I said, trying to smile and fend off his unwelcome hug at the same time. "I mean, I'm still in a lot of pain and I can't take it."

Little Ricky never knew a social cue, but the look in my eye told him to back off and do it quickly.

"Come on over here," I said, trying to make my voice sound both friendly and interested. It was a stretch. I led him to a booth, the same one the Italian Stallion had occupied the night before. Ricky slid across the seat and patted the leather space next to him. I pretended not to notice and slid in across from him. I had the advantage. He'd called me before I'd had to call him.

"So, you said you had something to tell me about Marla?"

A confused look crossed Little Ricky's face, then he smiled, as if remembering.

"That I did," he said, "but let's relax a bit first, get to know each other." He raised his arm and snapped his fingers in the direction of the waitresses. They were not impressed. One of them recognized me and stood up, wandering slowly toward the table.

"Ricky," I said, "etiquette demands that you do not snap your fingers at the barmaids. A, it is rude. B, one of them might decide to hurt you, as a morality lesson to other customers. And C, you don't know what they do when they make your drinks and they're pissed."

Ricky took this in, not sure at first if he should believe me, but finally deciding I might know more about barmaid habits than him. When the girl stepped up to the table, she found a humble Little Ricky waiting on her.

"Darlin'," he said, "I don't know what came over me there. I did not think. See, I was in New York City yesterday, promoting my new professional wrestling video, and I guess I got swept up in northern rude behaviors that are far from my own gentlemanly manners."

The waitress, a short blonde with a tiny chest and a wad of gun stuck in her mouth, regarded him as if he were a common species of toad.

"Bullshit, Little Ricky," she said. "I seen you in here yesterday afternoon and you were just as rude. Now whatc'hu want?"

Little Ricky looked nervous, thinking about his personal safety and drinks that were the least prone to staff tampering.

"Well, honey, bring me a long-neck, twist top, but don't open it. I need the exercise."

The waitress nodded and turned to me. "What're you doing here?"

"Slumming."

The little barmaid nodded again, looked at Ricky, and smiled back at me. "You want coffee or somethin'?"

"Coke'd be nice, if it's no trouble."

"Uh-uh," she said, "it ain't no trouble at all."

She flounced off and Little Ricky watched her, his eyes tracking the way she moved, calculating the odds of ever improving his options.

"You got one hope," I said.

Ricky looked back, puzzled.

"Tip her more than the cost of the beer and you might be safe." He frowned, then smiled. After all, what was a three-dollar tip when you might get lucky later?

"Now, tell me about Marla."

Ricky knew he was on the losing end of getting to know me better, so he retreated.

"Marla couldn't have killed that girl," he said finally.

"And why is that?" I asked.

"Because I had her gun. She asked me to hold it for her so she wouldn't shoot nobody."

The music cranked up and another new girl strutted out onto the runway and began to work the pole. She was obviously a stripper; dancers have routines, they think about their art. This girl was doing her best impression of a work for hire, later, in a sleazy hotel room.

"What?" I said, trying to be heard over the music.

"Yeah, I held her gun because she was mad at that Venus for coming on to me. I took it because I know about her temper."

"Well," I said, "all right. At least we can give the gun to the police. They'll test it and see that it hasn't been fired, and Marla will be clear."

The day was looking up. The barmaid appeared with Ricky's beer, opened of course, and my Coke, complete with straw.

Ricky's face went blank, then fearful. I assumed it was because his beer had been opened, but I was wrong.

"Sierra, I don't have the gun."

"What do you mean, you don't have the gun?"

"Well, I went out to my car to get it and it was gone."

This was not news that I wanted to hear. In fact, it was the very last thing I wanted to hear.

"All right, Ricky. When did you last see the gun and when did you remember to go look for it?"

Ricky's foot slid slowly across the floor and bumped mine. When he didn't move it away, I moved my leg. The idiot was trying to come on to me and hang Marla, all at the same time.

"Ricky!"

"All right! I put it in my glove box directly after Marla threatened Venus. I went out to her car, took it, and put it in my car. I didn't recollect about it until this morning when Marla said the cops were looking for her gun and she couldn't find it. I said 'Well, baby, don't you remember I took it and put it in my car?'"

My heart sank. "Marla thought you still had her gun?"

Ricky nodded eagerly. "But Marla don't have it. It's gone."

The sap couldn't figure it out that the cops would just think Marla took the gun, used it, and lost it. Or, a second and third explanation arose, that Little Ricky or someone else took Marla's gun and used it to kill Venus Lovemotion. Better yet, maybe Marla's gun wasn't used by the killer at all. It would just help if we had it, then we could rule her out. But I had a feeling. When something can go wrong, it usually does, so the gun that killed Venus and winged me was probably Marla's. It just figured. It was just the way things tended to run in life.

I looked back at the worm and tried my best not to let my true homicidal feelings seep out. Ricky found my leg again and rubbed his foot up against it. He had kicked off his shoes and was running his sweaty, smelly toes all over my calf. I waited a second, until I knew for certain where his other foot rested, and then jabbed the point of my heel into the meaty flesh of his big toe.

Ricky screamed with pain and gained an audience. Even the stripper who was doing her best to wrap her tits around the pole had to stop and stare.

"Oh God, sugar," I said, "was that your foot?" Ricky couldn't answer. He was clutching his foot, pulling it up into his lap and moaning. I guessed steroids didn't dull one's pain threshold.

"I am sooo sorry. I thought that was the table base. Oh, is it bleeding?" Steroids did not add IQ points to Little Ricky's marginal intelligence. He looked up at me with big cow eyes, believed me instantly, and said: "That's all right, baby. I'll be fine."

But his foot was swelling and he couldn't slip it back into his fake leather cowboy boots. When he tried to signal the waitress and have her fix him an ice bag, she ignored him. I stood up, looking very concerned.

"You sit right here, Ricky," I said, "and I'll try and find something for you."

Ricky sat there like a big, hurting baby as I turned and walked off, right through the back hallway, out the back door, and to my car. The little blond waitress said later that when he asked for me, she told him I had run out to the drugstore and probably gotten into an accident while trying to rush back. This was right before she handed him a supersized condom from the men's room, filled with crushed ice, and told him to stick it where it could do the most good.

Eleven

Marla lived in a high-rise condo right out on the Gulf of Mexico in the center of the Miracle Strip, Panama City Beach's tackiest few miles of souvenir shops, bars, and gooney golf emporiums. Unlike me, Marla liked to flaunt that she made good money. She drove a hot red convertible and ate out every day. She was a local fixture, well-known in the tackier dress shops, the kind that sell clothing covered in beads and sequins.

I took the glass elevator up to her apartment, my stomach lurching with each floor. It was a long way down and I have trust issues with man-made equipment.

I pounded on her door and listened to her singing along to a Cher track. She sang off-key and loudly all the way to the door, and only stopped when she realized her caller was female.

The door swung open and she stood there in a flimsy white dressing gown trimmed with fake ostrich feathers. In the daylight, even with her makeup on, Marla is a scary-looking creature. I think it's all that makeup and the way she tweezes her eyebrows so that they're kind of triangular, like Dr. Spock's on *Star Trek*.

"What?" she asked. "Is it all over?"

I pushed past her, out of the thickly carpeted hallway and into her foyer.

"No, hardly. I need to ask you some questions, and this time you'd better be straight with me and not leave nothing out."

Marla widened her eyes. "Well, Sierra, whatever do you mean? I have shown you the utmost honesty."

"You ain't shown me shit, Marla. We're going to have a good, old-fashioned talk about guns, tempers, and boyfriends."

Marla tried to smooth it over. "Goodie," she cried. "Girl talk!"

"There ain't no girls talking here, Marla. Why didn't you tell me you gave your gun to Little Ricky? Why didn't you tell the police? In fact, you should've turned it right over to them. They have tests they can do, Marla. They can look at your gun and tell straight off if it's been fired."

The look on her face told me more than I wanted to know.

"You fired the gun, didn't you?" A bad feeling crept up through my gut. I never had liked Marla and the feeling was mutual on her part. Why had I ever agreed to help her? It just never occurred to me that Marla might have nobody in her life for a reason. She might have killed them all off.

She looked down at her toes, shiny pink lacquered ones, and said nothing.

"Marla, I have to ask you this: Did you kill Venus Lovemotion?"

Her head shot up. "No! How could you think such a thing?" Marla was holding to the letter of the law. She was pulling a Clinton on me.

"Marla, did you fire your gun in Venus Lovemotion's direction?"

She shrugged, cocked her head, and gave me a very hard look. She was cracking, but not fast enough. I stepped forward quickly, shoving her shoulders with both hands. She lost her balance and stumbled backward, fear replacing the hostile look. I went after her, grabbing a handful of her long black hair and wrapping it tightly around my hand, then I yanked, hard.

"Let go!" Her eyes filled with tears and I took another step closer, forcing her to pull back and hurt herself more.

"Don't dick around with me, Marla. I'm the only person playing on your team, and believe me, I'm not doing it for you. Did you try to shoot Venus Lovemotion or not?"

"All right, all right! Yes! But it isn't like you thought."

I let go of her hair and waited. She rubbed her scalp and looked at me like she wanted to try and even the score.

"When I found her with Ricky, I don't know, something inside me just started seeing red. Next thing I knew I was standing by my car and somebody had fired a shot."

"Then what happened?" I asked.

Marla shrugged and chuckled. "Well, Ricky ran over, grabbed my arm, and took the gun away. Venus ran like a rabbit back inside, and that's when I let Ricky keep the gun."

I stared at her. Was she telling the truth? Somehow I didn't think so.

"Let me get this straight. You fired a shot at Venus, but nobody heard it or reported it? I frankly find that hard to believe."

"As God is my witness," Marla said solemnly.

"If God was witnessing half of your shit, Marla, she would've struck you dead a long time ago. Now, where's the gun?"

"I don't know."

I looked past Marla, through the picture window in her living room, and contemplated throwing her off the balcony.

"Honest," she swore. "You have it all now. The truth. Me and Little Ricky, we've just been so frightened. We didn't know who to trust. Honest, hon, I didn't think you'd need to know about me trying to shoot that slut. I figured it would only make things worse, and frankly, they're bad enough."

She seemed so pathetically eager for me to believe her. For an entire moment I forgot Marla was a chronic liar. I started thinking that maybe it wouldn't be such a bad deal if Vincent lost the club to the IRS. Hell, with what I'd saved up, maybe I could buy the place and run it right. But, no, then I'd have headaches like Marla on a daily basis. It was best to deal with the current mess and never get stuck this way again.

"All right, you gave the gun to Little Ricky, and it disappeared sometime after the shooting. I'm accepting your premise. How much time elapsed between your encounter with Venus and her getting shot for real?"

Marla squinted, allegedly a sign that she was deep in thought. "I'm guessing two hours or so. We were all done for the night. The bar'd been closed for an hour or more and all the customers were supposed to be gone. That's why it was so weird that one of them was backstage and holding the door for me when I left."

I wanted to slap her. "There was a customer backstage when you left? Marla, why didn't you tell me that? That's important! You know Vincent's rule. Customers never come backstage!"

Marla stamped her foot impatiently and glared at me. "Sierra, I can't remember every little detail of life! When Venus got killed, it kind of drove the policies and procedure manual right out of my head. You just sort of forget that stuff in a time of crisis."

"Which customer was it, Marla?"

She gave me a frustrated look. "I don't know his name. He wasn't a regular."

"Then didn't it occur to you to call Bruno and have his ass bounced to the curb? He wasn't supposed to be there. What did he look like?"

"Oh, you know him," she said. "New guy. Sharp dresser. Italian-looking. Kind of looks like he's always in a bad mood. I figured he was waiting on somebody. I didn't figure he'd be back there if someone hadn't said it was okay."

I just stared at her. That's Marla for you, never thinking, always assuming, bury-your-head-in-the-sand Marla.

"Right, Marla. Maybe he was waiting on Venus so he could shoot her!"

Marla gasped.

"That's right, kid. You just keep coming up with those little tidbits. Don't trouble yourself to think back over the night or try too hard to help yourself. Hell, who knows, at this rate you might be next."

Her eyes widened.

"Oh, yeah, Marla. See, it's like this." I took a step closer to her and she started to back up. "Whoever killed Venus will kill again. After you kill your first victim, the second one comes easier. The third and fourth, well, it's old hat. So the killer, if it isn't you, is sitting around wondering who saw him. He's wondering if there are any witnesses he needs to dispense with."

Marla looked really frightened now.

"So, if you're holding back any little details, anything at all that I could use to help out here, you should tell me."

I turned around and started walking toward the door.

"Wait," she called.

I turned back around, my hand on the doorknob.

"There is one more thing," she said, her voice breathy with fear.

"What?"

"That Italian guy was a really bad tipper."

I looked back, wishing I could vaporize her. I pulled the door open, stepped out of it, and slammed it shut behind me. Marla wasn't going to be any help at all. If anyone was going to save the Tiffany from an IRS lien, it would have to be me. At least I had somewhere to go. I was going to track down a well-dressed Italian who hadn't finessed the fine art of tipping but may have perfected the craft of murder.

Twelve

Raydean and Fluffy were waiting for me when I returned home. They sat across the road from my trailer, at the top of Raydean's steps, side by side, and they didn't look happy.

I pulled the Camaro onto my parking pad and got out, thinking it might be better to ignore them than to try and cater to their obviously rotten moods. But it was Fluffy's sigh that stopped me short. I heard it clear across the two yards. It was the sigh of someone who has given up hope.

"You two look like you've been to a bad funeral," I said. I was hoping that if I sounded cheery, they'd lighten up, but it had no visible effect.

Raydean sighed and looked down at Fluffy. "It's a turrible world," she said. "My girlfriend, here, found true love, only to have it blow up in her face."

I looked harder and started walking slowly across the narrow street toward Raydean's yard. Fluffy did indeed seem dazed and lost.

"What happened?"

Raydean shook her head. "I was weeding." "Weeding" is Raydean's euphemism for checking the various traps and snares she's rigged throughout her tiny yard to keep intruders and aliens at bay. "I looked up when I heard the doggie door and saw Fluffy come running out of the house and down the steps, dashing into the arms of a most handsome young Chihuahua."

"Raydean, dogs do not have arms."

"Whatever," she sighed. "Anyway, when she reached the edge of the driveway, the dog blew slap up!"

"What?" The concern I felt edged into my voice and made Raydean jump. She reached behind her back and pulled out a few tangled pieces of tan plastic and some thin red and blue wires.

"See this here?" she asked. "It's a mechanical robotized dog. A toy, Sierra. Someone put this thing at the edge of your driveway while I was otherwise occupied. When Fluffy ran out, it exploded. Liked to have pushed my pacemaker into an early grave, girl!"

Raydean stretched out her arm and wrapped it around Fluffy, who had started shivering. "Girl, them boys ain't at all what they seem. Since the invasion, you can't take nothing for granted, especially love." Raydean, sensing a theme, started humming "Love Is a Many Splendored Thing" to herself. Fluffy moaned, and Raydean, taking this for approval, began to sing in earnest.

"Raydean!" I shouted. "Did you see who did this?"

Raydean shook her head, completed the verse, and turned to look at me. "No," she said. "Did you?"

I shook my head and my shoulders slumped in defeat. Did no one take this as seriously as I did? As if in answer, a car's engine came within earshot, loud and powerful. I knew that car. I looked up at Raydean.

"Well, at least I done one thing right," she said. "I called in the law. At least one of us is gonna find true love and happiness." In the distance, I heard the faint wail of sirens. He was bringing reinforcements in response to whatever it was Raydean had said when she called. This was not going to be pretty.

Fluffy stood, her tail wagging as she identified Nailor's car.

What was it about that man that just seemed to drive women wild?

His car whipped onto my street, jerking to a stop in front of my house. Nailor jumped out, his gun drawn and an anxious look on his face.

"Where is the bomb exactly?" he asked.

I suppose the rest of the afternoon would've gone better had I not laughed, but I couldn't help myself. He looked so officious and cute in his Kevlar vest and helmet. The safety glasses he'd pulled on were an extra-special touch.

Raydean reached over and held up the detonated dog, now a mass of wire and plastic.

"False alarm," she said calmly. "It was just another death threat, disguised as true love."

Nailor lowered his gun and glowered at Raydean.

"I'm taking you in," he said as the first patrol car pulled to a halt. "I'm having you committed to the state hospital and they won't let you see daylight for a hundred years!"

I turned on him. There was no call for scaring Raydean. She'd meant well enough.

"Now, wait just a minute," I said.

"No, you wait, Sierra. I've humored her and tried to be fair, but this just takes the cake."

"Listen to me," I said. I took a step toward him, hoping he would read the urgency of the situation in my face and realize this wasn't just a false alarm. "Someone left a toy dog in my driveway, and when Fluffy came outside, they detonated it. It's a miracle Fluffy wasn't killed."

Nailor looked back at Raydean and the mass of wires, then turned to look back at the two squad cars full of combat-ready officers and bomb-sniffing dogs. He signaled to them, and with obvious disappointment they departed. Nailor took a moment to remove his helmet and safety glasses, then the heavy ceramic-plated vest. When he walked toward us, it was with a calmer attitude. You just can't fight city hall, especially not where Raydean's involved. You just go with the flow and hope you don't drown.

Nailor knew all about Raydean's yard, yet he hesitated at the edge of her little patch of lawn and stared up at her, as if waiting for a bobby-trap update.

"Ain't nothin' a wise human cain't avoid for hisself," she said. "You've been through it all before."

He nodded and walked up the narrow paved path to her door, avoided the third stair step, and ducked under the nearly invisible fishing line that attached to a water-filled bucket tucked up just under the awning. Raydean reached behind her back and pulled out the detonated dog.

"Careful," she said. "Explosives can be dangerous in the wrong hands."

Nailor sighed and his back stiffened. I could imagine the many things he wanted to say to her, but saying them would've only caused Raydean to clam up.

"Thank you," he said in a tightly controlled cop voice. "Maybe y'all could tell me what you know about this"—he hesitated—"this . . . invasion."

That brought Raydean around to his side again, and his threat to hospitalize her was forgotten. With great care, she repeated everything she'd told me, with one addition.

"I didn't see the fella what done this, but I heard a car slow down in between our two houses, just about the time Fluffy come running out. I was around back, weeding. I am always alert to invasion potential, so I stopped, especially when I picked up on the tune playing on his radio." She had our complete attention. Raydean leaned forward, looked both ways up and down the street, and spoke in a conspiratorial tone. "You see, I ain't heard that tune in a long, long while, not since Dan Hicks and his Hot

Licks used to play the VFW up home and my dearly departed husband would request it."

"What was it, sugar?" I asked, hoping to stop her from straying down memory lane.

" 'How Can I Miss You When You Won't Go Away.' " Raydean leaned back and smiled. "I never took it personal. He was just a fool for a catchy tune."

Nailor was giving up. He turned to walk back down the steps, the wires and plastic cradled in his hands. Raydean let him get about halfway down the path before she dropped another bomb.

"Yep, them floral delivery folks must really love their music."

Nailor turned back around. "How's that, Raydean?" he asked.

"Well, unless I miss my guess, and I don't usually, it was the same car as what brought them flowers to Sierra. It was running rough."

Nailor obviously didn't give this much credence. How could an old woman tell the sound of one car's engine from another? He shrugged and started to turn away, but Raydean cleared her throat.

"Oh, and he was listening to that same song when he drove up to bring her the flowers."

Nailor looked at me. Once again, Raydean had come through.

Thirteen

Nailor didn't hang around to discuss the finer points of police investigatory technique. He was off for the forensics lab, dragging his broken toy dog with him. The only thing he would allow was that the dog had been meant as a warning.

"If they'd wanted to seriously hurt you or Fluffy, they'd have made a real bomb. This was just a little follow-up to the flowers. They want you uninvolved, Sierra, a sentiment I echo, though not quite like that."

He didn't make me any promises. He didn't even look at me with anything other than his cop's eyes. He was on the job. I was for later, a reward after a hard day's work. I could live with that. I had my own career to tend to. If I didn't show up at the club and make my presence known, who knew what lowlife dancer Vincent Gambuzzo would let try and take over my job?

I settled Fluffy down with Raydean for the evening, leaving them to a Braves game, a boxful of Moon Pies, and a pile of doggie treats. If Fluffy didn't die from an overdose of doggie junk food, she'd be fine, and safe. No one was going to bother Raydean, not without a hell of a fight. At least I hoped not . . .

"You go on, Sierra," Raydean said from her perch on the sofa. "Me and Fluffy will be fine. Besides, Marlena won't take no crap off invaders." Marlena the Shotgun leaned against the corner, fully loaded and ready for action. "Go on now, honey." Raydean urged.

I left her sitting on the sofa with Fluffy and yelling at the Braves' pitching coach. It was time to turn my attention back to the Tiffany. On a normal night when I'm driving to the club, I focus on Sierra, Queen of Passion. Tonight my thoughts were all over the place. I was worried about Fluffy and Raydean. I could take care of myself, but they were vulnerable. The killer knew this.

The killer appeared to be threatened by me, or maybe the killer had picked me as his next target. That thought was new. Maybe the fact that I was "on the case" wasn't an issue. Maybe the killer was targeting dancers. Maybe Venus had been only the first. Or worse, maybe the killer had been aiming for me and Venus had caught the bullet.

My mind raced as I crossed Hathaway Bridge. Below me, boats crisscrossed the bay, their running lights twinkling against the inky-black water. Stars hung in the early-evening sky, winking out one by one as they made their appearance. The night was clear and warm. On a regular night I might've lingered by the water as I headed into work, driving slowly to catch the spring breeze against my skin. As a dancer, I try to connect with my inner being; it brings me more in touch with my sensuality. Tonight it was all I could do to drive.

By the time I pulled into the parking lot and parked, I had pretty much given up on doing one of my regular theme-centered acts. It's hard to pull off Little Bo Peep when you're injured. No, tonight was red velvet and elegance.

Rusty the stage manager saw me step inside the back door and ran up, his eyes wide with surprise. He twitched and looked from me to the locker room. With a jerky leap, he positioned himself between me and the door.

"Hey, Sierra," he squeaked. "You're supposed to be home taking it easy. What're you doing? You need rest, lots of rest."

I raised one eyebrow, straightened up so I towered over him, and proceeded to push my way toward the dressing room.

"Sierra, I don't think—"

"Obviously," I said, and walked on into the room.

A strange woman sat in my chair, in front of my station, peering into my mirror. The other girls looked up and all conversation came to a standstill. It took the newcomer a few moments to realize that the room had frozen. She stopped, mascara wand in hand, and turned slowly around. She was blond, bottle color, a cheap brand if I had to guess from the brassy, home-done highlights. Her eyes were empty sky blue and she had a little baby-doll nose that tilted up like a miniature ski jump.

"Hi!" she said in a perky, cheerleader voice. "I'm Frosty Licks."

I just stood there, taking it all in, trying not to act out of my inner-child rage.

The blonde took it wrong and proceeded to ram her foot farther down her throat. "Oh, hon, I know. I'm a movie star, true, but really, sweetie, we're just people." She giggled and one of the regulars gasped. Frosty was clueless.

"Well," I said, "ain't that nice. My name's Sierra, just like it says on the back of that chair where you're sitting."

Frosty looked at the back of the chair and smiled. "Ain't that cute! They put your names on the chairs." There was a sudden swift change as her previously empty eyes darkened and flickered. "Well, I'm sure you can find another spot to roost. Mr. Gambuzzo said to sit here and here's where I'm staying. I mean, after all, I'm the visiting star. And I would appreciate it if you girls kept the noise down while I'm trying to do my makeup. I need to concentrate. After all, I am an artist, not a stripper."

I crossed the room in three, long strides, my ass no longer a factor. I wasn't feeling pain at that moment. I grabbed the back of the chair and yanked, dumping the cheery little guest star on the dressing room's comfy little concrete floor. I bent down, grabbed a hank of Frosty's hair, and pulled her head back so she could see me better.

"I don't care what Gambuzzo told you to do. I don't care what flat-backing flick you just got off doing, and I certainly don't give a rat's ass what you think. I'm the star here, and you are just a gnat in my galaxy. So while you're here, you'll be playing by my rules. You'll sit down at the end of the bar where there's an empty chair. You'll be polite and courteous to the staff, and you'll keep your little trap shut. Are we clear?"

"I'll tell my agent about this and you won't have a job tomorrow."

I let go, straightened, and looked at the others. "Hey, I'm frightened by that. Aren't youse guys frightened?" The others moaned in mock terror.

"Oh, yes," I said, turning to look at her. "We are definitely terrified. Oh, please, don't tell your agent."

Frosty struggled to get up, raising her hand and gripping my wrist. I grabbed her thumb and bent it backward until she screamed softly.

"You're not playing nice so far," I said. "Now, let's try this again. Whose rules are you playing by?"

Frosty didn't answer. I squeezed a little harder. "Yours," she gasped.

"That's right, mine. Now, play nice and we'll let you stay. Otherwise, you'll find yourself very unhappy. You are here as our guest."

Frosty glared at me, snatched back her hand, and rubbed her thumb and wrist. She picked up her makeup case and stalked off to the end of the bar. The other girls watched her for a moment and then went back to their normal activities. Tonya the Barbarian waited until Frosty wasn't looking and sidled up beside me.

"Listen, I got a heads-up for you," she said softly. I raised a questioning eyebrow. "She's hooked up. Rumor is she's got paid protection. You know, the film business is different than dancing. There's big money at stake. Sierra, they don't mess around."

I looked back at Frosty. She had pulled out a tiny cell phone and was speaking into it. From the expression on her face and the way she was flapping her hands all around, she was dropping a dime on me.

"Who's her agent?" I asked. Tonya, not the brightest light in the stable, straightened the chicken bone that held her hair up in a tight pigtail.

"It's that Barry guy, same as Venus. He reps all them film stars that work the southeastern circuit."

Barry Sanduski did not frighten me. I figured that in a fair fight I could take him.

Tonya went on. "Frosty was giving Barry the business earlier. She said the locker room wasn't up to her standards. She didn't like the security either and told Barry he should be getting her more money on account of the hazard."

Tonya kept watching Frosty, as if she wanted to make sure she wasn't overhearing us. This was unusual. Tonya the Barbarian was a dancer we'd hired away from the Show and Tails. She carried a caveman club as part of her act, and had been reputed to use it as situations warranted. She wasn't the type to scare easily.

"So where's the problem?" I asked.

"Well, when Barry said there wasn't going to be any extra jack, Frosty went off. She said he ought to grow a set of balls. She said if he was having to pay for protection, then he should be damn sure they got it." Tonya looked real nervous now. "Her agent said Frosty wasn't understanding, that it was protection for extreme emergencies. It's for if another 'family' muscles in, not everyday complaints. 'Protection,' that's what the mob calls it.

They don't actually protect you from anything other than themselves."

I couldn't believe what I was hearing. Protection rackets in little Panama City? Organized crime here, not just passing through but trying to make a home? Back in Philly, protection money actually bought you a service, whether you wanted it or not. It was a day-to-day reality. Was Barry Sanduski telling Frosty the truth? Or was the protection out of Atlanta only hooked to Frosty because she was part of the circuit? Was she getting protection on the film set?

I looked back over at Frosty. She was slamming her tiny phone back into her makeup kit and looking genuinely pissed.

"She told him not to pay the money then if they weren't getting nothing for it." Tonya's voice was rushed and breathy, as if she were trying to get two words in the space of one. "He told her that 'they' didn't play like that. He told her this is the way it is in the film business and that technically they owned her dance time, too."

"No way," I said.

"Oh way," she said. Tonya adjusted the tie on her leopard-skin breechcloth and tried to fit more of her breasts in her tiny bikini top by leaning over and tugging. What was the business coming to, I wondered, when protection money was a requirement? We were hardworking girls. If the protection racket was hitting the film stars, how long would it be before it touched us?

I walked over to my locker and pulled out my red velvet sheath. I couldn't take that worry on right now. It was time to center and focus. I had an act to produce and a point to make. No porno flick bimbo was gonna steal my thunder or take a chunk out of my tip money, not while Sierra Lavotini was alive and on the marquee.

Fourteen

Rusty dimmed the house lights and turned the smoke machine up high. Billows of thick white fog rolled across the stage, drifting up about four feet. The twinkle lights went on in the backdrop, bringing instant nightfall. When he touched the strobe light, little moonbeams circulated throughout the room. Annie Lennox started to sing "I Can't Get Next to You," and I stepped through the curtains and onto the stage.

I was wearing a long red velvet tear-away sheath, molded to my body with two long slits on either side that reached my thighs. In the center of the stage was a chair. I walked toward it, my hands caressing the velvet fabric, moving up slowly toward my breasts, then across my chest and behind my neck. The room fell silent and the men began to move toward the runway and the edge of the stage.

Bruno looked up in surprise. I'd caught him off guard, hanging with his girlfriend at the bar. With the other girls, his presence isn't usually necessary at stagefront, but with me it is a requirement. He slid his glass across the bar and moved down the house, walking quickly, but looking as if he were only out for a stroll. If one man so much as reached a hand out to touch me, Bruno would be there. And he would anticipate correctly every time which idiot was going to get out of line and go for the gold.

I reached the chair and with one quick move unfastened the sheath. It slid to the floor, leaving me to stand before my audience in a red satin and sequined merry widow. My 38 double D's were propped up in my bra like an offering, brushed with gold glitter powder. The men love this.

I propped one stiletto-heeled leg up on the chair and proceeded to run my hands slowly up and down my leg, toying with the snaps that held my stocking in place. That's when the money began to flow. Men crowded the edge of the stage, throwing bills and begging me to "take it off." God, I love it when they beg. I love the control of knowing that I'm in charge of what comes off and when, that I rule the fantasy not them.

I pulled the pin that held my hair up in a French twist and it cascaded around my shoulders.

"Sierra," a young salesman called, "please!"

This was followed by a chorus of men, all wanting to stuff bills in my garter. What could I do but oblige them? I was counting the tens and twenties and thinking how much of a bite this would take out of Frosty's evening when I looked up and saw the Italian Stallion enter the club and walk to his now customary booth.

With a quick turn, I returned to the chair and leaned over the back, giving my fans a little wiggle as I moved to unhook my corset.

"Oh, honey," a man moaned, "let me help you!"

I ignored him and slowly unhooked each little snap, making eye contact with every man who lined the stage. "This one's for you," I was saying, and they believed me.

I straightened and pulled the merry widow away, leaving only the G-string, the garter, and my stockings to go. Men were moaning, calling my name in tones usually reserved for their lovers. I strolled slowly down the runway, giving them a good look at the breasts that made the Tiffany famous. There, I thought. Now there's no doubt about who rules this club.

I looked over at the Stallion. Even he was watching. I brought my fingers to my lips, blew him a kiss, then let them circle my nipples on their way down to my G-string.

"Oh, man!" a young airman cried. "I've gotta have me some of that!"

No one seemed to hear him except Bruno. He moved like lightning as the boy started to scale the runway. The boy seemed to poise in midair for a moment, and then sail, his feet off the ground, back toward the exit. Gordon intercepted him at the mid-point, relieving Bruno so he could maintain his stage presence. With strength that I had never thought possible for such a skinny new-ager, Gordon propelled the offending client through the double doors and out into the parking lot. It was several moments before Gordon reappeared, looking none the worse for wear.

Rusty cranked up the smoke machine as I turned around and bent over to pick up a few errant bills. With a controlled move, I straightened back up, pulled the tie on my G-string and threw it out into the audience. It landed exactly where I'd aimed it, right in the Stallion's lap. The smoke covered me and the lights went down. It was a rock-hard performance, if I do say so myself.

Rusty helped me into my kimono and I rushed out into the house. The Italian Stallion wasn't going to get away this time. I passed through the crush of admirers with Bruno's help, acutely aware of being totally naked beneath my gown. Usually I take the time to dress, but not tonight. I was going to have a talk with that gentleman. I was going to find out what he was doing here and what he'd seen the night Venus Lovemotion died.

I reached his table just as he started to leave the booth. I blocked him, sliding in beside him and acting as if he hadn't been ready to leave. Up close he was better looking than he'd seemed from the stage. Dark features, wavy black hair, and eyes that sank into mine with an all-knowing penetration that both disturbed and intrigued me.

"I believe you have something of mine," I said softly.

He pulled the G-string from his pocket, caressing it as he dangled it in front of me. "I believe so," he answered. He smelled of cologne and his body radiated heat and energy. The gun was there, beneath his expensive wool jacket. Every time he moved, even slightly, I was aware of his powerful, panther-like build. Everything about him spelled danger and seduction, yet I ignored the signals. I was on the job, not on the make.

"I've been noticing you," I said. "You've been here for a few nights in a row."

He shrugged. "Maybe it's the talent," he answered.

"You haven't been in before or I would've remembered you," I purred. "You in town on business or pleasure?"

He laid his hand on my arm, a hot caress that left me a little breathless. "You could say it's a bit of both," he said. "A man can never have too much pleasure." His fingers tightened imperceptibly on my arm and I felt my stomach flip over in response. Not since Carmine "The Touch" Virillo, back in South Philly, had I met such a professional. I recognized something else about him, too, something that I hadn't run across in all the time I'd been living in Panama City: this guy was mob, the genuine, connected article.

"How long are you gonna be around?" I asked.

"As long as it takes to get my job done," he answered.

Behind us, Bruno stood off to the side, joined by Vincent Gambuzzo. Bruno was worried, that much I could see. And Vincent was aware that the Stallion was carrying and Bruno hadn't pulled his piece to hold for safe-keeping. Vincent was quietly giving Bruno the business, but not so quietly that I couldn't make out the occasional word, like *gun* and *idiot*.

"I'd like to see you while I'm around," the Stallion was saying. "I could use somebody to show me the town."

I looked deep into his eyes and decided to try my luck. "I work nights," I said, "and I don't make a habit out of associating with strangers. I don't know a thing about you. Why, I don't even know your name."

Up on the stage, the music was cranking up, signaling the beginning of another act. The Stallion's attention wandered away from me and I turned to see who was currently captivating his attention. Frosty Licks had wandered onto the stage, her hair done in two blond pigtails. She was wearing a transparent baby-doll nightgown and fluffy bunny slippers. She was sucking her thumb and holding a teddy bear. From where I sat, the majority of her act was silicone. They do a lot these days with implants, and not just in the places you usually expect to see them. I think they're even able to insert them in one's posterior region. At least that seemed to be the case with Miss Frosty.

The Stallion turned back to me, his fingers flicking gently along the inside of my arm, setting parts of my anatomy on fire. "It's Alonzo Barboni," he said softly, "at your service."

Jesus. The man had a talent. "I'm from New York," he added, "and I sell insurance."

Yeah, I thought, and I peddle lingerie. I looked back up at the stage just as Frosty was strolling parallel to the table where we sat. She looked out, saw me, and smirked. Then she saw Barboni and came to a halt. She lost focus, an anxious look crossing her face. Beside me, Alonzo stiffened and his eyes went dull and hard. When Frosty tried to move off, she stumbled. The rest of her act was a waste of time, not that it hadn't been to start with.

"You know her?" I asked.

"Not really. It's just business." The way he looked at me sent a chill down my spine. I didn't want to be on his bad side, and yet, I couldn't pull away. Every instinct I had was screaming "Get out! Now!" but I couldn't move a muscle. Instead, my mouth took over.

"So, did you have this effect on Venus Lovemotion, too?"

His eyes narrowed and sharpened. "What are you talking about?"

"Well, Venus and Frosty are imported talent, porn stars or what have you. I figured maybe you have this effect on all the movie stars." It was as clumsy as it sounded, so I went for damage control. "Or maybe you just have this effect on all women," I breathed. Then I gave him a look like maybe, just maybe, we had a short future in front of us.

Alonzo shifted in his seat, moving back and bringing his hand up to caress the side of my face. This was a definite no-no in Bruno's book, but at a glance from me, he stayed back. I was sitting just like that, with Alonzo's fingers leaving trails of fire down the side of my neck, when John Nailor walked into the club and out of my life.

Nailor and I had an understanding about my work. He knew my parameters, and he knew I didn't take any man's attention seriously. However, he also knew I had a hands-off policy. He knew they could look but not touch, and here one sat, touching me.

I don't know how long he'd been watching when I looked up. It wasn't for lack of Bruno and Vincent trying in their own clumsy way to alert me to the fact. Vincent had a coughing attack and then tried to use Bruno and himself as human shields, but Nailor isn't stupid. By the time I dragged my eyes off Alonzo and brought them to focus on Nailor, he had started walking away, out the door and into the night.

There was no sense in following him. He wouldn't have listened. He was too angry, that much I knew. And I would've blown my cover with Barboni. I was trapped.

"Someone you know?" Alonzo asked.

I stared helplessly at the door, saw Nailor look back and confirm that I had seen him and not attempted to pursue him, and then watched as he melted away into the parking lot.

"No," I said, looking back at Alonzo Barboni. "I don't know him."

Fifteen

I was a traitor. Worse than that, a Judas. Here I was, after months of working up to it, maybe about to fall in love, the real kind, not the make-believe, too-good-to-be-true kind, and I'd screwed it all up, as usual. I was thinking this as I sat with Alonzo, leading him to believe that I was genuinely interested. I'd done such a good job I'd even convinced myself for a moment. What a crock.

Alonzo Barboni was the kind of bad news I thought I'd out-grown—tough, seductive, in charge, and morally bankrupt. In the olden days, back in Philly, I'd fallen for his type over and over again, finally culminating in my long-term affair with Tony the Married Mobster. Tony walked out on me. Well, not exactly; he'd gotten himself whacked outside of a local restaurant after eating a Sunday dinner with his wife and kids, the very wife and kids he'd denied ever existed. He left me alone and pregnant. The baby never made it, probably because of the grief that I allowed to ruin my body. I left Philadelphia on account of men like Alonzo Barboni, and now, like a true idiot, I'd allowed one to screw up the one good thing I'd found in Panama City.

I let myself wallow in my trough of self-pity for all of three minutes before I realized that I had to get next to Alonzo. All the sorrow in the world wasn't gonna help me now. I could clear

Marla of murder, hand Vincent back his income, and then explain the real story to John. Hell, wouldn't he have done the same in my situation? Hadn't he done the same in the past? I threw it off like a heavy quilt on a summer night, and got back in the game.

"So, you've never been to Panama City before, huh?" I asked. "Well, you're in for a big time, Mr. Barboni, cause I know places even the locals can't find."

Barboni smiled. "I'll bet you do," he whispered. "Why don't we start with your place."

Freakin' snake. He'd see my place when hell froze over. I looked at him like an innocent, offended virgin, and he backed right up. I guess he figured I was worth playing.

"I mean, I'm sure you have a lovely home. It must be in a beautiful location."

Yeah, right, if you considered a trailer park romantic, then you were on the road to nirvana. The Lively Oaks Trailer Park was pretty much devoid of oaks and devoid of charm, but we were lively all right.

"Well, I'll look forward to showing it to you . . . sometime." Mae West couldn't have done it better.

"Sierra!" Vincent Gambuzzo had finally had enough. He stood just three feet away, beckoning like I was supposed to jump up and run through a hoop.

"Duty calls," I said to Barboni. "Don't be a stranger."

"Can I call you?" he asked.

I looked down at him, reached across the table and into his inside pocket. At first, instinctively, he flinched, protecting his gun. Then he relaxed and let my fingers wander inside his jacket pocket. The predictable pen was there, a silver Cross. I reached for Barboni's hand and slowly wrote my number on his palm. I put the pen down and folded his fingers shut.

"Shhh!" I whispered. "Let this be our little secret."

"Sierra!" Vincent called, impatient now. I whirled around and glared at him, reminding him that Sierra Lavotini moves at her own pace. I am not someone's trained show dog.

Bruno stood next to Vincent, chaffing to get to me. "Sierra," he said, as I walked up to him, "don't go messing with that guy. Word is he's—"

I cut him off. "I know exactly what he is and I know exactly what I'm doing."

Vincent frowned. "Then you didn't see *him* come in."

I looked him dead in the eye for a long moment. "No, I was watching the front of the house." I said, "I didn't see him until . . ."

Vincent was watching me with something that might've passed for compassion mixed with a healthy dose of confusion. I think he knew me well enough to know that I wouldn't blow Nailor off without a damned good reason. He just couldn't figure out the rest of the puzzle.

"Well, if you're back in the club, then I expect you to work. Get your ass into costume and cue the deejay. I don't have no prima donnas in my place." That was a joke and we both knew it.

"Speaking of which," I said, "where's Marla?"

Vincent frowned and looked over at Bruno, who frowned and shrugged.

"But she isn't under arrest or anything like that?" I asked.

"No." Vincent sighed, pulling out a black handkerchief and wiping his damp brow. "She ain't managed to get herself hauled in. I would've gotten a call. I guess she's just running late."

As if she'd heard him, Marla suddenly slipped through the curtains and began her act. She was dancing to a country tune: "I Want to Be a Cowboy's Sweetheart." This time she had herself all dolled up in a white cowgirl outfit, complete with hat and six-shooters. In light of the charges looming over her head, I thought the act was in poor taste and said as much to Vincent, but he just shook his head. To him, it was enough that she'd shown up.

I looked over at Alonzo. Marla had his complete and total attention. He even allowed himself a small, tight smile. Who knew? The Italian Stallion was human after all. Marla didn't miss his reaction. She homed in on it like a pigeon coming in to roost. She was playing him for the big money. Too bad she hadn't heard what a lousy tipper he was.

I would've stayed to enjoy their little moment, but I was up next. I left without waiting to see Marla's grand finale, when she'd tear off her bra and expose her Texas-sized bazooms. It was truly a picture, but not one I cared to have etched in my brain.

Instead I walked back to the dressing room, lost in thought. What act was I gonna do to ensure that Frosty Licks never darkened the door of the Tiffany again? What could I pull out of my costume trunk that would positively ace my ranking as the Number One Act? I was so lost in my own thoughts, that I almost didn't react to the open back door. As security conscious as we needed to be, it was unthinkable that someone had left the back entrance wide open to intruders, yet there it stood, open a foot and begging for someone to come along.

I stepped over to close it, still with my mind on my next act, but the shrill sound of Frosty Licks's high-pitched giggle forced me to snap back to the present moment's reality. I pushed the door open a little farther and peered out onto the dimly lit back stoop. There was Frosty, happily ensconced on Little Ricky's lap.

"You are the cutest thing!" she was saying. "I could just eat you with a spoon! You can't really be a wrestler. You wouldn't hurt a flea!"

Ricky must've thought that the heavenly gates had opened and ushered him right on in, because he was sighing and running his hands up and down her body like he might never pass this way again.

"Ricky!" I snapped. "Do you just never learn?"

Ricky jumped up like a thief, dumping Frosty once again on her perky little behind.

"Sierra, now, it ain't what it seems."

Frosty was glaring at me, slowly struggling up and brushing gravel and dirt off of her little baby-doll nightie.

"It is every bit of what it seems, sport," I said. "You're thinking with your dick, Big Man, and that'll mess you up every single time."

"Who do you think you are?" Frosty whined.

I was about to answer her, but at that moment something flew past me, knocking me into the heavy metal door. Marla had finished her act. Apparently, seeing the three of us in conversation, and Frosty in a see-through negligee, had brought back traumatic memories of Venus Lovemotion and Little Ricky. Or maybe Marla had finally wised up to her skunky snake of a boyfriend. Whatever the reason, Marla had totally lost control and had launched herself into battle.

A catfight between two well-endowed exotic dancers is the stuff male fantasies are made of, until you actually witness the real thing, with spit and blood and hair pulling. It is not a turn-on, not even to a pervert. Little Ricky stood back, clearly horrified, his knuckles jammed in his mouth. I was standing there, kind of dazed from my run-in with the door, still too unsteady to move. It was Bruno and little Rusty who broke up the action.

Bruno took Marla, and Rusty tried to grab Frosty. Marla gave Bruno a good tussle, but Frosty had nothing left to give Rusty. She buried her face in his scrawny little chest and bawled like a baby. Ricky, aware now that he'd been buttering the wrong side of the bread, came to Marla.

"Baby," he gushed, "you done took it all wrong. I wasn't doing nothing but minding my own business when this she-vixen came out and leaped at me."

Marla wasn't any too sure who to believe. She stood, her arms pinned behind her by Bruno, her massive chest heaving like two mountains in a full-strength earthquake. She was sweaty and her lower lip was beginning to swell.

We were starting to draw a crowd as customers in the parking lot wandered over to watch. This brought Gordon out from the front door, Vincent and several of the girls behind him.

Frosty seized her moment and turned it on for the audience. "Is this the kind of place you're running, Mr. Gambuzzo? A girl can't even make a decent day's wages without her life being endangered? Is this what you're offering when you say I could be a Tiffany girl?"

Vincent turned bright red and started stammering. Tiffany girl? Had Vincent offered Frosty Licks a job working with us? What was he trying to do here? And what kind of package had he offered?

Marla heard the same thing I did. Her face darkened and she went ballistic all over again.

"You mean to tell me you offered this slut a job?" she said. "Working here? With real talent?"

Frosty didn't know when to keep her mouth shut. "Real talent? With a movie star in the house, Panama City will finally see what exotic dancing is all about. You girls are just little backwater lowlifes. I was classically trained. I studied in New York."

"Oh, you gotta train to flat-back it?" Marla sneered. She tried to wrench herself free from Bruno's ironclad grip, but found it impossible.

Gordon stood next to Vincent, worrying the tip of his little goatee. "You really offered her a job?" he asked.

Vincent, seizing the opportunity to save face, began to stammer. "Well, now I, er, um, I merely said that, um, it was somewhat of a potential thing. Of course, that was only if Miss Licks pulled in a substantial increase in door take."

Gordon pulled a wad of cash out of his pocket. "Well, we made a ton of jack this week, but I think that's only because of the killing and the fans concern for Sierra's, er . . . well-being. After all, she's the star."

I flashed Gordon a smile and promised myself to do him an extra-special favor sometime real soon, like maybe making him a pan of Ma's Italian ziti. Gordon blushed and looked like the babe in the woods I knew him to be.

"Besides, this ain't nothing like what they make up in Atlanta." Gordon looked at Frosty. "I used to work Club 69. We made more than this on a weeknight."

Vincent glowered at Gordon, then regained his self-control and took over. "All right, all right! The last time I checked, my name was on the lease saying I own this place and I am in charge. I sign your paychecks, so what I do and whom I employ are not your concern. Right now I'm telling you to get back to work. And if there is one further incident, the entire lot of you will be seeking employment elsewhere!"

He looked like a black barrel about to bust. He was wearing his black wrap-around sunglasses, but they still couldn't hide the nervous twitch that starts up on the left side of his face when he knows he's out of control and we've bested him once again. His black silk shirt collar seemed to choke him, because his neck and face were a brilliant red. This was not Vincent Gambuzzo's best day.

Frosty stormed off, muttering something about her agent. Marla was staring at Ricky like she'd just uncovered a cockroach. Rusty scampered on into the building, his mind on the next act. Vincent turned to walk off, saw the gawking customers and dancers, and made a flapping motion with his arms, kind of like a big black goose trying fruitlessly to take off.

"Show's over, folks. Let's go inside where the real action is." One by one they turned and walked away, all but Gordon. He stood rooted to the spot, his hand inside his pocket groping the wad of door money.

"Gordon, you all right?" I asked.

"Man," he said, "Mr. Gambuzzo's making a big mistake if he hires that girl. She's nothing but trouble. I heard her talking to her agent. She has it all sewn up in her mind. She thinks she's gonna be the star here."

Poor Gordon looked worried, like he thought maybe she could do it. I shook my head. Didn't he know these kind of things happened every day in the business? Frosty Licks was no threat to me. There'd always be somebody breathing hard on one's heels, but true talent won out every time.

I watched him for a moment, then checked out the parking lot. Maybe Nailor hadn't left. Maybe he was sitting in his car, watching the action. I scanned carefully, hoping, but there was no Nailor. He was gone.

Sixteen

I danced my ass off. I spent the rest of the night pulling out all the stops, ignoring the warning signals my body was sending. It didn't matter that Alonzo Barboni was watching me, smiling as if we shared a secret. All I wanted was to hurt so bad I would forget about Nailor and Venus Lovemotion and sorry Vincent Gambuzzo's financial and legal problems. I wanted to be far, far away in a land where I called all the shots.

It got so bad at one point that I went out to the payphone by the dressing room and tried to call Ma. The phone rang longer than it should have, had she been home, and then clicked over to my parents' latest attempt at technology, an antiquated answering machine that Pa had picked up at a flea market.

"Hey," Pa's gruff voice barked, "leave your message. We ain't here."

The wait was endless, and then the long, shrill beep sounded. "Ma, it's Sierra." I don't know what took over then. I guess it was the kid in me, 'cause I started to cry. "I just wanted to . . . oh, shit, Ma. It ain't no big deal."

She was probably down at the Sons of Italy Social Club with Pa. Hell, that's where they had to be. It was bingo night. Ma would sit next to Pa, their cards in front of them, looking all serious. Pa would keep asking Ma to repeat the numbers on account of he couldn't hear too well. Years of fire calls and sirens had finally taken its toll on the Chief.

Ma would act all irritated, but on the sly, she felt needed when he did that. Pa would drink Chianti while Ma actually watched the cards for both of them. She'd allow herself one small glass of wine, and that was only if the band was gonna play afterward and there'd be dancing. Ma loved to dance, but she lacked courage.

I stood there, holding the receiver and thinking of them dancing. Pa is a real tough guy, but not when he holds Ma in his arms out on the floor. She has a way of nestling her head right in the crook of his shoulder. Pa wraps his big arms around her and holds her in close. She whispers to him when they dance, all her little secrets and thoughts. And I've noticed Pa don't seem to have any trouble hearing her. He leans in close, his eyes closed, and there's a soft smile on his face. He's listening.

Nobody at the Sons of Italy Social Club bothers Pa when he's dancing with Ma. It is an unspoken contract between him and his buddies, a bond that transcends all the times they bitch about their wives. Pa's buddies look the other way when he's loving Ma, because if they ever acknowledged how good Pa has it, they'd have to examine their own relationships. They'd come up short, and for all their bitching, Pa's buddies long for a love like he has with my mom.

I stood there, holding the receiver, tears rolling down my cheeks, so homesick I thought I would die. Then I realized that the machine was still on and recording my nervous breakdown. "It's just love, Ma. I just . . . needed to talk I guess."

There was a click and then a voice broke in. My oldest brother, Francis, had been sitting there listening.

"Sierra," he said, for once sounding gentle and sincere, "is there something wrong, honey, 'cause Ma's not here." I knew

Francis felt desperate. He was cut from the same cloth as Pa, a fireman, all brawn, no emotion.

"Hey, Francis," I said, my voice weak and husky with tears. "I'm all right." I meant for it to sound definitive, like I was truly sure, but instead I only started crying all over again. "It's just one of those days, I guess. You know, you want things to go one way and they end up all jammed into a big mess."

Francis didn't know what to do, but he gave it his best shot. "Honey, did someone hurt you? Are you in trouble again?" Again. Francis assumed I lived in a perpetual state of trouble. He hated the fact that I danced. I had tried to explain it to him, but he always felt embarrassed. His sister was a stripper. He couldn't see that I was a performer working a trade and doing a damn fine job of it.

"No, Francis, I'm not in trouble. I'm just going through some stuff with a guy, that's all."

"He'd better not be hitting you!"

"Francis, give me some credit! Do you really think I'd date a lowlife beater?"

Francis didn't answer for a minute, because either he didn't know or he didn't know what to say.

"Francis," I said, "just tell Ma I called. And thanks for the vote of confidence." I hung up. I know it wasn't right, but I felt too messed up just then to do anything but escape. I'd call him back and apologize, later.

"Sierra, you're on next!" Rusty was standing at the end of the hall, calling me. There was no more time for thinking about home or love or anything other than dancing. After all, what better way to forget about my troubles? Dance, and if that didn't do it, dance harder. Work the crowd, take control, and make money.

I ran into the dressing room, grabbed my jungle Jane costume, and threw it on. Then I looked in the mirror. My eyes were puffy and swollen and my face was all red, streaked with tears and smeared makeup.

"Thank God for pancake and concealer," I muttered. I coated my face, pinned up my hair, and ran back out just as the deejay cued up my music.

Rusty grabbed my kimono and looked up at me. "Are you all right?" he asked. "You know, if you're hurting, Vincent will understand if you don't go on. You shouldn't push yourself like this." He blushed beet red and looked embarrassed, like maybe he'd overstepped the bounds of our working relationship.

"I'm all right," I said, and kissed him on the cheek. "Thanks for asking."

"Sierra, I'm telling Vincent to let you go home early."

I shook my head and walked past him, up the steps and onto the stage. Rusty wasn't going to tell Vincent Gambuzzo anything. I was the only one in the club who got away with that, and that was only on account of him thinking that I was connected to the "Big Moose" Lavotini arm of the Syndicate.

I cleared my head of anything but the music, letting the beat lure me out onto center stage. I surveyed my audience, picking out the big wallets and the first-timers. I smiled slowly, like I needed coaxing, and began the routine.

Alonzo Barboni was still in his booth, but he was angry. Barry Sanduski sat across from him, listening, now and then offering a word or two with his palms raised up as if saying "What could I do?" or "This is all I can offer." Alonzo was speaking in a low voice, leaning forward, his dark eyes boring into Sanduski. A vein pulsed out on the side of his head. His face was reddening, yet his features appeared calm and impassive. I tried to watch, but I had to dance at the same time, so I missed it when Sanduski left. Alonzo was suddenly alone, leaning back, not even noticing that I was onstage. He reached into his coat pocket and pulled out a cell phone. It was a brief conversation, and when it ended Alonzo Barboni stood up and walked out of the club.

I had stripped down to my tiger's head G-string and was following Barboni's progress by strolling down the runway. I tried to see him walk to his car, but the door swung shut too quickly and Gordon blocked what little I could see of the parking lot.

By the time I walked offstage, Rusty had actually made good on his promise. Vincent Gambuzzo stood waiting for me, a dark look on his face.

"I try to do what is in your best interest, Sierra," he said. "Frosty Licks is here to help, not to take away. Look at you." Gambuzzo was geared up for a lecture. "You're obviously hurting. You got concealer on your ass, but even I can see them two little stitches, and you're bruised. You can't keep it up like this. You'll knock yourself out of commission. Go home. Rest. Come back next week."

I glared at him. "I take off a week and Frosty Licks will have her name up on the marquee. She's no good, Vincent. I don't trust her and I don't want to leave her alone in my club."

Vincent shooed Rusty off and stepped closer to me. "I am trying to run a business here, Sierra, and you got a job to do. I will handle Frosty. You got bigger fish to fry." He looked over his shoulder. "You making any progress?" I shook my head.

"Then a week off will help the both of us. I'm not askin', Sierra, I'm telling. Nailor didn't come in just to say howdy-do to you. He stopped by to see Marla before he came out here and caught you with Mr. Slick. He jacked Marla up and told her he's closing in on her."

"Police technique," I scoffed. "He ain't got squat. He just wants to make her nervous."

"Yeah," Gambuzzo said, "well it worked. Between him jacking her up and Little Ricky acting like the fool he is, she's over the edge. She left, said she couldn't work. So where's that leave me? I got one basket case and one gimp. I need Frosty Licks and I need you to get Marla off the hot seat. I don't just gotta maintain income here, Sierra, I gotta come up with some extra jack for the government or they're shutting me down. I have only a week to cough up a large chunk of change. This ain't helping, Sierra."

I couldn't tell him not to worry. I didn't have any idea of where to go next. I needed a plan.

"It don't help, you pissing Nailor off," Vincent continued. "I told you that at the very beginning. I told you not to mess with a cop. Now look. You need to be on his good side. We need him to look favorably upon us, but no, you gotta go play lovey-face with a customer."

Vincent paused to take a deep breath. He was getting his second wind and I didn't want to hear it. I spun around and walked off, my ass burning like fire, hurting.

"Hey, where are you going?" he called after me.

"Home," I said, not bothering to turn around. "I've got something important to do. This could be crucial."

Vincent took it how he wanted to hear it. He figured I was taking his words to heart. Be that as it may, I was figuring to go home and crawl into bed. This was one day I wanted to see end.

I changed into my street clothes, all the while watching Frosty Licks giving me the evil eye. I was thinking about going down to the end of the counter and helping her to understand my position better, but I just didn't have the energy. The quicker I cleared up Marla's mess, the sooner I'd be showing Miss Licks the door.

Tonya the Barbarian walked up and caught me staring. "Sierra, you say the word and she's yesterday's lunchmeat."

Tonya meant it, I knew, so I turned around and hugged her. "Not yet," I said. "If her karma don't catch up with her in the next couple of days, I may call on you, but not yet." Tonya did only one routine involving her club and the pole at the end of the runway. She wasn't going to help Vincent maintain the club's status. Unfortunately, right now we needed Ms. Licks, but it was only a temporary situation.

I took off, using the drive home to cool down. Bruno and Gordon had both insisted on walking me to my car. Bruno knew I felt lousy and said as much, telling me I shouldn't be working in my condition, telling me I shouldn't worry about a visiting porn star. Gordon echoed him.

"I can't stand to see you hurting, Sierra," he said. "Not you. Go home and rest."

Bruno chimed in. "Yeah, put everything out of your mind. Let us handle the club, baby." Then he hugged me, slipping his arm around my shoulder and pulling me in close. "You're one of us, Sierra. You're family."

"Yeah," Gordon said. "You look like you could be my sister. I wouldn't let her work if she was hurting. Don't worry about some loser porn star. Let us handle that."

Right, I thought, if only it was that easy. I drove the whole way home, worrying. Fluffy ran out of Raydean's newly installed doggie door when she heard the Camaro hit the parking pad. She pranced and yipped and turned circles, overjoyed to have me home.

I looked down at her and had to smile. "So am I to understand from this that you're cranked on sugar and that the Braves won? Or should I figure you're just glad to see me?" Fluffy bounded up the steps and waited for me. She was glad to have me home.

We crashed in record time. I don't think it was five minutes before we were both asleep and snoring. It couldn't have been more than a half an hour later that company arrived.

Seventeen

*N*o one ever knocks on my door and then waits politely for me to come and answer it. No, they bang, they pound, and they generally yell out my name, as if I didn't know who they were looking for, or as if it would make me move any faster. At five A.M., Detective John Nailor was in no mood to make an exception to the rule.

"Sierra!" he yelled, pounding away. "Open up!" I waited for him to add "Police!" but he didn't.

Fluff flew off the bed, heading for her buddy. I was slower. I'd been lying down just long enough for all my muscles to stiffen up. Dancing had been a huge mistake.

I pulled on my robe and shuffled slowly down the hallway. Nailor never let up. The pounding got louder the closer I came to the door. It eclipsed my attempts to call out to him. This just seemed to make him all the more anxious. Finally I pulled the chain off the door, unfastened the dead bolt, and stood face-to-face with one distraught cop.

"Why didn't you answer me?" he demanded.

"Why didn't you listen, instead of pounding away like a jackhammer?"

Raydean's lights came on and I knew we were under surveillance. Nailor ran his hand through his hair and just stared at me.

"When did you get home?" he asked.

"You mean you haven't already felt the hood of my car and made a scientific determination?" Nailor wasn't in the mood for my sarcasm. "All right. I guess I got in around three. Vincent made me come home early."

"I know," he said.

"Then why did you ask? And how do you know? You mean you came back looking for me?" This was a positive sign. He'd decided to let me explain.

Nailor ignored my questions. "You're saying you left at three and came straight home?"

I looked at him like he was some kind of freak. What was the matter with him? Did he think I'd run off with Barboni?

"Would you like to come in, or do you want to stand on my stoop, disturbing my neighbors and making me look like a criminal?"

Nailor brushed past me. He was still dressed in the suit he'd worn to the club, but his shirt was rumpled and the tie was loosened. He smelled of something I couldn't quite identify, maybe deodorizer and cigarette smoke, chemicals and old copper pennies. It was a strange smell, but not unfamiliar.

I shut my eyes, the memory almost on the tip of my tongue. Nailor interrupted.

"So you came straight home? No stops? You didn't stop at the store or buy gas or anything? No one saw you?"

"What's this all about, because if it's about that guy you saw me with, I can explain."

He shook his head again impatiently. "Just answer the question."

"No. How about you tell me why you're asking, instead."

I took a step away from him and pulled my robe closer. The kitchen was dark, lit only by the pale light of dawn creeping through my bay window and a tiny light over the stovetop.

"Sierra, Frosty Licks is dead. Someone shot her and dumped her body in her hotel pool."

That was the smell on his clothing. It was the smell of a murder scene. I'd been around it before, a couple of times. But it was no wonder I couldn't quite remember. My brain hadn't wanted to remember. Dead bodies, blinding camera flashes, the stink of decomposition mixed with fear and blood, the odor of the chemicals the forensics team uses to process the scene. My brain never wanted to remember that smell. Now it clung to Nailor, haunting me.

"I don't understand," I said, still not really wanting to hear what he was saying.

"Sierra, she's dead. What's to understand?" He was cold, removed, still angry with me or worse, hurt.

"Who? What? When? The basics, John, I need the basics. Why are you treating me this way? Why're you checking up on me, as if I were a suspect?"

Nailor watched me. His face was closed, tight with some unnamed emotion. I was frightened by his withdrawal.

"Sierra, you fought with Frosty earlier in the evening. You were there when Marla caught her with Ricky. I've gotta wonder if you're holding out on me. I come into the club, I see some punk touching you like he owns you. I've gotta wonder what's going on here."

I stood there, forcing my body to relax, making myself look him in the eye. I wanted to spill my gut, and yet he was standing in front of me, virtually saying he didn't trust me. So I waited.

Nailor hung himself. "What do you have on Marla that you're not sharing?" he asked. "And who was that guy? If you're screwing around, Sierra, I need to know."

I nodded slowly, like I was really listening. If he had more poison inside his system about me, well, let it go. It was better to find out now than to give my heart away and get burned. But

Nailor was done. He folded his arms across his chest, leaned back against the wall, and prepared to listen to my statement. And what a statement it was going to be.

When I get mad, really mad, I start off slow and quiet. I was beyond mad. I hurt so bad I felt like my guts were squeezed up inside my head. I couldn't see or feel anything but pain. You start to trust a guy and where does it get you? Right back where you should've been all along: alone.

"All right," I said, "so you have concerns about me. Fair enough. The guy, Alonzo Barboni, says he's an insurance salesman, looking to show me a good time. I think he's mob-connected and wanted protection money out of the circuit girls. So I was working him, not screwing him."

Nailor nodded, pleased that the subject was coming through. He had no idea how I felt.

"And Marla? Marla don't have the brains to kill off all her competition, but I believe I've told you that in the past. She didn't kill Frosty or Venus. I know her gun is missing. I know she made threats, but it's a setup. Going with what seems most logical to me, I figure Barboni's your man to watch."

Nailor listened patiently, his arms still folded across his chest, still distancing.

"I'd have to differ with you there, Sierra," he said. "According to Vincent, Marla left early. She had the opportunity to set up and wait for Frosty to come back to her hotel. She was already mad as hell at her. This wasn't a close-range pro hit like the mob would do. She got hit three times, and only one bullet was lucky enough to kill her. Same caliber as the bullet that hit you. And Marla has no alibi."

I didn't say anything and he went on. "I'm glad you came across with that information about Barboni. We'll look into it."

He took a step toward me and I stepped aside. He was feeling better, but I was just starting.

"Good, so you have everything you need from me, right?"

"Yeah. I just needed to check, that's all. You can understand my position, right?"

"Yep," I said, passing him on my way to the door. "I sure can. You didn't trust me enough to know where I stood with you. You don't know how I feel about you after all the time we've known each other. You don't trust me. That's all I read coming back from you."

"Sierra, you're not remembering that I have a job to do."

I opened the door wide and stepped aside. "And you're not remembering that I have a job to do, too, but I know who my friends are. You need to leave."

We were hurting each other, slashing away, and neither one of us could stop the process. It was a pattern, a familiar life dance that we were doomed to repeat time after time, always hoping that it would change, always feeling hopeless when it didn't.

He walked past me and down the steps, pausing once and almost turning back, but I closed the door and he continued to walk away. I leaned with my back against the door, then I turned to further twist the knife in my own gut by watching him drive off.

So now there were two murder victims. The cops would be focusing their search on looking for the gun and completing the circle of evidence to link up Marla to the murders. They might run Barboni's ID through the National Criminal Identification Center, but it would come up clean. No, Barboni was mine. Nailor wasn't going to help. It was just me, just like I liked it.

Fluffy stood at my feet, intimating that she might want breakfast if I was in the mood to serve it. She did this by dragging her bowl over and setting it down on my left foot.

"I know, you're trying to tell me that I'm not alone. I have you." Fluffy yipped in agreement and went to stand by the pantry door. I followed her and reached for the can of dog food. "We can do this," I said. "I've got Raydean and Pat. I can hook this up." Fluffy no longer cared. She was lost in the ecstasy of her meal.

"I'm going to bed, girl. When I get up, we're on the job."

Fluffy belched, which I took for implicit understanding. I looked over at the counter where Pa's Chianti sat. Ma swears it's good for whatever ails you. I figured I had too many ailments to name and poured a short tumbler full of the cure.

I took it back down the hall with me and climbed under my satin sheets. The sun was just beginning to streak across the sky when I finished my drink and sank deep under the covers. Despite Pa's remedy, it took a long while to fall asleep. And when I did, I had vivid dreams of Venus Lovemotion and Frosty Licks, laughing and mocking me, their arms around John Nailor and Alonzo Barboni.

Eighteen

*A*lonzo Barboni called at noon. I was finally sleeping, the deep kind where, if you wake up, you don't remember any of your current life, only the faraway past. I rolled over, pulled the phone into bed with me, and muttered, "Hello?"

"Ah," he murmured, "you're in bed. I hear the sleep in your voice and I am sorry to have awakened you."

For a moment I didn't place him, and then it rushed back to me. "Oh, it's you. Thanks for calling. I needed to get up anyway."

"I wanted to reach you early," he said. "I want to see you."

My stomach started to churn. "Good," I said. "I want to see you, too."

Alonzo practically purred with satisfaction. "Do you work tonight?"

I stretched, trying to wake up enough to think straight. God, he had a sexy voice. "No, I'm off tonight."

"Good, I have a dinner reservation in Grayton Beach at Michael's. I'll pick you up at seven."

Alarm bells went off. No, not my place. I didn't want him coming to the trailer.

"Wait," I said, "that's way too far out of your way. I'll come into town." Grayton Beach lies twenty-six miles to the west of

113

Panama City, a long, isolated drive. The town is a tiny beach community, frozen in the fifties, but not undiscovered, just too expensive for all but the most wealthy to own property. It is the Martha's Vineyard of the Panhandle. How had he heard about it? Why there? Why not in town, around people, on my turf?

"I don't mind coming to get you," he said, his voice a little more forceful.

"Well, thanks, but my roommate will be here and the place is a mess." I looked over at my roommate, peacefully sleeping all curled up on my other pillow. It did the trick for me, though.

"All right," he said. "I'm in the Moongazer, room fourteen-fifteen."

"I bet you have a lovely view," I murmured. "I'll meet you in the bar downstairs at seven." Before he could say anything else, I hung up.

I stretched and lay in bed thinking. Alonzo Barboni was gonna give it all up to Sierra Lavotini. The trick would be in escaping before I had to give any of Sierra Lavotini up to him. If he was mob, then I had an entirely different set of rules to play by. I had to leave him smiling . . . or else. But I also had to find out where he'd been when the murders took place, and why Marla had seen him backstage in the moments before Venus Lovemotion's death.

The phone rang again, but I ignored it, waiting for the machine to pick up. On the fourth ring the message began to play, then the tone, and finally a voice, muffled and indistinct: "I'll take care of you," the voice murmured. "Don't try and stop me."

Fluffy growled low in her throat. I reached out for the receiver, but the connection had been lost. The caller was gone. I hung up and almost instantly, the phone shrilled again.

"Who are you?" I demanded, the adrenaline controlling my reactions, every nerve on fire.

"Sierra?" It was Ma. "Sierra, that is no way to answer a phone. Where are your manners?"

"Ma," I breathed, my heart racing up into my throat. "I thought you were someone else."

"Humph!" she said sniffing. "Is that how you talked to Francis last night? Is that why he was so upset?"

I sighed and stared up at the ceiling fan, silently counting the revolutions as it slowly whirred around.

"No, Ma. It was just a bad night, that's all."

Ma's tone softened. "You want to tell me about it, sweetie?"

I thought about it for a moment. "Nah, Ma, it's just my love life. It stinks."

"No! Sierra, what's with you and that boy? He's a good boy, Sierra. He eats good when I feed him. You cook for him and he'll plump right up. He's not sick, is he?"

I laughed softly. "No, Ma, he ain't sick, he's just a little . . . controlling, I guess. He's gotta have it his way or no way."

Ma cackled. "I knew it! I knew it! The hens have come home to roost. You finally got ahold of one you can't wrap around your little finger! Praise the saints, Mother Mary, and the heavenly Host. I was about given up on you."

"Ma, that's not it at all."

"Oh, I think it is," she said, smug now. "I watched him when I came down there. He's right on the money." I started to argue with her, but she cut in. "Oh, dear, I guess I should've discouraged him, but I was so worried."

"Discouraged who, Ma? Nailor?" What had she done now? If she'd sent Pa or Al down . . .

"No, Sierra. Don't be silly!" Ma paused, obviously deciding how to phrase the bad news. "Like I told you, Francis was worried to death. So when he asked what did I think, I said by all means."

"By all means what, Ma?"

"That he should go. He left early this morning, before Pa could go wake him.

"He's coming here? Ma, tell me Francis isn't coming here!"

She snorted. Obviously I'd pissed her off. "Sierra, must you always think about yourself? He's concerned. That is a good thing. He cares about you, Sierra, no matter what he says or how he acts, he cares."

"Ma, Francis thinks everything I do is wrong."

Ma ignored this. "He needs to get away, Sierra. You should see him. He's pale. He ain't had a vacation from the fire department in four years, and if it takes him coming down to see about you to get him to relax, well, I think it's mighty selfish of you to be resentful. What am I always saying, eh?"

"I know, I know, Ma. Blood is thicker than water. If you ain't got family, you got nothing."

"Exactly! Now you should be about making up the guest bed for him. And while you're at it, make sure he eats good. In fact, you should invite John over. They're two peas in a pod. This could be very good, Sierra." Ma sighed with satisfaction. Her job was done. Both kids were seen to, and she was once again in charge.

"All right, Ma. Thanks for warning me."

"When your own brother drives for twenty hours to see you, I would not expect you to be thinking you needed warning. Honestly, Sierra! It's for your own good!"

Ma hung up and I rolled over and closed my eyes. This was all I needed. Francis. If there was a man alive more opinionated and uptight than him, I had yet to meet him. Damn.

Fluffy opened one eye and watched me, never moving from her spot on the pillow.

"If he left at six," I said, "he'll be in sometime late tonight. Maybe early tomorrow morning." Fluffy stretched one paw until it touched the tip of my shoulder. She'd never met my brother, but I could tell she was feeling anxious. "Of course, that's if he drives straight through. He might not. He might stop somewhere."

No, Francis wouldn't stop. He might pull over for an hour or two, but if he smelled a way to tell me "I told you so," he'd keep plowing on through until he reached me.

I lay there a little while longer. I wasn't being fair. Francis loved me, but like a brother eight years older. Ma was right. He needed to relax, have a good time, and still feel useful. The tiniest seed of an idea began to germinate in my head. It would mean getting Francis to play along, but what the hell? He'd be helping his baby sister out of a jam.

I lay there for another moment and the voice on the phone flooded back into my awareness. Francis and Ma had been a distraction. *I'll take care of you. Don't try and stop me.* Barboni first, the voice second. I tried to compare the two voices. Could the second caller have been him? I didn't think so, but it was hard to say. It had sounded so muffled. It could've been anyone, male or female, young or old.

Fluffy jumped off the bed and ran out of the room. She clicked away, running down the hallway, slipping through the doggie door and into the outside world. She had it easy. You didn't see her family coming to visit her. Easy come. Easy go. I should've been born a dog. I rolled over onto my stomach and clutched my pillow! As I lay there, thoughts of Nailor crept into my head, just images of him, flashing through my memory banks in a slideshow.

I closed my eyes so I could see him better and gripped my pillow. He was such a sexy, hardheaded man. Then I remembered how he doubted me, hadn't trusted my motives, hadn't wanted to let me work the case with him. That doused the flames. I rolled over and sat up. No more sleeping. No more lying around waiting for the world to come to me.

Fluffy came running back in through her doggie door, scampering down the hallway. I started the shower and turned back around. She stood at the edge of the bathroom, too cautious to approach in case the shower was for her. In her sharp little teeth she held a rolled-up slip of paper.

"That would be for me?" I asked. Fluffy dropped the note at the edge of the tiled floor and ran. She was not taking any chances.

"*Pat made cinnamon rolls and I got the coffee. Get yourself over here asap.*" It was signed, "*The War Council.*" In other words, Raydean's Prolixin had kicked in and she was ready to ride.

"Tell her I said fine," I called out to Fluff, and stepped into the stall.

There is nothing like a hot steamy shower to stimulate the thought processes. I closed my eyes, leaned my head back into the spray, and began to line it all out: suspects, motives, and plans. Venus and Frosty were circuit girls using Barry Sanduski as an agent; that was the only connection between the two. And they'd both fooled around with Little Ricky, but that was just a measure of their collective low IQ. It wasn't a murder motive. No, Barboni was the man voted most likely to be in town on an enforcement mission. I just needed to link him up.

I lathered up and shaved my legs, standing under the water until it began to run cool, then cold. That's one thing about trailers: they've got tiny hot-water tanks. A girl can't solve every problem in the world without freezing her ass off. I was wrapping myself in a thick Egyptian cotton towel when someone started pounding on the door. Fluffy barked and I headed for the back door.

"Hold on! Hold on! I'm coming!" I was swearing to myself that Raydean had the smart idea when she booby-trapped her yard. No pounding doors, no intruders.

I looked through the peephole and froze. Flowers, masses of flowers. I couldn't make out a face, but if it was the same delivery boy, we were going to have a talk.

"Who is it?" I called.

"Sierra?" a male voice asked.

I looked around for a weapon and as usual, came up short. I'm just not a weapon girl. I grabbed up a knife from the counter, hid it behind my back, and prepared to do business.

I opened the door slowly and said: "For me? How lovely." The man thrust the flowers forward, and I pulled the knife. With one hand I grabbed his wrist, and with the other I stuck the knife up against his side.

"Don't move, wiseass, or I'll cut your heart out and stuff it in your mouth!"

The man froze. The flowers started to tremble as he panicked, and then dropped as his arms became weak with fear. At least, that's how I chose to view it.

We were face-to-face, me and . . . Gordon.

"Gordon, what are you doing here?" I pulled the knife back and stepped aside to let him in. He didn't move, just stood on the doorstep, staring.

"Me and the guys, well, we all figured you were having a tough time and um, well. . . . Here." He picked up the flowers and shoved them into my arms, then turned to leave.

"Gordon, wait." I felt like a total heel now. Gordon spun around with an expectant puppy-dog look on his face. "Come on in a sec," I said. "Let me throw something on and I'll get us a cup of coffee."

He hesitated, then stepped inside the kitchen, looking from the flowers I held in one hand to the knife in the other.

"I promise, it's safe." I buried my nose in the bouquet of tulips and roses. "This was so thoughtful," I murmured. "Guess I'm just a little gun-shy."

Gordon's features relaxed. "Well, that's understandable, I reckon."

I shoved the flowers into his arms and walked off down the hallway. "Make yourself at home," I called back to him. It was

119

beginning to occur to me that Gordon was an untapped source of information. He'd been working the door. He knew what Vincent was paying the guest stars. He knew what money was coming in. And he hadn't taken Barboni's gun away from him when he walked through the door of the club, or alerted Bruno. Now what was that about? One night I could see an oversight, but Barboni had been in night after night.

I threw my robe on and walked back down the hallway. Gordon had made himself at home all right. He'd found a vase and was carefully arranging the flowers.

"You want me to do that?" I asked.

Gordon jumped, not hearing me walk up behind him.

"No, ma'am. I'm used to this. I worked in my sister Lori's flower booth in Atlanta before I moved here."

I settled onto a stool and watched Gordon work, trying to figure the best way to get to what I wanted.

"You went from arranging flowers to working the door in a strip club? That must be some adjustment."

Gordon smiled softly. "Not really." He snapped the end of a stem and stuck it down into the warm water.

"So, Gordon, why'd you let that man, Barboni, into the club with him carrying?" I figured, what the hell, might as well shoot straight. Otherwise I'd be talking flower arranging all night.

Gordon's fingers slipped and the flower he was working with took a direct hit, the stem cracking and petals flying everywhere.

"Like I told Mr. Gambuzzo, I didn't see it."

I stretched. "Yeah, Gordon, but unlike Gambuzzo, I ain't stupid. What's the real deal? Come on, you can tell me. I won't rat you out. I'm just curious."

Gordon wouldn't make eye contact, something that would've had the nuns at St. Mary's on him in a flash, rulers at the ready.

"Flowers are really easy to work with," Gordon said, "but so fragile . . ."

"Gordon, cut it out! Why'd you let Barboni in carrying? Who is he?"

He stuck the final flower down into the vase and turned around to face me.

"Sierra, stay away from that guy. He's bad news. He hurts people for entertainment."

If Gordon was trying to frighten me, it was working.

"Who is he?"

Gordon brushed his hands off on the front of his shirt and started heading for the door. "Sierra, I didn't come here to get into all this. I'm doing my job. I'm not going to let you get hurt or nothing, but you can help us all out if you stay away from Barboni. Them other girls may have to do what he says, but you don't. Let me handle this."

"What are you talking about? If that guy's as dangerous as you say, can't nobody handle him. Is he mob-connected? Did he pay you to let him in with a gun?"

But Gordon wouldn't say another word. He walked out the door with me right behind him, calling his name. He jumped in his battered heap of a car and roared off down the road, his good-will gesture forgotten in his rush to get away.

I turned and saw Pat and Raydean across the way, watching.

"You coming for coffee or have you got other fish to fry?" Pat called. The smell of fresh cinnamon rolls wafted out of Raydean's trailer, curling across the narrow street and seducing me.

"You bet," I answered. "Besides, I think I'm gonna need your help tonight. I've got a hot date."

Raydean spit off the porch into a bush, triggering her hyper-sensitive intruder-alert sprinkler system to turn on along the edge of the sidewalk.

"Honey, if that's your idea of a date, you got more problems than this here team can handle. That little feller couldn't last a round with the likes of you!" Her eyes narrowed as she squinted off in the direction of Gordon's departing car. "Maybe he's one of them Flemish. Never can tell what guise they'll take."

Fluffy apparently agreed. She uttered a low growl and crossed the street to Raydean's house, skirting the booby traps and making her way up onto the steps. Trouble was brewing all right, but it was way worse than a scrawny beatnik with a flower complex.

Nineteen

*T*here was going to be a full moon. The barest outline of a white circle stood out in a corner of the sky, waiting to make its full appearance later. I slipped the T-tops off of the Camaro and prepared to do battle. The troops had been briefed. The plan was in place. They were to stay right behind me, but out of sight. They were to approach only if I was in obvious trouble, or if I gave the signal. If it worked, Barboni would be putty in my hands. If it failed, well, I didn't want to think about that.

I looked over at Raydean's place and noticed that her old Plymouth Fury was missing. She and Pat were in place, I hoped. Pat's pickup truck was gone from her driveway, too. Good. I left a note on the door for Francis, telling him to make himself at home. He'd have a fit when he found the door unlocked, but it was that or leave a note with a key in it. No one bothered my trailer anyway, they were all afraid Raydean would come out and shoot them.

I slid into the driver's seat, popped in a Stevie Ray Vaughan tape, and headed for the beach. I was looking good. My hair fell around my shoulders in soft blond waves. I wore a subdued, but nonetheless sexy, black sheath. My makeup was sophisticated to-night, not like the stage makeup I piled on to do my Queen of

Passion routine. I looked elegant, like Audrey Hepburn meets Grace Kelly, the younger years. I held that thought and listened to Stevie Ray howl about being in love for a few moments. The outside package was one thing, but inside, I needed to feel like steel, like I didn't give a shit whose back I climbed to get where I was going. Stevie Ray was the man to put me in that mood. I was invincible, just like him before the plane crash.

I roared down the Strip, no easy feat in the spring. Usually tourists and spring-breakers crowded the narrow road, but not this week. There was a temporary lull in the action. School was back in session, summer hadn't brought its crowds from L.A. (Lower Alabama), and the snowbirds had all started heading back to Canada or Michigan. The concessions and gooney golf emporiums were all open, but few people played. Big plastic sharks and whale floats flapped on their trap lines outside the convenience stores. I was the cowboy at high noon, driving down Highway 98, my hand on the butt of my gun, all ready for the big showdown. Too bad I didn't actually have a gun.

The Moongazer loomed ahead of me, a tall white hotel with a big fountain in front. The word had always been that Syndicate money was behind the huge palace. It wasn't one of the chains. It charged a pretty steep price, even by Panama City standards, and it was always fresh and bright, despite rarely being full up with paying customers. And the word also added that the regular working girls on the Strip were not welcome. The Moongazer provided its own, beautiful, nonlocals who came in for a brief stint, usually during conventions or peak tourist season.

I pulled the Camaro up to the front door, Stevie Ray wailing at the top of his lungs, and counted the milliseconds until the valet attendant came to take her from me. The door opened, I stepped out, and a fresh-scrubbed, dark-haired young man slid in behind the wheel. In an instant, Stevie Ray fell silent.

"No taste in music, huh?" I said.

He smiled and pulled away from the curb. I was left holding a blue parking tag and watching my baby slide into the darkened concrete tomb of a garage. It was seven o'clock on the very dot, nothing left to do now but head for the lounge. Barboni would be waiting. Before I stepped into the revolving door, I looked over my shoulder, surveying the Strip for a sign of the team. Either they were very good, or they'd blown it already.

I went through the door and stepped out onto plush carpeting patterned with leaves and red swirls. Classy. The lounge was to the right, a ton of mahogany and brass, etched glass and darkness. I stepped through the door, waited for my eyes to adjust, and spotted him immediately. He was in a corner, facing the door, his back to the wall and a martini glass in his hand.

I let him take in the Lavotini package for a moment, then slowly began my walk to his table. I smiled and started to slip into the chair across from him, my back to the door as if, unlike him, I didn't care about covering the exits or having an escape route. I'd scoped the bar on my way to the table. The back exit lay just to my right, a small door by the ladies' room.

Barboni rose immediately, moving around to pull my chair out, leaning down and letting his lips brush the side of my face in the barest of kisses.

"You smell like a sun-ripened, summer peach," he whispered, "warm and sensuous, like a woman stretched out naked in her bed on a hot August evening, waiting."

Oh, bite me. Like I haven't heard that line before. Actually I hadn't, and for a moment I was once again tempted by his strong masculine presence, by the raw sexuality that seemed to surround him. Then I shook myself and remembered Salvatore Minuchin and Carmine Virillo. They were snakes, all of them, even Tony the Married Mobster. Barboni was one of their kind.

Alonzo, thinking he was on a roll, motioned to the waitress.

She came instantly and smiled a smile that was all teeth. I figured Barboni tipped better here than at the Tiffany.

"May I order for you?" he asked. I hated to see him disappointed so early in the game, so I nodded. "A cosmopolitan," he said.

The waitress looked at me and her smile faded. Her big tipper now had a no-vacancy sign flashing all over her prospects. Oh, well, easy come, easy go. Someday maybe she'd thank me.

The drink materialize in no time at all, along with another martini for Barboni. I barely had time to check out the rest of the room, hoping maybe one of my team members was sitting in a quiet corner, watching. They were nowhere in sight.

"So, when are we due for dinner?" I asked.

Barboni smiled. "Nine," he answered. "I thought we'd sit here for a little while and then ride out there."

I ran a finger up his arm, feeling the muscle ripple underneath his suit coat. This was no insurance salesman. We sat there for maybe ten minutes, at first saying nothing, and then making small talk. Eventually I figured it was time to gather a little information. I needed to try and contact Pat and let her know the plan as soon as possible.

"So we're going to the Red Bar for dinner?" My hand caught the edge of the glass and almost sent it reeling.

Barboni cut right to the chase. "Sierra, I sense some apprehension on your part. You're looking over your shoulder. Your hands are trembling. You seem, I don't know, frightened, maybe?"

A million thoughts and sensations seemed to hit me at once. The vodka in my drink settled into my belly, I felt scared and intimidated but somehow also reassured and stimulated. What in the hell was going on with me? I looked at my drink and back at him.

"What's in this thing?" I asked. "It packs a hell of a punch."

Barboni shook his head. "It's not the alcohol, Sierra. Now what's going on with you?"

His eyes were dark pools of concern. I was starting to doubt myself just a little bit. All right, so I still didn't think he sold insurance, but maybe he wasn't such a terrible guy.

"All right, you've got me," I said, "but it has nothing to do with you. I am concerned and I am frightened, but it's my mother I'm thinking of." God, Sierra, you do spin a line of crap when you have to.

Barboni frowned, like maybe he had a mother, like maybe he remembered back in the old days when being Catholic counted for something and guilt was a virtue not a sin.

"Sierra, is something wrong with your mother?" His voice was thick with Old Country concern. It was the New Yorker creeping back into him.

I mentally crossed myself, said a Hail Mary, and proceeded to tell a huge, whopping lie.

"Well, she had surgery today." I raised my hands, palms extended, at his alarmed expression. "It was minor, you know, kind of exploratory. She didn't even tell me until last night, and even then she didn't want me to come up. She said it was routine, but I'm not so sure. I tried to call before I left home, but no one answered in her room."

Barboni eased ever so slightly. This was fixable. He could handle this problem and maybe still score. I could see it in the back of his eyes.

"I would just feel so much better if I could call before we leave, you know, check on her. After all, since Pa died, it's only me." I crossed myself twice more and added a rosary for good measure. "I'll just be a minute."

"But of course, my dear," he murmured. "Take your time."

And so I did. I took my time and the hotel's elevator right up to the fourteenth floor. I walked straight down the hallway to the

127

door to room 1415 and tapped ever so softly, my heart thudding against my rib cage.

"Be there," I whispered.

The door swung open slowly and Raydean stood there grinning, her hair in pink foam rollers.

"Took yer time, lady," she said.

I looked back at the corridor, just to be sure, then stepped inside Alonzo Barboni's room.

"I know," Raydean sighed, looking around the immaculate room, "there ain't nothing to be said for it. I couldn't find a thing, and believe you me, I looked. That housekeeper what let me in said she hadn't seen my 'son' anywhere." Raydean chuckled then her eyes narrowed. "I swept the room for bugs, but them Flemish must run this place. There ain't so much as a gnat in here."

I walked around the room peering into corners, gingerly lifting the edge of the bedspread and letting it drop again. There was no sign that Alonzo Barboni had ever spent so much as one moment in the room.

Raydean let me look until I was satisfied. "I did find this," she said, producing a small gray business card: GRANTHAM INSURANCE, ALONZO BARBONI VICE PRESIDENT. "So, I guess he's been here, all right. Unless, of course, and why I didn't think of this I'll never know, it's an alien plant."

"Raydean, you watch too much TV," I said. "Let's go. He thinks I'm making a phone call."

Raydean reached for her huge purse. It whimpered.

"You didn't," I said.

Raydean looked down at the tips of her shoes and smiled softly. "I had to," she said softly. "She was just a 'beggin'."

I opened the hallway door, checked the corridor, and motioned for Raydean to follow.

"Raydean, if anything happens to Fluffy . . ."

Raydean snorted. "This dog's got more sense on a bad day

than you do on a good. She's my lookout. Besides, if it comes down to a battle, the little booger's got teeth like rusty needles. I want her in the foxhole beside me, don't you?"

"Raydean, where's Pat?"

"On lookout. Don't you worry, we've got you covered."

I was standing by the elevator watching the light hop from floor to floor. "Our reservations are at nine," I said softly. "I'll go down first. You wait and take the next one."

Raydean nodded. The elevator doors opened and Alonzo Barboni stood staring out at me.

For a moment neither of us said a word, then Raydean's purse started to growl, diverting our attention.

"God, I'm hungry!" she cried, and hopped into the elevator.

"You coming, dearie?" she asked.

I stepped into the car and shook my head. "I don't know what happened. I thought I pushed Lobby but I must've hit the wrong button." Alonzo said nothing. "That drink really went to my head."

Raydean was humming to herself and ignoring the both of us. Her purse, however, was very angry and growled throughout the short trip to the first floor.

"Have a nice day!" Raydean said, and stepped out into the lobby. She seemed to melt into the potted plants, disappearing in seconds.

I was not so lucky with Barboni. He smelled a rat.

"Did you call your mother?" he asked softly, his voice dangerously calm.

"Sure did," I said. "Turns out she had hemorrhoids. Go figure."

"I wondered," he said, heading for the front door of the hotel. "You were gone for quite a while. Which phone did you use?"

The trap, but I was ready. "Well, that was part of the problem," I said. "I didn't want to use the one out in the lobby, you know. I figured with Mom's condition being what it is, we'd need privacy. Took me forever to find a private phone."

"Which was where?" he asked. We'd stepped into the warm evening air and Barboni was signaling the valet. His arm gripped my elbow like a vise.

"Um, well, actually, I tried to find the health club. They said it was on the fourth floor, but it must've been somewhere else. You know, I thought about using the locker room phone, but I never did find it."

Barboni's attention was diverted for a second as a silver Porsche Boxster drew up to the curb. The valet stepped out and left the car running, ran over to the passenger side and opened the door for me.

"Damn," I said, looking over at Alonzo. "I didn't know Hertz rented these things. That must be costing your company a pretty penny in expense money."

The boys in white shut the doors and we were closed in again, pulling out of the brick driveway and onto the street.

"There is no health club in this hotel, Sierra," Barboni said. "What were you doing in my room?"

He couldn't have known; he was guessing. A part of me knew this, and yet I suddenly felt as if I were back in Sister Mary Margaret's office explaining that it hadn't been me down at Giardello's Drugstore, sipping a vanilla soda during school hours. It had been my evil twin, Monica.

"Now you look here, Barboni," I said. "I don't know what type of floozy ditzbag you're used to running over, but you don't get to talk to me like that. In fact," I said, as Barboni hit the edge of town and ran the speedometer up to eighty-five, "you can just turn this thing around and drop me back at the hotel. Our evening is over."

Barboni laughed and punched the accelerator. He had no intention of going back. I turned and looked behind us, knowing what I'd find. The road stretched like a long, black snake out the rear window. Pat's pickup would be no match for a Porsche.

The moon rose over the Gulf. Now and then I caught glimpses of the waves crashing onto the beach with phosphorescent white trails that followed them back out to sea. I was afraid for the first time in a long while. What had I been thinking? What sort of plan was it that involved two elderly women and a dog as backup?

I tried to relax. They knew where we were heading, but what if he'd lied? I tried thinking of escape plans and alternatives, but when you're moving down the highway at ninety-plus miles an hour, escape becomes a life-threatening option.

I knew we'd pass through Seaside, a tiny, ready-made neo-Victorian village. He'd have to slow down there, but it wouldn't be enough for me to roll out to safety. No, I was trapped. I watched him for a moment. He was intent on driving, one hand on the clutch and one on the wheel.

"All right," I yelled over the engine's roar, "look at it from my point of view."

He glanced at me and snickered. "What's your point of view? You're a stripper trying to rip me off. Fair enough. You wanna act like a whore, I'll treat you like one."

Shit. Which was worse, him guessing the truth, or him thinking I was common dirt looking to rob him?

I laughed. "That's what you think?"

The car slowed a tiny bit. "Yeah," he said, "that's what I think." But there was a tendril of doubt in his voice.

"So, what are you, just stupid or flattering yourself?"

Now we were only doing twenty miles over the speed limit. Barboni was spending as much time looking at me as he was the road.

"Man, you have brass ones. You break into my hotel room and then you have the nerve to deny it?"

I laughed again, like I was delighted with our little game. "Barboni, you spend too much time up north selling insurance. The smog must be getting to you. Of course I broke into your room, and actually, I didn't technically 'break' in. The maid opened the door."

"So you admit it?"

We crested the edge of Seaside and blew right on through to the other side in less than a minute. The place needed a speed trap. Barboni hit the accelerator again as soon as we left the last gingerbread cottage behind and pushed on for Grayton Beach.

I favored him with a withering glance. "Of course I was in your room. What else could I do? Do you think a dancer goes out with just any customer? Do you think, in fact, that I have *ever* gone out with a customer?" Barboni was listening. "No. I have never, ever, crossed the line, until I met you." Oh God, this was crap, but it was working.

"Did you really think I would leave a public place with a man I hadn't checked out? No. I went up and looked through your room. I don't need your jewelry or your money. I need information. I need to know you're not maritally affiliated. I need to know you're really a businessman and not a dope dealer or a serial killer. So I went up to your room to check you out. You've got some explaining to do, big guy."

Barboni shook his head slowly. He couldn't believe it.

"I have explaining to do?"

"Absolutely," I said. "Like, where's your suitcase? Where are your toiletries? Why is there no sign that you've ever slept in that room?"

We were coming up on Grayton Beach. If he stopped I was in good shape. If he kept on going, I was dead. He stopped two minutes later at the only five-star restaurant on the Panhandle. Michael's is perhaps Florida's best-kept secret, and yet the tiny parking lot was full, leaving only one space beside the trash

Dumpster. NO PARKING AT ANY TIME, read the sign. Barboni couldn't read.

"You know what?" he asked, turning to look at me.

"What?"

He smiled slowly. "You're full of shit. I like that. Let's eat."

He wasn't going to answer my questions and he wasn't going to kill me. At least, not until after dinner.

He unfolded himself from the tiny sportscar and stood waiting expectantly. Apparently waiting for him to open my door would've been pushing it. I stepped out onto the sand and gravel lot and pointed to the No Parking sign.

Barboni shrugged. "Don't look like a fucking law to me. Do you see any trash trucks coming to make a pickup?"

I walked around the front of the car and started up the wide wooden steps to Michael's. The building was low-slung, with a tin roof. If you'd dropped it down by the beach it would've passed for an elderly vacation cottage. There were rocking chairs on the porch and a huge beveled glass door that swung open as an unseen hostess spotted us and opened it.

"Welcome to Michael's," she whispered. She was a reed-thin blonde with a long black skirt, a white form-hugging polyester blouse, and a need to please.

"Barboni, party of two," he said, smiling like he approved.

"We're expecting you, sir." Her eyes were only on him. "Right this way. I believe you requested the private room?"

"I did."

She was walking across the pine floors, past quiet tables with flickering candles and white linen tablecloths, out onto a small screened porch. One table waited in the middle of the tiny room, banked behind it was a chintz sofa. Intimate dining at its best.

The hostess pulled the table out and waited for us to sit down before she pushed it back, trapping me against the wall. Barboni sat beside me, a foot away, turned slightly so he could face me.

The way I figured it, I was right where he wanted me.

"Bring us a bottle of Taittinger," he said, smiling at the hostess and slipping a bill into her hand. Funny how the guy tipped everywhere but the Tiffany.

I studied the porch. There were bookshelves behind us, filled with old novels. An elderly ceiling fan whirred, producing the barest breeze, pulling in warm sea air. Glass windows were folded up like shutters waiting for the truly hot weather of summer, or the occasional thunderstorm. In any other circumstance, this would be my kind of place. Tonight, however, it seemed two-dimensional, a façade that, should I allow it, would lure me into a false sense of security.

A waitress returned with the champagne and two flutes. She popped the cork slowly and poured, all the while rattling off the evening's specials. Barboni waited until she finished.

"Just bring us two good salads with a balsamic vinaigrette, two filets, medium-rare, two baked potatoes, fully loaded, and then finish up with two coffees, regular, a piece of key lime pie and"—he looked over at me appraisingly—"a chocolate mousse. You got that?"

The tiny waitress nodded, her dark-haired bob jumping up and down. How New York provincial, I thought. Order your usual, don't consult the lady, just take charge. Whatever. I needed to arrive home alive. What was making a stink over steak and potatoes compared to my personal safety?

Barboni watched the waitress walk away, picked up his glass and then motioned for me to do the same. I figured he was going to make some crass toast and was surprised when he didn't. Instead he drank thoughtfully for a moment and then looked over at me.

"Sierra," he said, "I like your style. You're a liar and you make no apologies for it. Even your explanations are lies. Fair enough." He took another sip of champagne and I fairly gulped mine. "You and I come from the same background. Things aren't always what they seem and you learn not to ask a bunch of questions that might cause an otherwise lovely evening to turn ugly. Am I right?"

I nodded. I was listening, but I was also casting about for my eventual response. I needed a don't-fuck-with-me policy, something that would ensure my safety.

"So, here's how it's gonna work," Barboni continued. "No questions. No lies. Just a good time had on a casual basis between two consenting adults. It ain't gonna last because I'm not sticking around this hellhole any longer than I have to, and if you were looking to return up north, you would've done so by now. Understand?"

I nodded, took a sip of my champagne, and prepared to knock his dick in the dirt. I set my flute back on the table and turned toward him.

"I'm guessing we come from the same, shall we say, family structure?" I said. "And just so's you can feel more at home, I should tell you that my family has a long connection with New Jersey." I looked at him like he should be catching my drift and saw that he was listening carefully. "To be specific, my uncle Moose lives in Cape May."

Ah, the lights were on and the Barbonis were home. His eyes widened a little. I saw him thinking that he'd been about to mess seriously with a member of another family, a family that would not take kindly to someone hurting their little girl in any way, shape, or fashion.

"Your uncle is 'Big Moose' Lavotini?" he asked.

I shrugged like maybe he was slow on the uptake. "What do you think?" I said. "In fact, his son's due in town to visit me tomorrow. You know, take in the sights, relax a little. That might jam up my free time a bit, but I could still probably work in a lunch or something."

Too late, I saw the wheels turning. Little Moose would be due in tomorrow; that left all of tonight.

"Actually," I said, sneaking a peak at my watch, "he says tomorrow, but he's so precise. I figure him to arrive in town sometime shortly after midnight."

If I didn't miss my guess, Barboni gulped. What was it about that syndicate that scared the piss out of everybody? Someday I'd have to do some more careful research into those Lavotinis, but for now, it was enough that I used them to bail me out of any and all difficulties where a mobster would be a helpful contact.

"Of course," I said, eyeing the waitress's approach, "I'm sure you got family back home, too. Have you met my uncle?"

Barboni laughed. "Ain't nobody seen Big Moose. Not for years. Word is, after the big one, he decided it was better to lay low."

What big one was that? I wondered.

"Aw," I said, "I saw him just last year. I was up for the holidays. He's big on family togetherness."

Barboni was looking at me like I had two heads. "Your dad must be the other brother," he said softly. "The one the Moose didn't kill."

Shit. What could I do? I nodded and dug into my salad. I had a very dangerous family.

"So, set me up to meet Little Moose," he said suddenly.

I dropped my salad fork, sending it crashing to the floor between us. "What?"

"I'd like to meet your cousin," he said. "Maybe we share some common interests."

"Oh, I don't think so," I said. "He's a quiet guy. He don't even drive fast. Besides, when he comes to see me, he just wants his rest and relaxation."

Barboni laughed. "That's not what I hear," he said. "Word is Little Moose does his thinking with the little head and not the

136

big. I figure he's coming to see you so's he can try the variety at the Tiffany without having to pay for it. I hear he ain't big on relationships. I hear he's left a trail of dead pros. I hear he wears them out and then . . ."

Barboni stopped, probably realizing he shouldn't be talking about my cousin in such a cavalier fashion. He was right.

"Little Moose ain't like that," I said. I was starting to warm to my role. "Little Moose may have his problems with the opposite sex, but that is because he's a thinker. He don't spend a lot of time with feelings, henceforth, he misconstrues the signals his women give him. If he's turned to pros, it's on account of he don't want to get hurt any further. Little Moose is a sensitive guy."

Barboni chuckled softly. "If you say so," he said. "I've just seen the mess he leaves when he's on a tear, and believe me, it ain't pretty." He raised his left hand in defense. "No disrespect intended, understand. I'm just saying, people shouldn't cross him, that's all."

I took my opportunity and looked Barboni right in the eyes. "Nobody should cross a Lavotini," I said. "Nobody."

Barboni refilled our glasses and raised his in a toast. "Here's to not crossing any Lavotinis without mutual and informed consent."

I tossed mine back, never taking my eyes off his face. "So," I said, "are you here on business or not?"

Out of the corner of my eye, I caught something white moving, just behind Barboni, outside the porch, level with the floor. My team had arrived. I smiled and sat back, waiting for Barboni's answer.

"Like I said, and I mean no disrespect to you and yours, but ask me no questions and I'll tell you no lies."

He wasn't budging, not for the Big Moose or for the little one. Oh, well.

"Just like you got the word wrong about my cousin, I thought you would welcome the opportunity to set the record straight on the rumors about you."

"What rumors?" Barboni asked.

"Like that you're here to teach a lesson to certain circuit girls who won't pay to play, so to speak. I hear you're the muscle to enforce a certain, shall we say, insurance policy."

Barboni's face reddened.

"Word has it, sometimes you gotta do that to set the others straight. Sometimes, when you're looking after people, you've gotta keep them in line."

Barboni seemed to be wrestling with himself. He sat there, a faraway look in his eyes, and said nothing. When he roused himself, he looked back at me and shrugged.

"Everybody needs insurance," he whispered, and drained his flute dry. "If my company has a customer and they don't pay for the service we provide, well, sometimes I have to step in. I guess you could call me a customer-relations sort of guy. Likewise, if my customers are in need of assistance, I'd be the man to call.

The waitress picked that moment to arrive with our steaks, effectively cutting off any response I could've made. At least I had him on the run. I was one of *those* Lavotinis.

Twenty

$\mathcal{D}$inner was lovely, so long as you didn't think about the company or the circumstances of said dinner. The mousse was lighter than air, but it was the key lime pie that did me in. A dancer is not supposed to indulge in indiscretions like dessert, but I've never had to worry about my figure. It takes care of itself; the Lavotini genes, I guess.

Barboni was having an equally nice time. He smiled continuously, at everyone, including me. Every now and then his beefy hand would slide over and rest on my thigh. After a couple of glasses of champagne, I began to think I rather enjoyed the attention. By the time he paid the bill and we started to leave, I was having ideas that maybe I wouldn't mind kissing him. Crazy, I know, since I was fairly certain he was a hired killer working to ensure that the visiting porn stars paid their cut to their mob protectors.

We stepped out onto the porch and he slipped his arm around my waist. We walked at a leisurely pace toward the car. I could practically taste the man, so that was an indication of my level of sobriety. I was chalking it up to the Courvoisier we'd had with our coffees. He stopped just short of the Boxster and grabbed my arm. Here it comes, I thought, and turned to face him.

"Holy fucking shit!" he yelled.

This was not exactly the effect I had worked to engender, but then, different men react differently in the throes of passion. However, I did open my eyes. He was staring at his car. It had four flat tires.

I knew they'd heard him from inside, but I guess the little blond hostess knew it wasn't her job to deal with an irate ex-patron. The door remained firmly closed. We were in the middle of almost nowhere, with four flat tires and no hope of salvation. So when the tow truck pulled into the driveway mere seconds after our discovery, I was not only shocked but delighted. The fact that the tow truck was the twin of Pat's pickup, with a yellow flashing light hastily stuck on the roof, only further peaked my euphoria. The team was working.

Pat hopped down from the truck, left it running, and strode forward. She was wearing her work clothes: faded overalls, a bleached-out ball cap, and a tool belt. She walked up to the Boxster, kicked one of the tires, and turned to face Barboni.

"Reckon you don't have four spares, huh?" she asked.

Barboni barely stopped himself from exploding. I squeezed his arm and stepped in front of him.

"No, ma'am," I said. "Can you help us out?"

Pat grinned. "Sure can," she said. "My sister's on her way with a cab. Way I see it, we gotta call for a flatbed from over in Destin or P.C. Cain't get aholt of one before tomorrow morning. We'll have you good to go by then. In the meantime, Geniveve'll run you on home. You folks staying nearby?"

I managed to look disappointed. "No, we're at the Moongazer back in Panama City."

Pat just nodded and looked at the car. Barboni stepped away and pulled out a tiny cellular phone. We watched in silence as he paced back and forth across the lot, talking, gesturing with his hands, and venting. He paused, he listened, and finally he gave up, slamming the little phone shut and walking back to face down Pat.

"This is the best you can do?" he said, as Raydean's Plymouth Fury pulled into the lot. "You don't even got a real tow truck?"

Pat nodded. "That's right," she said. "Best we can do this time of night. See this?" she said, motioning to the winch mounted onto the bed of the truck. "That's my multipurpose tourist-hauler. I can pull you outta the sand when you attempt to four-wheel. I can haul you outta the water when you're fishing and don't know the tide tables. And I can haul you back to the garage when you break down. But I cannot haul a fancy foreign car with four flat tires. What're you people doing out here anyways? Ain't no restaurant worth paying a gagillion dollars for food that don't fill a plate. And to drive twenty-something miles just to get here?" Pat shook her head. "Why that's just asking for trouble."

Raydean pulled up beside Pat, stuck her head out the window, and spit. At least she'd lost the curlers. It was taking a hell of a chance that Barboni wouldn't recognize her as it was. But it was dark, and to some men all old ladies look alike.

"Genieve's Giddy-Yaps," she called cheerfully. "You two need a ride?"

"Can you take us to the Moongazer in P.C.?" I asked.

"That place is overrun with aliens," she said, "but, yes, if you insist, I can take you there."

Barboni looked at the mint-condition 1962 Plymouth Fury and scowled. It was not a limo. It was not even the yellow cab I knew he was used to, but it was transportation. He didn't give Raydean more than a cursory glance.

"Let's get the hell out of here," he muttered.

We slid into Raydean's backseat and I quickly pulled on a seatbelt. Barboni, never having ridden with her, didn't. Poor baby. Raydean floored it, chirped the tires out onto Highway 98, and took off like a bat out of hell. With one hand she reached over and switched the radio to a country station and cranked up the volume.

"You lovebirds enjoy yourselves," she yelled from the front. "Nothing like country to put you in the mood."

"Can you turn it off?" Barboni boomed.

"What?"

"Turn it off!"

Raydean reached over and turned the volume up. "Anything you say, sir!"

Barboni groaned and leaned back against the seat. His evening was clearly ruined. Tammy Wynette started crooning "Stand by Your Man," and I laughed.

"Aw, lighten up, Barboni," I said. "Look at it like this: you're in the backseat of a car with a beautiful woman on a lovely evening. Relax."

Barboni took my advice. He turned to me, slid his arm around my neck, and started to pull me toward him.

Raydean jerked the wheel and Barboni lurched sideways.

"What the fuck?"

"Possum!" Raydean yelled.

Barboni tried again. This time he cupped my chin with his fingers and tilted my head. His lips brushed mine and Raydean ran off the road, onto the shoulder. We bounced around like rubber balls as Raydean fought to regain control of the car.

"Antelope," she called back to us. "Feisty little critters."

"Don't you mean armadillos?" Barboni asked.

"Nope," Raydean answered. "Have a nice day."

It took Barboni only three tries to figure that whenever he made his move, Raydean would be watching. If she was watching us, she wouldn't be watching the road. He gave up.

We rode along with Raydean humming to the golden oldies, country-style. Now and then I peeked through the rear window and saw a comforting pair of headlights following us. My team was working their magic.

Raydean slowed down as she approached the edge of Panama City Beach.

"Y'all sure you want the Moongazer?" she asked.

"Absolutely," Barboni said. He was counting down the seconds until he would escape the backseat of the Fury.

Raydean drove on, making a beeline for the hotel. She turned into the sweeping expanse of cobblestoned driveway, narrowly missing the fountain itself, and screeched to a halt in front of the revolving doors. She then jumped out of the front seat and pulled my door open, bowing like a servant as I stepped out of the car.

"How much I owe you?" Barboni growled, pulling some twenties from an overstuffed billfold.

"How much you got?" she asked.

"I don't think it works that way," he said, and stuffed four twenties into her outstretched hand.

"Charity," Raydean muttered. "I'm working for charity."

Barboni didn't hear her over the noise of the traffic out on 98-A and the loud splashing of the fountain. He was darting back and forth, scoping out the front of the hotel. His hand slid into his jacket and pulled out an ugly black gun. Then he moved to the edge of the fountain and leaned forward, shielding himself in a crouch behind the fountain, staring intently through the multicolored lights that tinted the spray. My heart started pounding against my chest and my body was needled with a pepper spray of anxiety. What was going on? What was with the gun?

Barboni straightened abruptly and seemed to try and duck behind the tiers that stood in the center of the water. There was a popping noise, like firecrackers, and I realized someone was shooting. I froze, unable to make my body respond to the sensory input that my brain was receiving. We were in danger. I needed to get away, but I couldn't move. As I watched, Barboni jerked and fell forward into the fountain, his body dancing like a dolphin as it was riddled with bullets.

Twenty-one

I screamed. Everyone was screaming, running away from the entrance to the hotel, away from the awful sight that was playing itself out just in front of us. I grabbed Raydean, pushed her head down, and shielded her with my body as I propelled her around the Plymouth and took cover.

Raydean had seen everything, the way the bullets stitched across Barboni's chest, the way the water in the fountain turned to a dark red. She was beginning to shake, trembling in my arms as the waves of fear overtook what tender hold she had on sanity.

"Ohhh," she moaned. "Oh God, Sierra!"

I couldn't leave her. Even though the shooting seemed to be over, I couldn't risk running to try and help Barboni. It didn't really matter now anyway. He was dead.

In the distance the sirens began to wail, drawing closer in response to the hotel's 911 call. The hotel security guards, four of them wearing navy blazers with gold buttons and carrying guns and walkie-talkies, came blasting out of the hotel, running for cover behind the brickwork that sheltered the building. Fat lot of good those goons would do. The gunplay was over and whoever had shot Barboni wasn't hanging around just on the off chance he might take out a hotel security guard.

I looked up and down the strip for Pat, but I didn't see her.

If she'd been there I could've sent Raydean home, saved her from the questions that were bound to follow. As if reading my thoughts, the first patrol car squealed into the drive, sealing it off. Five other cars followed, closing off the driveway and preventing escape. It would only be a matter of time before the brown Taurus showed up. If the first detective on the scene wasn't Nailor, the second one would be. All he'd have to hear was my name, or Raydean's license plate number, and he'd be across town and down my throat.

Raydean started to cry softly. I stroked her hair and pulled her closer as the first uniform walked up to us. We must've looked pitiful because he squatted down next to me, his eyes blue pools of concern.

"You aren't hurt, are you, ma'am?" he asked softly.

I looked over her head at him. "She saw him get shot," I said. "It was a shock."

He nodded. He was tall and lean, with thick black eyebrows. I figured him to be in his mid to late thirties, too old to be a rookie.

"Why don't we get her inside. We're going to use one of the meeting rooms for our interviews. She might be more comfortable there." He looked over at Raydean again. "I'd sure feel better if an EMT looked her over."

I nodded, starting to feel a little cold and shaky myself. "That's very kind of you."

We stood up, each of us taking one of Raydean's arms. In my high heels, I was almost as tall as he was. So intent was I on walking Raydean inside, that I almost didn't notice Nailor's arrival. But it's like a sixth sense with me. I don't have to see him actually pull up; I feel him long before he's there.

The cop led us through the door of the hotel and I felt Nailor watching me walk away. I turned back and saw him standing by the fountain, pulling on a pair of latex gloves and issuing orders.

He'd be inside soon enough; in the meantime I had Raydean to attend to. I also needed to think fast about how much Nailor needed to know of the events of my evening.

I let the uniform lead us to the meeting room. The hotel staff was bustling around, hauling in chairs. Someone offered us coffee and I looked at Raydean.

"I think she needs hot tea," I said. "And if you got any cookies back there, that would be nice." It materialized in a matter of minutes, but Raydean was having none of it.

"Poisoned. I told you there were aliens here." She seemed resigned to it. She looked around the room at the other witnesses and nodded to herself. "That's them, all right." I didn't want to know who "them" was, so I let it go. She sat with her tea on her lap, tears rolling silently down her cheeks. She was terrified. What had I been thinking, dragging her into something so dangerous?

We waited for almost an hour before Nailor made his appearance. When he walked into the room, Raydean gasped. Two streaks of drying brown blood crossed the front of his chest. He hadn't noticed, but seeing Raydean point to his chest made him look and swear under his breath.

"All right," he said, when he reached me, "this is what I've got. You and the victim arrived in the driveway at eleven thirty-eight P.M. Raydean, here, was driving. The victim appeared to give Raydean some money and then stepped away. Thirty seconds later someone shot him and he fell into the fountain."

"That would about sum it up," I said. I didn't have the strength to put on an act.

"So, what's the deal? Why did he pay Raydean?"

I stretched my legs out in front of me and tried to get more comfortable in my seat. "She was our taxi driver," I said. "We went out to dinner."

"He left in a Porsche Boxster," Nailor said. "Where's that?"

"In Grayton Beach. Raydean and Pat flattened his tires because they were worried about me."

This brought a curious response from Raydean. She coughed, suddenly slurped down her lukewarm tea, and turned on me. "We did no such kind of a thing!" she said.

"You and Pat didn't slit his tires?"

Nailor was watching, not certain if this was part of our act or what.

"No! We were surveilling you from behind that porch. We weren't sure what he was up to, but Pat thought you had it under control. It wasn't until you guys settled into dessert that Pat went around front and saw your tires. That's when we decided to rescue you ourselves and not leave it to redneck chance." Raydean snorted, her old self. "Tire slitters! Why we're a whole heap brighter than that!"

"What I want to know," Nailor said, his voice neutral, "is why you and Pat felt the need to follow Sierra."

Raydean raised an eyebrow. "Why to protect her, of course! I didn't see you running in to save the day. There she was, trying to catch a murderer and where were you? And it wasn't just me and Pat acting like the Lone Ranger, neither."

"You had help?" Nailor asked.

Raydean nodded. "Of course we did. Fluffy wouldn't have missed it for the world! She was all tucked up in Pat's truck, waiting, just in case we needed our secret weapon."

Nailor sighed. He hadn't missed Raydean's mood shift or overlooked the tears that stood wet upon her face. In short, he had compassion.

"Why don't you take Raydean home," he said. "You need me to get a uniform to drive you?"

I knew he knew my car was in the hotel garage. The cops would've checked it long ago. So maybe it was concern on his part. Maybe it was his way of trying to make up for doubting me.

Or maybe it was further evidence of his lack of faith. Maybe he was testing me, trying to see if I'd lie about my car.

"I'll drive Raydean home in her car," I answered. I hesitated, watching his face for a sign. He was, as usual, unreadable. "That'll leave my car here, in the garage."

"How about I bring it out to you when we're done here?"

"I wouldn't want to trouble you."

He was staring at me, right into my eyes like nobody else was even in the room. "It's no trouble. It'll take me awhile here, but I'll be out when I'm done."

I nodded. For a moment I didn't trust myself to speak. I couldn't tell him that I needed him. I would never tell him that.

Twenty-two

*R*aydean said nothing on the way home. We rolled into her driveway at one-thirty. The rest of the trailer park was dark, except for the streetlights and the occasional porch light. The full moon was hidden by clouds, and a restless wind blew back and forth, changing directions to signal the approach of an impending storm.

I cut the engine and we sat there, neither one of us saying a word or moving to get out of the car. A moment later, Pat's old pickup pulled in behind us. The rusting door swung slowly open and Pat hopped down to the ground with a slow grunt that signaled her arthritis was kicking in. She moved like she hurt. Fluffy, feeling forgotten, jumped out of the driver's side window and ran ahead of Pat, leaping up and into the window of Raydean's Plymouth. She settled into my lap and began licking my hand.

"Is she all right?" Pat asked. Raydean didn't look up. She was staring out of the window, up at the thin outline of the moon.

"I don't know. Let's get her inside and into bed. Maybe she'll feel better after she's slept."

Pat seemed doubtful, but she walked around to Raydean's door and opened it anyway.

"Come on, honey," she cooed softly. "Let's get you into the house. You'll feel better after you've had a little rest."

Raydean allowed herself to be led inside. Pat took her back to the bedroom, helped her into a nightgown, and then returned, a worried look on her face.

"I'm staying," she announced. "I'll sleep here on the sofa, just in case she needs me."

I sank down into a chair at the kitchen table and put my head in my hands. Pat stepped closer and rested one of her work-roughened hands on top of my head.

"It isn't your fault," she said. "You couldn't have anticipated this."

"But I should've known something might happen," I said. "After all, you two were my backup." Fluffy barked like she objected to not being included.

"All right," Pat said with a sigh. "You should've known. Now, what does that get you? Guilt on top of grief? We've got a situation. We took a risk. Raydean, for all her non compos mentis behavior, was sane enough to understand that this was not a game. We've been in some tough spots before and we'll see them again. But don't you see what it does to include her? Raydean spends her days alone. We're all she has. And she's all we have."

Pat stopped, realizing as she spoke what a huge admission she was making about the quality of our lives. We were the outcasts: two old ladies and a stripper.

"When you make her a part of us, you're saying we need her. Sierra, no one has needed or valued Raydean for years. Sit there and guilt-trip yourself if you want, but pull your butt up off your shoulders long enough to see things as they really are."

I couldn't think. I was too tired to figure it out. Maybe in the morning, I thought.

"I'm going home," I said. "Nailor's coming later to bring my car. Francis'll be getting in sometime. I need to try and catch a couple of hours of sleep before they're on me with a million questions. The team can reconvene for a debriefing in the morning."

At the word *team*, Pat smiled.

I left her there in the kitchen, sitting at the table with the lone source of light casting a pale yellow circle around her as she sat drinking a cup of coffee and listening out for our friend.

I walked across the road and up onto my stoop where I sat for I don't know how long, contemplating nothing more than the way the grass bent as the wind swept down over the trailer park. The sky sparkled with distant lightning and the air trembled with thunder that drew closer as I sat waiting. I could smell the rain in the air, feel it becoming heavier and full of moisture. It smelled like home on a hot summer night.

In Philly the rain was our only salvation during the summer. We didn't have air-conditioning until I was in the seventh grade and Pa broke down and bought three window units. Before then, we would sit out on the stoop, waiting for the rain, our sweaty kid bodies reeking of exercise and dirt. When the storm approached, we'd stop playing and sit like stone statues, gargoyles maybe, hoping to feel the first cool drops on our skin. In Philly, in the summer, the rain was a second chance. It cooled you and washed the salty moisture from your skin, replacing it with the grassy smell of a country summer, even though we lived miles from the rolling hills of Chester and Bucks counties. In the rain you could be anyone, even yourself, because everything started over.

I sat waiting for the first fat drop, and felt it plop down beside me, then another and another. Fluffy, who'd trotted up beside me, didn't share my enthusiasm. She scampered through the doggie door and sat whimpering on the other side. She wanted me to come in. She didn't understand that I needed the rain.

The drops came faster, melding into a steady stream. The

lightning pierced the nearby sky and the thunder shook the trailers. I stayed on my stoop, the rain drenching me like a cool shower, my black sheath clinging to my body like a second skin. I took off my heels and slung them inside through the doggie door, stretching my feet out in front of me, and leaning back on my arms. The rain stung my face, slapping at the images that refused to leave my head.

I sat there until the tears came, crying through the peak of the storm, my sobs carried off by the wind and hidden by the thunder. I was so alone and so afraid. I hadn't seen the attack coming on Barboni, hadn't anticipated it, hadn't known what to do when it arrived. In short, I'd been completely vulnerable. It could've just as easily been Raydean or me that took the hit. This wasn't a game. There was a killer out there somewhere and he could strike at any time and hit anyone. Who was I to think I could stop him?

The rain had eased, moving off, the thunder rolling in the direction of the beach. The temperature had dropped by a good ten degrees. What had been refreshing and cleansing now felt like stinging icicles. I stood up and looked around. He could be watching me. He could realize that I was here, alone, and come after me. Wherever I was, he seemed to follow, killing off the people around me. I shook my head, trying to clear that thought from my head. Now I was paranoid. It only seemed that the killer followed me, shooting over my shoulder, killing the people in my path. In reality, I just happened to be there when he struck.

The danger was that he knew I was trying to find him. Maybe that was why Barboni died. Maybe the killer was trying to taunt me. No, that didn't make sense, either. Nothing about this situation made sense. I was too tired to think clearly. I turned and went inside, peeling off my sodden dress and leaving it lying on the kitchen counter. I unhooked my bra and left it lying on the bathroom floor, along with my panties. I pulled back the covers and crawled in between the sheets. Fluffy hopped up, turned a complete circle twice, and flopped down at the foot of the bed. We fell asleep within seconds it seemed. When I awoke, Nailor was sitting on the edge of the bed.

Twenty-three

I was dreaming about him. In my dream we were riding on a motorcycle. I sat behind him, holding on, my head resting on his shoulder. We were happy, the troubles of the present forgotten. We were going away and no one was chasing us. We were driving down 98-A, the beach road, laughing at the seagulls that chased along the shore, outrunning them.

Suddenly Nailor hit the brakes, trying to avoid something in the road. The bike veered and Nailor battled for control. I looked out in front of us, trying to see. Alonzo Barboni's body lay in the road, soaked in blood, his face picked away by scavengers, decaying. Road kill. We slid, hitting the pavement and traveling, the road tearing at our skin as we slammed, inevitably, into the rotting, heat-bloated body that lay before us.

I sat up in bed, terrified, breathing hard and sweat-soaked. When I saw the figure sitting beside me, I screamed and Nailor grabbed me.

"It's all right. Sierra, it's me." He pulled me to him, his arms wrapping around me, stroking my hair, shushing me with soft whispers. I shuddered as the images kept coming, a slide show of blood and gore.

"It was a bad dream," Nailor said softly.

"No," I said. "It was real."

"Okay, okay," he whispered. "It will be okay. I'm here. You're not alone. Shhh. We're going to be okay."

He held me for a long time, not saying a word. Fluffy jumped down off the bed and walked out of the room, figuring this was one situation that required privacy. I felt the nightmare fade into the distance and the horror of the evening recede. I was home and I was safe. My body relaxed and for a while I let go, resting in a safe harbor.

At some point Nailor's touch changed and I responded. His breathing quickened when my fingers moved across his back, drifting up his neck and into his hair. He kissed me, his hands pulling me closer. I felt my body tense as he touched the nipple of my left breast. His tongue started moving down my neck and I knew what was next.

"Stop!"

"What?" He straightened, pushing back a little so he could look into my eyes.

I felt like an idiot in some way, because it was finally here, the moment I'd been waiting for, and I was about to spoil it, again.

"You and me," I said, "we've got stuff to figure out here. You can't just come barging in here and take advantage of the moment."

His eyes glittered dangerously. His body tightened ever so slightly, but enough to let me know he was on guard again.

"Sierra, this thing with Marla, you can't let that come between us." His hand tightened against my back and for a second I was sorely tempted, but then I remembered that the only thing standing between Marla and a railroad trip to hell was me.

"You think I'm a flyweight," I said. "You don't want me to talk to you about your murder investigation, even though I have access to information that you could never get in a million years, but it's fine for me to get naked with you."

"That's not true, Sierra, and you know it." Nailor pulled away and my heart sank.

"Then what is true? What is with this here?" I said, gesturing to the two of us and the bedroom.

"Sierra, have you ever thought that I want to be able to take care of you every once in a while?" I started to argue, but he put his fingers to my lips. "Not all the time. I'm in no way saying I think you're helpless or stupid or incapable of holding your own. I'm just saying that this is a very dangerous situation. Someone has threatened you. I hear what you're saying, but you have to trust me to take what you give me and use it my way."

For a moment I was speechless. No, I had never once stopped to think that Nailor would want to take care of me. I'd gone right past that. People didn't take care of Sierra Lavotini. That was my job.

He read me. "Is it so inconceivable that I would care about you, Sierra?" He reached up and brushed a lone curl away from my cheek. "Is it so hard for you to trust me?"

It felt as if every wall, every defense I had was suddenly being stripped away, and I was vulnerable before him. To further complicate matters, tears began rolling down my cheeks, betraying me.

"Don't cry, honey," he said, and pulled me into his arms. "It's all right."

There was so much I wanted to say, and yet I couldn't make the words come out. I didn't dare do that. What was I going to do? Tell him about Tony? About how he'd hurt me and left me so dead inside I could hardly breathe? Was I supposed to tell him about all the bad choices I'd made or the people who'd hurt me in the name of getting their own needs met? I didn't think so. And I certainly wasn't going to tell him there were times I just wanted someone to hold me, just like he was holding me now. No, Sierra Lavotini was not in any way spineless and weak.

Instead I let him hold me. I let whatever doubts I had about him fade into the background. I lingered on the edge of diving in, still reluctant to swim in what could only end up becoming dangerous waters.

But Nailor must've sensed all of this. His touch never changed. He never stopped caressing me and holding me close to him. He didn't back away, but he wasn't going to push himself on me. If anything happened between us, it would have to be my move, and perhaps that's what made it all right.

I pushed back and looked up at him, our eyes meeting and holding there, the questions asked and answered without a word being spoken. There was something there, something that I just didn't want to fight any longer; and so I smiled and the Sierra he knew returned.

"Okay," I whispered.

"Okay, what, Sierra?" He was going to make me say the words out loud.

I reached up and touched his cheek, my fingers trailing slowly down his neck. "Okay, so maybe you don't think I'm stupid. And maybe you were trying to look out for me."

"Maybe?" He smiled.

"Yeah, maybe." I leaned forward and kissed him, my lips brushing his softly. "But I'm at a disadvantage here," I murmured.

"How do you see that?" He looked around the room, then at me sitting there with the sheet bunched around my waist. "We're in your bedroom, on your turf, and you're calling the shots."

"I'm at a disadvantage because you're dressed. Look at you. You're in my bedroom wearing a suit, and I'm completely naked."

"Completely?" He reached over and slowly drew back the sheet. He whistled soft and low. "Well, so you are."

"My point exactly," I said. "Stand up."

He rose slowly from the edge of the bed and stood in front of me. I smiled and moved my pillows back against the headboard. It was show time.

"Unbutton your shirt," I whispered.

His eyebrow went up and he smiled. He reached for the top button and very slowly started to undo his shirt. His eyes never left mine. The shirt fell open, revealing his broad, muscular, tanned chest. I felt my stomach flip over and my heart begin to pound against my rib cage. He unbuttoned his cuffs and slipped the shirt off.

"Unbuckle your pants," I said.

He stepped out of his loafers and began to undo his pants. They fell to the floor, carried by the heavy buckle on his belt. He stood there, wearing dark gray boxers, obviously very happy to see me.

"All right," I said, "come here."

Nailor laughed softly. "Oh, Sierra," he said. "What's this? You turning shy on me? You don't want it all off?"

The tables had turned. He'd read me again. His eyes burned into mine and he slipped his fingers under his waistband. With one fluid movement he pushed his boxers to the floor, stepping out of them and standing before me. Oh God! I looked at him, really looked at him, and he laughed.

"Take your time," he said.

I was not going to look away. I was not going to give him the satisfaction. I couldn't possibly . . . and on the other hand, I couldn't possibly *not*. . . .

He took a step closer toward the bed and instinctively I moved back, suddenly uncertain. He sat down beside me, stretched out one hand and ran it down the length of my side. This could be a good thing, I thought, a very good thing.

I moved away from the pillows to reach for him. "Come here," I said. I ran my hand across his chest. "Kevlar implants, or is that the real deal?" I asked.

He laughed, and pulled me halfway onto his chest. "Guess you'll have to find out for yourself," he said. But I couldn't think.

He moved, rolling me over onto my back and poising himself above me, his tongue flicking across my nipples, moving from one breast to the other.

Stop that! I thought. But thank God he wasn't reading my mind. His tongue made its way slowly across my belly, moving down my body like a Geiger counter homing in on the mother lode. And then he was there. My back arched, my hands gripped his hair, and I lost touch with reality. Oh God, I couldn't remember ever feeling like that. I moaned softly and he chuckled but didn't stop. I could feel my body heating up.

"Please! Now! I want you inside me! Now!"

Nailor chuckled again but paid no attention to me. Instead he slowed down, which only made matters worse. I moaned and pushed up against him. Then he stopped! He pulled back and looked up at me. The bastard was smiling, enjoying prolonging my agony.

"What are you doing?" I reached for him, tried to pull him up on top of me, but he was going nowhere. I was so close!

He kept his eyes locked with mine, but his fingers took over, slipping inside me, moving everywhere, slowly building me to a point where I felt the rest of my reality slipping away. I was going to lose it. I was going to explode while he watched.

"Please," I whispered. But I was hatching a little plan of my own. He shifted sideways and I slipped out from under him, using one of his own close-quarter combat moves to take him off guard. He landed on his back with a soft thud and this time I was on top.

"Well, how do you like that?" I said. "Looks like I'm in the catbird seat now."

"Oh, yeah?" He reached up and pulled my breast into his mouth. For a moment I froze, then slipped out of reach, sliding down across his chest, reaching out for a little taste test of my own.

162

He groaned as my tongue found the little line of pleasure just behind the tip of his shaft. I began getting better acquainted and Nailor stiffened. Gotcha, I thought to myself.

"Sierra," he moaned softly, "stop."

I lifted my head and let my fingers do the talking.

"No!" He pulled me up to him and slipped his fingers in between my legs. "No!" he whispered, as he rolled me over, "it goes like *this*. . . ."

Oh, yes! I thought as he moved in between my legs. *It goes exactly like that.*

Twenty-four

The sun was streaming through the trailer windows when I awoke and someone was yelling my name. From the sound of it, the person was inside the house and moving closer. For one split second, I nestled closer to Nailor, feeling his hot body wrapped around mine, but then I sprang fully awake. Francis! My big brother was in the trailer and moving at a rapid clip toward the door of my bedroom.

"Hey!" I called out. "I'm coming! Go make coffee!"

The footsteps stopped. "That freakin' figures, Sierra! I drive twenty hours, with only two short stops, and you're busting my balls for coffee!"

But he was moving back down the hallway, heading for the kitchen. Nailor was awake, lying there and looking at me. He didn't seem at all concerned about the other man in my trailer. No, his look was more like that of a man with unfinished business. When he pressed up against me, he left no doubt about what was on his mind.

"That's my brother," I said. Nailor showed no signs of backing down. "My big brother, Francis."

I wanted to jump out of bed, but Nailor's fingers were doing the most interesting things. I moaned and rolled back toward him, biting the edge of his shoulder softly.

"Oh God! No! I've got to get up."

I pushed him away and sprang out of bed. This was all I needed, my big brother and Nailor, face-to-face. Who knew how that would go? Francis already didn't like me dancing. He had a set of rules for himself and a set of rules for me, and they were very different, and they probably didn't include having Nailor in my bed.

I pulled on my purple terry robe and sprinted down the hallway, stopping just short of the living room to run my fingers through my hair and compose myself before I walked into the kitchen.

Francis was pouring the water into the coffeepot, his back to me, when I stepped up behind him.

"Hey, bro," I said.

Francis turned around, scowling. He looked like a Marine, ramrod-stiff posture, black hair clipped close to his head in an almost buzz cut. He looked like a larger version of Pa, handsome, black-eyed, and not an ounce of fat on his well-muscled, fireman body.

"Hey yourself!" he said. He didn't hug me like he usually did. Instead he looked behind me, his eyes wandering from the floor where my heels lay to the counter where my black sheath lay tossed like an afterthought.

"Must've been a wild night," he said, his voice tight with displeasure.

"It was," I said, "but not at all in the way you think."

He looked at me. "Really? 'Cause I think you should look in the mirror before you go saying that. Your eyes have black circles from where you didn't take your mascara off. Your lips are all swollen. And your hair looks like you sat out in a windstorm."

I might've had a shot at convincing Francis that I was not the lascivious wild woman that he just knew me to be, but at that moment Fluffy and Nailor strolled into the kitchen. Nailor grinned at me like we shared some kind of secret and Fluffy broke wind. Not at all the impression I was trying to create.

" 'Morning," Nailor said, extending his hand to Francis. "Welcome to Florida."

Francis stared at the outstretched hand, then up at Nailor, who smiled genuinely and looked my brother right in the eye. There was one awkward moment where Francis sized up Nailor and then shook his hand.

"Francis Lavotini," he said. "Sierra's brother."

I was watching a tribal rite. It couldn't have been clearer had there been drums, headdresses, and a campfire.

"I'll have coffee ready in a minute," I said, supremely wishing I had a faster coffeemaker. Moments such as this were meant to be endured only when one has had enough caffeine to function. I was sorely in need.

"Babe," Nailor said, enjoying the new familiarity, "can you make mine to go?"

Babe? Did I look like somebody you'd call babe? Oh, I think not.

"Sure," I said, and smiled. I wasn't giving Francis any ammunition.

Nailor reached for the wall phone and dialed a number. He waited, grunted a series of commands, and finally seemed to reach a human voice.

"Whatc'hu got?" he asked. There was a long pause, more grunting, and a large frown. Nailor nodded and began barking orders. "Serve the warrant at the apartment. Now." He heard something he didn't like. "What? When was that?" His frown grew deeper and I noticed that he had Francis's undivided attention.

"All right, then. They're idiots and I'll deal with them later. For now, issue a BOLO. Go to the Tiffany. Post a guy there. Page me when you have her. Oh, and send a uniform to pick me up. I'm at the Lively Oaks Trailer Park, lot thirty-eight." He hung up and turned around. The man who had made love to me was gone. The cop was all the way back.

"Would you excuse us for a minute?" he said to Francis.

Francis didn't like that one bit, but he walked into the living room anyway. Nailor waited until he was out of earshot and then turned to me.

"I don't want to tell you this, because it's going to cause problems, but I figure you'd rather hear it from me. I've issued a warrant for Marla's arrest. We recovered the gun used in last night's shooting. The initial ballistics report matches it to all three murders." He was watching my reaction, hitting me with fact after fact. "The gun is registered to Marla and we recovered one of her prints from the barrel. Honey, I'm sorry."

I went numb. If this was true, the Tiffany Gentleman's Club was sunk. It also meant I was a seriously bad judge of character.

"Well, just because it's her gun —"

He interrupted. "We had someone watching her condo. Somehow during the night, she gave them the slip. She doesn't have an alibi for the time of this murder either. She's it, Sierra." His tone of voice said, "end of story," but I couldn't let it go.

"I stand by what I said before: Marla's no murderer. You're looking right past Barboni and the protection-money angle. This has something to do with all of that, I know it does." I wasn't going into it with Francis possibly listening. It wouldn't have served a purpose anyway. Nailor's mind was made up, and I'd have to prove him wrong. "So what's next?"

Nailor reached out and touched my shoulder. "When we find her, she'll be arrested and arraigned. She's going to need a good lawyer." He looked back over his shoulder in Francis's direction. "Why don't you just try and put this out of your mind for the day? Take some time off with your brother. If I need any more information about last night, or if we apprehend her, I'll let you know."

He pulled me closer and wrapped me in his arms. "Don't wander off too far," he said.

I had other plans, but there was no point in telling him that, either. Instead I walked him to the door and kissed him good-bye. A patrol car sat just behind my car, so I made it a good kiss, just in case there was any question in the young officer's mind about what the detective had been up to. Nailor laughed and walked off.

"I'll call you later," he said.

I watched the car pull out and drive off, visuals from the night before running through my head. I could still feel his fingers on my skin, the way he felt as he moved inside me, the way he sent me screaming out of control when the orgasms shook my body, one after another. It was going to be a long day and, hopefully, an even longer night.

Francis didn't let me linger. He stepped up behind me, a steaming mug of coffee in his hand. "Here," he said. "Thought you might need it."

I looked across the street and saw the curtains flutter in Raydean's living room. Pat's truck was still sitting in the driveway, so I figured the team was sending smoke signals.

"So what's going on here, Sierra?" Francis asked. "You call home, crying to Ma. You get us all worried. I come down here and what do I find? You with a guy in your bed. Is that the guy that made you cry? 'Cause if that's him, I gotta wonder what's up."

The questions were coming in a steady stream. I took a large swig of my coffee and tried to come up with a policy statement. Fortunately for me, my response was delayed by the phone.

"Ms. Lavotini?" The voice rumbled like the train coming in to Reading Terminal.

"And you are?"

"Let's say I'm a friend of the family." The way the voice said *family* made a chill start at the base of my neck and work its way down my spine.

"A friend of what family?" I asked. Francis stopped drinking and looked up with a frown.

"The family representing the newly deceased, Alonzo Barboni. We would like to speak with you and your visiting cousin at your earliest convenience."

My throat went dry and my head started to pound. How did this person know about my "visiting cousin"? Barboni was the only one I'd told. Then I flashed to Barboni's last phone conversation in the parking lot of Michael's. Had he called New York?

"Which cousin would that be?" I tried to sound innocent.

"Don't fuck with me, girlie," the voice continued. "I am giving you the opportunity to speak with our affiliates and explain how Mr. Barboni died. Because of our respect for your family, we are asking that Little Moose be present. We want to assure him of our good intent. We merely need information."

What choice did I have?

"All right," I said, "here's the setup. Meet me on the deck at Ernie's this afternoon at three. I'll have my cousin with me, but understand your business is with me. If he declines to come, you've still got me."

"If he declines to come, we'll *have* you."

Shit! What was with this guy? Surely they didn't think the Lavotini syndicate was looking to take out whatever group Barboni had represented? This was just what I needed, a family holy war.

"How will I know you?" I asked.

"You won't," he answered, "but we'll know you." The connection went dead and I turned to look at Francis.

"Okay," I said. "You've probably got some questions about that, so I'm going to give it to you straight up: I'm in trouble and you're the only one who can help me."

Bingo. Francis tried not to look pleased, but he stuck his

tongue inside his cheek, a childhood thing he always did when he wanted to appear cool and was secretly excited.

"What's up?"

I told him, leaving out minor details. I tried to play down the entire thing, but in the end, he caught on.

"So basically, you're saying you want me to act like Big Moose Lavotini's son. You want me to keep you from getting your ass kicked by muscle from New York?"

"Right. See? It's simple. You say the Lavotinis have no beef with whoever it is in New York City, and before you know it, we'll be on our way home."

Francis stood up and slammed his coffee mug down on the table. "Bullshit, Sierra! Nothing's ever that simple with you. There are parts you've left out, things you've covered over, and just plain lies here. But, yeah, I'll do it. I'll do it because you'll wind up dead if I don't. They'll assume this is a family war, then." Francis shook his head and walked to the coffeepot. "Honest to God, Sierra, you need professional help."

"All right, granted I owe you big for this," I said. "But there are reasons and explanations you don't even get here. I owe Vincent a helping hand. He gave me a job. He took me in when I moved here and he made me the headliner. We were raised to help people who help us, Francis, or didn't you come up in the same family? And Marla? She's an asshole, but she don't got nobody to help her out."

Francis wasn't saying anything.

"You look down your nose at me, Francis. You think I've got a cheap profession. You think it's next to whoring, and nothing I can say will change your mind. Be that as it may, but you're wrong. I'm an entertainer and a therapist and a priest to the men I dance for. I'm their sister and their mother and their wife. I'm the one who listens when nobody else will. And they think they own me. No way. I'm good, Francis. This is what I do. So, yeah,

I'm in a scrape. But tell me you never got in a situation before."

Francis drank his coffee, his eyes clear and dark. He was listening.

"It's funny," I said. "Nobody respects a dancer, but you come watch us. You tell us your secrets, your hopes, your failures, and you feel better for it. So what's that about, eh? And don't tell me you never visited the Beaver Club in Upper Darby, 'cause I know you have."

Francis put down his coffee mug, stretched his hand out across the table, and took my hand in his.

"Truce," he said softly. "I'll do it and you don't owe me. I'm your brother and I love you. You know how I feel about this dancing thing. I don't approve, Sierra. But maybe it's not my place to give approval. Still, I don't understand it. I don't like the way they look at you."

"They can look any way that they want, Francis," I said. "I'm the one who empties their wallets. I'm the one who walks off the winner."

He shrugged and I let it go. We sat there for a while, drinking coffee and staring out the bay window at the empty street. Finally, he spoke again.

"So, what's your basic wardrobe for a New Jersey mobster on vacation? Were you thinking Hawaiian shirt and dark glasses? Or were you wanting a suit and tie?"

He laughed and I did, too. Then I got up from my chair, came around the table, and hugged him.

"I love you, Francis," I said, my voice muffled by his shoulder.

"I love you too, honey," he said.

Twenty-five

$\mathscr{E}$rnie's Restaurant and Bar sits touching the waters of St. Andrew's Bay. It is a small, well-heeled watering hole that caters to the local business population. It is nestled close to the in-town old Panama City homes and draws a crowd of locals who come for good food and microbrews. The tourists overlook it, making it all the more attractive to those in the know. It is a favorite of mine, but that's not why I chose it for the meet.

I picked Ernie's because at three o'clock in the afternoon it is well-lit and sparsely populated. Less chance for a large loss of life should there be gunplay, and less chance for gunplay because a lot of the local law-enforcement officers stop by for an afternoon beer on their way home. We could sit outside, overlooking the water, and discuss business with relatively few worries. At least, that's the way I hoped it would run.

Francis chose a suit and a pair of aviator-style dark glasses for his first, and in my best opinion, only appearance as Little Moose Lavotini. He walked up the wooden steps and through the doors of Ernie's like a man who knew where he was going and was used to being in charge. He stopped just inside the door, took stock of the main room, and then breezed right on through and out onto the deck. Once there, he looked out at the water, took in all the possible routes of escape, and settled for a table that faced both the front door and both exits. Something told me Francis had been watching TV all of his life, just waiting for a moment like this.

I was wearing a bright little sundress splashed with tropical colors, a royal blue, big-brimmed straw hat, and a matching pair of high heels. I looked the exact opposite of the way I felt. Francis looked tough. When the waitress approached, he ordered coffee and I ordered a mai tai. A stupid drink, I know, a waste of alcohol, but it matched my outfit and this was a time when appearance counted more than desire.

The drinks arrived and I had worked my mai tai halfway down the glass before the New York contingent showed. They pulled up in a dark black rental, tinted windows, the whole incognito bit played to the hilt. But the guy who stepped out of the car didn't look the part. He had greasy brown hair pulled back in a ponytail, wore moccasins without socks, faded blue jeans with worn-through spots in the appropriate places, and a polo shirt. He looked like a Hollywood producer more than a family man.

The car stayed by the front door with the engine running, so I figured the true muscle was sitting behind the wheel and maybe also in the backseat. Francis tensed and took a long draw of his coffee. From the looks of it, Mr. Hollywood wasn't carrying. This was a good thing, as Francis and I weren't armed either.

Hollywood spotted us and walked directly through the bar and out onto the deck. He walked to the table, rested a hand on the back of a vacant chair, and smiled.

"You look a little like your picture," he said. It was the voice from the phone, ugly and deep, no match for the smiling man who stood looking down at me.

He turned to my brother, who rose slowly and stuck out his hand.

"Mr. Lavotini, it is an honor."

Francis looked at the outstretched hand and ignored it. "And who might you be?" Francis asked.

"Packy Cozzone, out of—"

Francis interrupted. "I know where you're from. Have a seat." He waited until Packy sat down, then sank back into his own chair. Packy didn't seem at all uncomfortable with Francis. If I'd been on the receiving end of my brother's behavior, I'd have been shaking, knowing I was on thin ice.

"Let's get this little matter cleared up, shall we?" Francis said. "You're disturbing my vacation. You've added more unpleasantness to what is already a traumatic situation for my cousin, and you have cast a pall over an otherwise lovely afternoon. So what is it, exactly, that you think Sierra can help you with?"

Packy stretched and signaled to the waitress. He ordered a dry martini, onions, straight up, then he turned his attention back to us.

"Alonzo Barboni was here to conduct a little business survey for me. He called me from the parking lot of a restaurant last night to complain about his tires being slit and there being no one available to rectify the situation. He was hoping we could do something from New York, but of course we don't have connections in such an isolated part of the country." Packy turned and looked at me. "That's when Barboni mentioned your name. He wondered why Little Moose here was really coming into town."

Packy looked at Francis. "Imagine our distress when an hour later our friend is killed. Put yourself in our place. You'd have to wonder. Two New York families with overlapping interests, and suddenly one of the families sends a representative into the other's territory. So I start thinking maybe somebody wants to squeeze us out of an area, such as the Panhandle. I'm thinking maybe it's you and your family." Packy's eyes were ice cold and his voice thick with anger. "So you can see why I needed to speak to you."

Francis betrayed no visible emotion. He took a sip of coffee, leaned back, and stared through his glasses at Packy. My brother was a natural. I was starting to wonder why he hadn't taken up acting as a professional venture.

"What exactly was Barboni sent here to do?" he asked.

Packy's eyes glittered. He probably figured Francis knew all about Barboni and was playing him for a fool, testing him.

"Same thing he did in New York," Packy answered. "He was just insuring our investment in Florida. After all, we wouldn't want anything to happen to our actresses when they go out on tour. It costs money to provide protection. A few of the girls happened not to understand that. Barboni was only in town to explain it to them. To cut their fucking tits off if they didn't come around."

The last sentence was so harsh and so unexpected that I jerked at the raw venom in Cozzone's voice. He assumed we knew. He probably figured that was how the Lavotini Syndicate dealt with holdouts, too.

Packy looked up as the waitress approached, took the martini, and flipped her a twenty-dollar bill. She went away pleasantly surprised.

"Now, to cut through the bullshit here, I figure the Lavotinis want a piece of the travel circuit, but Panama City's ours, as is Pensacola, as is Tallahassee. That's the way it's been for two years. Why're you choosing to fuck with the arrangement now?"

Francis leaned back in his chair and merely stared at Cozzone. The silence grew and with it went whatever peace of mind I had left. I sucked down the rest of my mai tai and hoped for a buzz. All I got was a fruit-juice aftertaste.

Packy looked back toward the waiting sedan, then out at the water. His eyes were slowly lowering, like he was maybe in deep thought. He was probably figuring out when and how to kill us both. I glanced over at Francis, stealing a glance from under the brim of my hat. I couldn't see his eyes, so I had no idea what in the hell he was thinking, but if he didn't come up with something fast, the North Florida Lavotinis would be history, bad history.

Finally Francis spoke. "We're not after the protection angle," he said. "Frankly, that's small potatoes. We've never done much with protection. We look at that as chump change for losers, no offense intended." Damn! Why didn't he just reach over and slap the boy?

"We had nothing to do with your guy taking a whack. That's not to say he didn't deserve it, or that he didn't piss people off, but we didn't see taking him out in such a public manner and with such fanfare as being worthwhile."

Packy Cozzone was steaming, but perhaps out of respect for a larger family, he held his temper in check.

"Barboni was fucking with my sister's—cousin's—club. He was completely too high-profile." Francis shook his head with distaste. "Very unprofessional. If you were looking to issue a warning, then killing the girls was carrying things way too far. You lose your valuables that way. If you got nothing to protect, then you got nothing to lose. You see what I'm saying here, Packy?"

Packy's face went from red to white to a bluish purple. Francis was slapping him publicly and it felt bad. I looked over at Francis, trying to warn him that he was getting a little carried away, but he wasn't taking his eyes off Packy.

"It is one thing to teach a lesson," Francis continued, obviously warming to his role, because his tongue was stuck firmly in his cheek. "You scar a face, you cut up a body part, but you do not kill the girl, let alone two of them."

Packy couldn't help himself. He was brimming over with his desire to set Francis straight, and that was just what Francis wanted.

"Alonzo Barboni did not button those two bimbos," Packy said. "The Cozzone organization may be significantly smaller than you Lavotinis, but we are every bit as professional. We supply film producers and dance clubs with girls. We make sure the client gets quality entertainment and the girls get taken care of. To that end, Barboni was trying to figure out who was taking out the girls down here. It is our first venture into the Panhandle area, and we expected some resistance, but we didn't expect this kind of trouble. Barboni said he was getting a pretty good bead on the problem"—he looked over at me, long and hard—"but then he got killed. Makes you wonder, huh?"

Francis clearly took offense at Packy's implication. He stood up, towering with all of his Marine presence over Packy Cozzone. He leaned across the table, his knuckles biting into the wooden surface in front of Packy's empty martini glass.

This brought a response from the sedan. The two front doors swung open and two gorillas stepped out and turned to await a signal from Cozzone. Packy looked at them, looked like he wanted to ask for help but couldn't quite bring his vocal cords to act.

"You don't wonder about a Lavotini," my brother said. "There is never any doubt about where we stand. If I tell you that we had nothing to do with your pissant operation and the loss of your goon, then you'd best believe it. If we wanted the business, we'd have it, and you and I would not be having this conversation."

Francis gave this time to sink in, then continued. "Now, you owe my cousin an apology." Francis backed up a little and waited, apparently oblivious to the muscle that stood touching bulges under their thin windbreakers.

Packy Cozzone fumed. He was about to kiss my ass. We all knew it. It was just a matter of swallowing enough bile to make the job possible. He gulped, looked over at me, and brought forth the most disingenuous smile ever shown on the back deck at Ernie's.

"I don't know what came over me, Miss Lavotini. I suppose I was overcome by the grief entailed in losing a cherished member of our organization. Whatever the reason, my behavior was inexcusable and I beg your pardon."

Spoken like a boarding-school graduate, but his eyes told me how he planned to hurt me if ever given the chance, and I fought to suppress a shudder. I smiled right back, bigger and broader and much more genuine than his pitiful attempt.

"Apology accepted, Mr. Cozzone. We all lose our heads from time to time." My look told him I was praying for the loss of his little head, just as soon as I had the opportunity and a dull knife.

Francis smiled. Packy's smile was still frozen in place on his face, and I was smiling too. We looked like one big happy threesome, but murder was the only thing on our minds. Packy pushed his chair back and started to stand. The muscle by the car moved imperceptibly closer to the deck and I started having a bad feeling. Once Packy was gone, what was to keep the goons from mowing us down, especially in light of Francis having pissed him off so bad?

I shouldn't have worried, though. Pat and Raydean were on the job. In the distance sirens began to wail, drawing closer by the second, joined by other sirens that seemed to converge on Ernie's all at once. A large ambulance pulled into the driveway, followed by a firetruck and three squad cars. It was a full demonstration of Panama City's fire-and-rescue capabilities.

At the sight of the police cars, the muscle quietly withdrew to the car. Packy seemed alarmed and looked anxiously at the exits from the parking lot. There was no way he was going anywhere. The EMTs rushed the deck, followed by a couple of burly firefighters and two cops.

"Just have a seat, sir," the female paramedic said. "These things happen all the time. We'll take good care of you."

Francis and I stood up and backed away from the table. Packy looked like a trapped animal.

"What are you talking about?" he asked. His voice shifted an octave higher. "There's nothing wrong with me!"

"Sir, we all want what's best for you. Now, if you'll have a seat and let the paramedics check your vitals, we can be on our way."

"I'm not going anywhere!" Packy said. "I got a car right out front and I'm leaving with them."

Francis stood just behind Packy, slowly shaking his head. The cops saw him and nodded ever so gently.

"Dr. Slayback said you might try that, but she assured us that the hospital is the best place for you."

"There is nothing wrong with me!" Packy roared. "Now let me go!"

The smallest cop was a blonde. Her arms were thicker than Arnold Schwarzenegger's neck. She was beautiful, but she wasn't about to let Packy Cozzone go past her.

"You wanna go easy or hard?" she asked him softly. The rescue squad and the firemen backed away slowly.

"I'm not going fucking anywhere with you!" Packy said. "I'm going to leave this restaurant, get in my car and fly the fuck back to New York."

The blonde looked at him and smiled. "So I guess that means we do it the hard way."

Packy may have started to move. He appeared to move, but just as quickly dropped to his knees, then sagged forward onto the deck. The blonde had brought forth a stun gun from behind her back, and poor Packy lay in a stupor on the ground.

The blonde looked at me, her face screwed up with concern. "I'm sorry to have to do that to him, especially in front of y'all, but an order's an order. We've got involuntary commitment papers issued from a Dr. Slayback in Tallahassee, but I guess y'all know that, huh?"

Francis didn't miss a beat. "Well, we were just hoping to hold him long enough for someone to arrive and pick him up. I guess you'll be taking him straight to the state hospital, won't you? The sooner they get him back on his medication, the sooner he'll lose his delusions. I mean really, New York? Come now. He's a school maintenance worker from Wewahitchka."

I started to laugh but bit the inside of my cheek. Packy Cozzone was about to take a one-way trip to Tallahassee, courtesy of the Panama City Police Department. They'd drive for an hour and a half, all the way to the hospital, only to find out that Dr. Slayback had no idea who Packy Cozzone was.

As I watched the police carry Packy to the waiting patrol car, Raydean's Plymouth drove past the front of the restaurant. A gnarled hand fluttered out of the passenger-side window in a mock salute. The team had accomplished their mission and were heading back to squadron headquarters.

"Well," I said, turning to Little Moose, "our work here is done."

"Yes," said Francis, tossing another twenty onto the table. "I believe it is. Now we can go home and relax. It's vacation time!"

I let him have his fantasy. After all, his bubble of denial would burst soon enough. And when the golden moment arrived, I planned to have him too full of Pa's Chianti to care.

Twenty-six

$\mathcal{T}$he team was waiting when we pulled back into my driveway. They were already inside and, from the sound of it, were ready to party. We'd pulled one over, but I had to worry about the eventual cost of said maneuver. Inside, the coffee was perking, Pa's Chianti was sitting out in the middle of the kitchen table, and Pat was shuffling the deck of cards.

"Dr. Slayback?" I said. "I know I said come up with a distraction, but how'd you come up with that?"

Raydean grinned. Fluffy sat curled up in her lap. "Honey, by now you oughta realize that I know the ins and outs of the state hospital system."

"Yeah, but when we talked about it earlier, you just said you'd call the police and have them pick him up."

Raydean laughed. "The system don't work like that, sug. They gotta have their paperwork. They gotta call you back and double-check you're who you say you are. Otherwise, people'd be committing their neighbors and anybody what ticked 'em off."

Pat and Francis reached for Pa's jug at the same moment and I could guess why. Francis reached because he dreaded what would come next, the obvious commission of a felony by an elderly woman. He didn't know yet how insane Raydean was. Pat reached for the jug as a matter of celebration.

Raydean's smile grew. "That's why I faxed them the papers earlier. I keep all the ones they done on me. You just white-out my name and put in any old thing. They don't really check. They just want the paper. Besides, can you read a doctor's handwriting? Then I called my friend Verna Slayback out at the hospital and told her to take the call when it came in. Told her to tell 'em the papers were on their way."

Francis couldn't stand it. "You got a psychiatrist to commit someone she didn't even know? She lied to the police? She could lose her license."

Pat smiled and took a deep swig of Chianti. Raydean turned to Francis and looked at him like he had to be either an idiot or an alien.

"You can't lose your license to be nuts," she said. "Verna's grandfathered in. She's done been in the Big House so long they let her work in the kitchen. You try it. Call up there and ask for Dr. Slayback, extension four-twenty. They'll give you the kitchen every time. Everybody knows old Verna."

Francis tossed back the entire tumbler of Chianti, shook his head like it hadn't done the job, and poured another glass.

"You got money?" Raydean asked him.

"Enough," he answered, not knowing what was coming.

Raydean looked at Pat, nodded, and slapped the table as Pat began to deal the cards. "Then hit me, Little Big Man! I feel lucky tonight!"

I felt a little sorry for my brother. He played cards down at the Sons of Italy Social Club. He played with gentlemen. He never lost big because he was used to being the young son, the sharpie, the winner. Raydean and Pat were about to show him how the game of poker was played. Fluffy settled deeper into Raydean's lap, and Francis smiled at his two accomplices. If I knew him at all, he was thinking benevolent thoughts, like, "I'll be kind to the old bats," or "I won't take all their money. Wonder where their penny jug is?"

I shook my head and wandered off to get ready for work. It was going to be a long night. I'd be working my tail off and Francis would be losing his.

I didn't bother putting on all of my makeup or curling my hair like usual. I figured it would only freak Francis out to see me in my glamour-girl getup. So I pulled on jeans, pinned my hair up in a twist, and walked back through the trailer with my gear bag.

"I've gotta head in," I said to him, but it was wasted air. Francis was drinking Chianti and playing cards. His stack of chips had gone down significantly in the short time it had taken me to shower and change, and he looked worried. He kept glancing over at his Chianti glass like maybe it was responsible for his lack of luck.

"You guys keep an eye out for trouble," I said. "You never know when the Cozzones will be back."

Francis grunted and Raydean looked up. "Marlena will be on the alert," she said, nodding to the shotgun by the door. "We've always got our guard up. You never know when the Flemish will choose to invade."

"That's a roger," said Pat.

"Jesus!" my brother said, under his breath. "What is it with these cards?"

I left, not even certain that they noticed.

Vincent Gambuzzo was waiting for me when I walked through the back door of the Tiffany Gentleman's Club. He stood there, his jaw twitching, his black wraparound sunglasses reflecting the backstage lighting.

"Thank God you're here," he rumbled. "That would be all I'd need. This place is in a freaking mess, Sierra. There's no customers out in the house. I got girls calling off, right and left. They're spooked on account of we lost them two others. And with Marla not here, we got nothin'. I've got a call in to get another girl from off the circuit, but I don't got much hope. The agent wants an arm and a leg now anyway. You'd better get those other girls back in line."

No "please" or "could you," just "you'd better," as if I were in charge, not him. Of course, I was in charge. I could get them motivated when he couldn't. But still, a "please" would've been nice.

"Is Marla in jail?" I asked.

"Not the last I heard. Nobody knows where she is. Do you think you could round them others up and get them out front?" Ah, there was Vincent's "please," or the closest he could come to the actual word.

Rusty wandered up, wanting Vincent for something. I brushed past them and decided to check out the front of the house first. Was it as bad as Vincent seemed to think? It was early yet. The customers wouldn't begin filing in until after nine, and anyway, the curiosity factor would draw in a lot of newcomers as well as the regulars and the press.

Gordon stood watch over the door, collecting money and carding the questionables. I stood next to him for a few moments, watching the roll of bills that flashed in and out of his pocket every time he collected a cover. Gordon looked tired and strained. His face was pale and his eyes sunken in his head. Bruno was working the stage area, so it was only Gordon covering the front.

"You not getting any sleep?" I asked him.

Gordon turned to me and smiled softly. "Gambuzzo worked me two straight weeks without a break. I called in sick last night because of my stomach, and he still made me come in at midnight. He said it didn't matter if I was dying, none of the others were here. Bruno can't cover it all."

"What's wrong with your stomach?" I asked. He looked bad.

"Ulcer." He turned and took two covers off of a businessman and his friend. "Can I buy you breakfast when we close?" Gordon asked. He looked so pitiful.

"Well," I said, "let me see how the night goes. I'm still a little sore and my brother's visiting. I might just be too tired."

He nodded and seemed to lose hope. "Some other time, then," he said, and turned back to the door. I walked off through the paltry crowd, past Bruno, who only grunted, and the waitresses, who watched the exits with nervous eyes. The place was coming apart, all right. They were scared and desperate.

There was only one person who seemed to be not bothered at all by the tension that hung over the club. He reached out as I walked by and pinched my ass, just by way of saying hello.

"Sierra!" Little Ricky yelled. "Gotcha!"

I whipped around, smarting, and glared at him. "Pinch me again, asshole, and I'll rip your short hairs out one by one."

Ricky drew back on his stool protectively and smiled. "Where you been, baby? We've all been missing you, haven't we, boys?" He turned to include the others sitting near him, but they ignored him. No one wanted to be caught dead with Little Ricky.

I took a step closer, lowered my voice, and spoke to him again. "Where's Marla?" I asked.

"My lips are sealed," he said, straightening on his stool and raising a smug eyebrow.

"Ricky, I'll seal your freaking lips to your ass if you don't tell me." Sometimes tough is the only approach that works.

Ricky looked hurt but not frightened. "Honey, I'd tell you if I knew, but she done run out on me too." Well, who wouldn't, I thought?

"Ricky, you do know that the cops have a warrant out for her arrest, right?"

He nodded, then favored me with a sly, cockeyed look. "Your

boyfriend's one of the main ones looking for her. What makes you think me and Marla would trust you?"

"Oh, that's the pot calling the kettle black," I said. "As soon as Marla turns her back, and sometimes even when she's staring straight at you, you've got your dirty little hands all over anything that wears a skirt. Oh, you're real upstanding and true, Ricky. I make no bones about the fact that I don't particularly like Marla, but at least I'll tell her to her face. I'm helping her out because we dancers stick together, no matter what our personal feelings are. You, you swear up and down you love her, but you can't be left alone for a minute."

Ricky ducked his head but just as quickly brought it back up. "I've got a problem with intimacy," he said, like maybe it was a badge of honor. "I'm working on it."

"Oh, really and truly bite me, Ricky! Don't hand me that psychobabble."

He swept his ball cap off his head and tried to look hurt. "Obviously you haven't read *Men Who Can't Love Enough*. It would explain everything."

"No," I said, "but maybe you should read *Women Who Don't Give a Shit About Total Idiots*."

I walked off and left him. He was worthless.

The dressing room was practically empty. The strippers were there, the girls Vincent kept on only for a body count, the ones who worked the pole for a buck and never thought about having a routine or style. They were there because they wanted money more than they valued their lives. They were working to support a habit or a drug-addicted boyfriend. I kept trying to get Vincent to quit hiring strippers, but he kept telling me good talent was hard to find, he had to supplement. With strippers you don't look for talent because all you get is trouble.

I ignored them and went to the phone. It took me twenty minutes to convince three of the regular dancers to agree to come in, and that was only after I guaranteed them a bonus from Vincent. He wouldn't be pleased about that part of things, but then, he authorized me to take charge. After all, with a full house and a bevy of real dancers working the crowd, Vincent would more than make up the amount of any bonus he shelled out. It was good business, pure and simple.

I started lining up outfits for the evening. I figured I'd be doing twice as many numbers as usual, so planning was essential. We don't have a house mother at the Tiffany like a lot of the clubs do. They keep on an older dancer to help out, to keep the girls in line and train the new ones. At the Tiffany, I filled the role even though I was by no means an older dancer.

I brought out my newest costume, Princess Leia, and started gathering my accessories. I figured to do a salute to *Star Wars* and let the gentlemen imagine themselves with only their trusty light sabers and me, alone on a spaceship. Vincent walked into the dressing room just as I started to change.

"Okay," he said, "what you got?"

"Jolene, Tonya, and Markie are coming in. How about you?"

"Barry Sanduski is sending some bimbo named Candy Barr. He swears up and down she's one of his biggest acts, but who knows what that means?"

I stepped out of my jeans and began pulling my T-shirt off over my head.

"So when will she be here?" I asked.

"He said he's putting her on the ten o'clock flight out of Atlanta. He wants me to make sure somebody meets her at the airport on account of he don't think she can manage to take a cab here."

I grabbed the costume off the hanger. "He said that? He said she couldn't even find her way out to the cab stand? I mean, Vincent, come on, the airport's tiny."

"No, that's not what he said, but that's what he meant. See, he said she oughta have an escort. He said he was worried for her safety, and with good reason since the last two girls he sent ended up dead."

"So why's this one coming and why did he send her?"

Vincent shrugged. "She's coming on account of she probably can't breathe and chew gum at the same time. Remember, she's from Atlanta. Up there, they got murders two and three a day. Whacking a dancer ain't no big deal. It's more an occupational hazard. Barry's sending her because money talks and because I told him the police had issued a warrant for Marla's arrest. I told him she did it and the club was safe."

I whirled around. "But, Vincent, that's not true."

Vincent wouldn't look at me, not even through his dark glasses. "We don't know that for certain," he said. "Maybe it's time to start believing the police. They got her fingerprints on her gun. She's got a past history of losing her temper and popping off. She could've thought her job was in jeopardy. You just don't ever really know with these things, Sierra. If we could tell a murderer just by looking at him, if they all had certain and true profiles, then we could lock them up before a crime ever occurred. But you watch the news. How many times have you heard some killer's neighbor interviewed? What do they always say? 'He was such a nice guy . . . so quiet . . . who would've thought?' "

Vincent walked over to the makeup table and started fingering the doodads I'd laid out to wear as Princess Leia.

"Sierra, Marla acts like a murderess on a good day, even I gotta admit that."

He sighed deeply, like it hurt him, and I knew it did because I was realizing something else about Vincent, it was written all over his pudgy little face. Vincent Gambuzzo was in love with Marla the Bomber.

It was suddenly clear. Vincent making her a headliner, even when she had little true talent. Vincent sticking up for her, even when everyone else was against her. Vincent never taking someone else's side against her in an argument. It had to be love, true-blue, all-American, Cinderella love. I was shocked, but go figure.

I walked up to him, put my arms around his neck and gave him a big hug. Hugging Vincent was kind of like bouncing off Teflon, but I hung in there and eventually felt his arms attempting to encircle my waist.

"You don't believe she killed them people," I said softly into his ear.

He smelled like sweat and the remnants of strong cologne. I could feel his big heart beating against his chest like he'd climbed twenty flights of steps.

"I don't want to believe it, Sierra, but I don't want to be taken for a fool, either." He broke away and struggled to maintain his tough side. I knew what he meant to say. He meant to say that nobody takes Vincent Gambuzzo very seriously, that he comes off like a big buffoon most of the time. He meant to tell me that he didn't think Marla would ever love him back, if indeed she ever knew. He just couldn't bring himself to voice those fears. If it were up to Vincent, Marla would never know his true feelings. He would love her for the rest of his life and never let on that he cared.

I felt part of my heart break for him. He deserved better than what he'd set himself up to take.

"Vincent," I said, "you can't give up on her. You owe her that much."

Vincent cocked his head and gave me a look. "How you figure I owe her?"

"Look at it from a pure business standpoint," I said. "She brings in the bucks. Up until this business happened, she was here every night. She was giving more than a hundred percent. She always takes your side in a fight. She's loyal to you, Vincent.

I don't know why, given what a grouch you are, but she's loyal. Now, are you gonna walk away from that?"

He didn't even hesitate. "No," he said, his voice stronger than it had been. "A Gambuzzo don't run out on loyalty."

"Good," I said, braiding my hair into a Princess Leia head-wrap. "Then we won't have any more discussions about turning our backs. Call the attorney and line him up. I'm going to finish proving she didn't do it."

Rusty saved us from any further display of emotion and affection by walking in and yelling, "Sierra, you're up!"

"Help me, Obi-Wan," I muttered under my breath, and walked out of the locker room.

I adjusted my gown, patted my hair, and walked backstage. The *Star Wars* music started up, the smoke machine belched, and Princess Leia went into action. I stepped out onto the stage flanked by some aging cardboard cutouts of Storm Troopers. I've seen the video of the number, and believe me, it's impressive: life-sized, three-dimensional-looking men with guns, and me, in a see-through gown.

I walked to the edge of the runway and let her rip. "Help me, Obi-Wan," I said, stretching out my hand in an exact replication of the movie, but then I couldn't remember what came next. "They're after me," I ad-libbed.

A farm boy, obviously too young to remember the original movie, stepped up to the edge of the stage, concern filling his eyes. I smiled softly and tossed him a garter. He turned to his companion, an older man, weather-roughened by work and more time spent in the fields. "I told you them girls are white slaves," he said. "Lookit there. Prime example."

His buddy looked at him and laughed, then handed him a bill. "Slip that in her other garter," he said, "maybe you can help buy her freedom."

The boy looked uncertain, then took the bill and held it up.

I pulled the Velcro tab at the top of my gown and let it slip to the floor before I stepped up to him. He blushed and averted his eyes.

"Hey," I said, moving to the pulsing throb that Rusty slipped in to replace the movie theme. "I'm up here."

The men who heard me laughed. The farm boy glanced at my leg, just long enough to zero in on the garter, and stuck his hand out to slip the bill under the elastic.

"Hey!" I said again. He looked up, trying to keep his eyes on my face, but losing the battle as Sierra, Princess of the Night, took over. "Don't you like me?" I said softly.

He stuttered. "It isn't . . . I shouldn't . . ."

I chuckled like we were sharing a secret. "Oh, yes, you should," I teased. "Come on, baby, it won't hurt you to take a little peek."

He was at war with himself. All of his shoulds and shouldn'ts were in the way.

"I like it when you look at me," I said, my voice dropping to a husky whisper. "Look at me."

From that moment on, he was mine. "You're beautiful," he breathed.

"Have a little fun, sweetie. Look all you want. Sierra's gonna take good care of you." Before he could look away, I unhooked my bra. The man next to him slipped a five-dollar bill into my garter, and I wiggled down into a half-crouch. "Am I the best girl you've ever seen?" I asked.

"Oh Lord, yes!" my farm boy cried.

"Hell, Lester, she's the only girl you've ever seen," his friend crowed. The men clustered around the stage broke into laughs, and finally Lester did too. Another first-timer inducted into Sierra's fold.

I straightened and began giving my regulars some attention. Little Ricky kept trying to catch my eye, but I ignored him. He never tipped good, anyway. I found myself scanning the crowd, not for tippers the way I usually did, but for troublemakers, people who looked out of place, anyone who looked like they'd pull a gun and mow me down while I moved. It was dark and smoky, but I was doing good to see through the crowd to the front door. Rusty let another round of smoke billow out across the stage, a signal to remind me to wrap up the act. The music would end in another thirty seconds.

I pulled away the little breechcloth that hid my G-string and got ready to do my final stretch. I pulled my hair loose and let it fall to my shoulders. I turned around, bent over, and stretched my hands out to touch my ankles. Even hanging upside down, I could see the familiar shape of John Nailor as he walked across the room toward the edge of the stage. He was smiling, as if he remembered a similar view, only up closer.

I straightened, still facing away from my audience, pulled the G-string off, and waved it over my head just as the smoke reached up to cover me. The curtain swung shut and I walked off, the sound of war whoops and applause ringing in my ears.

I slipped into my robe and turned to find John waiting for me backstage, something he'd never done before.

"How did you—" I started.

"Bruno said he could tell from the way we were looking at each other that I should come back and say hello."

"He did, huh?" I stepped up to him and sighed as his arms encircled my waist.

"He most definitely did."

I should've known something was wrong. My alarm system was sounding, but I thought it was hormones and chemicals. The guy was too happy. I let him nuzzle my neck. I forgot about everything for a minute and let my body respond to his. Oh, this was going to be a long wonderful night; I could just feel it.

"How about I meet you back at your place later," he said, his fingers moving deliciously across my back.

The alarm bells got louder. I pushed my head back and looked at him. "Aren't you in the middle of a murder investigation?" I asked.

"Not any more," he said. He smiled like he had other things on his mind, like he didn't want this moment to fade.

"You arrested Marla, didn't you?" I asked, taking a step back. The spell was broken. "Yes, honey," he said, "we did."

He hadn't listened to me. Marla looked like the killer, the evidence pointed her way, and he hadn't taken the trouble to take it any farther. Well, what did you really expect? He was a logic-driven man. He took the course that offered the least resistance.

He must've seen my thoughts mirrored in my eyes because he started talking immediately. "Sierra, I know you don't think she did it, but all the evidence points to her."

"Then someone's setting her up."

"No."

"You're not listening to me. Marla couldn't be the killer. I know it looks bad, but you know Marla. She's a chicken at heart. She gave Ricky her gun."

Nailor just stared at me, and in the back of his eyes I began to see frustration mixed with pity.

Dancers moved past us, rushing up the steps and out onto the stage. Rusty pushed past, a headphone and microphone glued to his head. To me it seemed that time slowed to a crawl, but the others were going right on about the business of running the club.

"I've got to get back to work," I said. We were at a stand-off and he knew it.

"Fine." His voice was tight and his shoulders stiff with tension.

I made myself turn away and walk off. It felt like I carried a forty-pound sack of concrete on my back. Why did things always have to turn out like this? Why wouldn't he listen to me?

Vincent waylaid me as I started into the dressing room.

"They've got Marla," he said. His jaw was pumping overtime with anxiety. "I called Ernie. He's on his way. The arraignment's in the morning. Ernie says he might be able to get her out on bond, but I'm gonna have to put up the club."

"Can you do that, I mean with the IRS fixing to come after your money?"

"There's no lien yet," he said. "They can't take away what I don't got. Ernie's on top of it. All's you gotta do is worry about finding out who really did this. Maybe it's time you called in . . ." He looked over his shoulder, making sure he wasn't overheard. "You know, *him*," he said.

Something came over me, or maybe it was just my mouth moving before I could slip my brain into gear. "Oh, I know that, Vincent. You think I'd try to catch a serial killer by myself? I called and he sent someone. In fact, he sent the next in line, the second biggest guy."

Vincent seemed very impressed and reassured. He smiled, patted me on the back, and said, "Why didn't you tell me? I would've relaxed."

"Yeah," I said, "you can relax. The Lavotinis are in charge. Don't worry about a thing."

Easy for me to say, I thought. Relax. Take a load off. Leave the driving to us. Vincent obviously bought it. He walked off whistling and I stood behind him worrying. Who would kill dancers and a mob guy? Why were they killing the dancers at this club? Who stood to profit from them being dead? Who wanted the club out of business? I wandered toward the back exit, thinking that fresh air might clear my head. My hand was on the bar, pushing the door open, when a light tremor shook the building.

I pushed against the door, opening it as a second smaller explosion echoed through the parking lot. My own words to Vincent echoed in my head: *You can relax. The Lavotinis are in charge. Don't worry about a thing.*

Twenty-seven

I pushed the heavy door back and ran out onto the dock. The explosion had occurred somewhere near the front entrance to the Tiffany, that much was evident by the way people seemed to center in that direction and from a thin flicker of orange that cast a fiery glow against the far wall of the building.

The screaming had stopped almost as soon as I'd heard it, replaced now by the sounds of approaching firetrucks. A cruising police car pulled into the parking lot just as I rounded the corner and saw the source of the explosion. An unmarked police car, a brown Taurus sedan, was almost fully engulfed in flames, the shell quickly turning black as the flames ate their way from the front to the back of the car. The screaming started again, but this time it was me.

I ran until the heat singed my face and strong arms held me. "It's all right," he said. "It didn't get me. I'm right here."

I turned away from the car and buried my face in his chest. I felt his arms tighten. I wanted to run away then, to take him with me and go, forget about the murderer, forget about everything but keeping this man safe and staying safe myself.

His hold on me loosened as the emergency vehicles pulled into the lot. The firemen rushed to the car while Nailor moved toward his colleagues. I stood and watched him take charge.

Vincent Gambuzzo wasted no time getting to my side. "You know what this means?" he said excitedly. "She didn't do it. She couldn't have done it. You can't blow up a car from a jail cell!"

I looked at him, not getting for a moment what he was saying. "What makes you think this has anything to do with the murders? Vincent, that's John's car. He could've been killed."

Vincent stopped, looked at my face, then out to the burned shell of the car. "Jesus, Sierra! I didn't know. I'm sorry." He stepped up to me and moved to hug me, saw me pull my arms across my chest, and let his hands drop to his side. I couldn't have done anything else that would've hurt him as much as I did with that one gesture. The worst part was knowing that I'd hurt him and feeling powerless to undo my cold withdrawal. It wasn't him, it was me.

"Vincent, I'm . . ."

"Don't worry about it," he said. "You gotta take care of your guy. This is getting too deep for us. I'll worry about Marla; you just stick here with this." He turned and walked off, flapping his short arms and yelling, "Show's over, folks! There's a better one inside."

Was there a connection here? Two porn stars, a mob guy, and almost Nailor. What was the deal? I watched the firemen douse the car one more time, even though the flames had vanished and there was nothing left to burn. John and a fire official in a white car spoke. I watched them talk and figured the other guy for an arson investigator. Other police officers in vehicles rolled through the parking lot, stopping, lowering their windows, and chatting with each other. A voice called out to Nailor.

"What, you too lazy to fill out the requisition form for another car?" This was followed by a chorus of male laughter.

I realized Nailor was really okay and where he belonged for now. I could leave him and know he was safe. The music cranked back up inside the Tiffany, calling me, reminding me that I had a job to do, two jobs, maybe three if you counted fence-mending with Vincent Gambuzzo.

Gordon held the door open as I walked inside, his eyebrows and goatee looking faintly scorched from the fire.

"You all right?" I asked.

He looked at me and smiled. "Never better, ma'am," he answered.

"Well, that makes one of us."

Tonya the Barbarian was out on the runway wearing some kind of animal costume. She was breaking in a new routine. She pounced around the stage growling and swiping at people, biting the money out of the customers' outstretched hands. She was actually attracting more attention now than the burned-out Taurus. I gave her the thumbs-up and moved on back to the dressing room. Another explosion had taken place there: Candy Barr had arrived and the Tiffany was once again in pandemonium.

Candy stood in the middle of the floor, looking around the room, a tentative expression on her face. She was stunningly beautiful with long black hair that reached to her waist, clear blue eyes, and a smattering of freckles. She had to be also almost seven feet tall.

She had a perfect figure, but oversized to fit her huge frame. She dwarfed me by a good foot and I like to think I'm the tallest girl working the Tiffany. If this girl could put on six-inch stilettos and actually walk in them, Rusty would have to consider moving the stage lights to accommodate her.

The other dancers were flat out staring at her, and the strippers barely hid smug grins that told all. She was a freak, an anomaly of female anatomy. What in the world were we going to do with her? And where would she dress and shower?

Sierra the House Mom took over. I figured there was no approach better than taking the bull by the horns, so to speak.

"Hi," I said, stepping forward, "I'm Sierra Lavotini. Welcome to the Tiffany."

Candy Barr looked down at me and her eyes brimmed with tears. I looked over at the strippers. "All right," I said, "which one of you told her?"

Nobody said a word. In fact, it was pin-drop silent. Vincent chose that moment to barge in, but he stopped in the doorway, his eyes widening as he took in the enormity of our situation.

"Jesus! That's what Barry sent us?"

Candy Barr cried in earnest now and her nose began to run.

"She'll be just fine, Vincent," I said. "She's just a little scared, that's all." I pitched my voice to carry across the room, signaling with my eyebrows and facial expression that he should go along with me. I looked at the rest of the girls and jerked my head in Candy Barr's direction. The dancers took the cue and surrounded the sobbing newcomer.

Candy Barr raised her head, her eyes swollen and bloodshot, mascara running in a black river down the sides of her face. "It's not so much that," she said between sobs. "I've just never been so far away from home, and then, to get here and find out Frosty and Venus were the ones that . . . that . . ." She dissolved into another torrent of tears.

"They were your friends?" I asked.

"The best," she said. "I hadn't seen them in a couple of months because Mr. Sanduski made them travel, but we were close."

"But you didn't know they'd been killed?" I asked.

Candy Barr's eyes widened. "No! Nobody said a word to me. I don't watch the news or read the paper or anything like that. It's just too confusing, and it always gets me upset. I guess Barry didn't tell me on account of I get emotional sometimes."

Sometimes?

"I guess I'm all heart," she said. "I mean, I think with my

emotions and not with my head." Candy Barr wasn't impressing me as a Rhodes scholar, so I nodded and let her go on. "But we actresses are like that. We have to live in the scene, be with the inner core. What good is a brain if you can't push it aside and use your gut instincts?"

I shook my head. Candy was the missing link that separated man from the lower animal kingdom.

"Candy," I said, stepping up and putting my arm around her waist, "do you ever find it helps to dance out your feelings? You know, put them all into your act?"

"You can just call me C.B.," she said. "And, yes, that's exactly how I see it." She looked down at me and smiled just a little bit, but enough for me to know she was workable.

"Well, I was thinking," I continued, squinting my eyes and focusing on a far corner of the room, "maybe taking your feelings out on the stage in the very place where your friends died would be like a tribute to them. A memorial."

C.B. lifted her head, tossed back her long hair, and smiled. "Oh, that would be lovely," she breathed. "A tribute. That's real nice." She cocked her head sideways and looked at me, a shy smile beginning to cross her face. "You know, you favor this girl we all used to dance with in Atlanta. I mean, you really look just like her." Candy's face clouded and tears began to brim again.

"Well, lots of girls leave the business," I said, and started to move away. But Candy's next words gave me shivers.

"She got killed, too. And nobody up there even spoke her name again, much less gave her any kind of tribute."

"It's kind of the Tiffany way," I said, not wanting to let Candy slip into the details. "We always honor those who have fallen in the line of duty. I mean, after all, who will do it if we don't?"

"Damn straight!" Tonya the Barbarian said.

C.B. straightened her shoulders and looked toward her gear bag. "All right," she said. "When should we dance?"

I looked over at slack-jawed Vincent and said, "Right now would be ideal. The club's filling up, we've had a hell of a commotion outside, and people are thirsty and looking for another thrill. You would be perfect."

Vincent smiled to see the Lavotini system working its magic.

"All right, then," C.B. said, "let's get a move on. I'll be ready in ten minutes."

I turned to the other dancers. "Let's make this big," I said. "There isn't time to call in any of the girls from the other clubs, but let's show them how the Tiffany Gentlemen's Club faces down fear and salutes the girls that have gone on to their just rewards."

I was really milking it, but a part of me believed what I was saying. We needed to do something not only for the girls who'd died, but for ourselves. We needed to reclaim our turf and this was the perfect way to do it.

Tonya and the four other dancers started rummaging through the costume closet. The strippers stood around for a moment, looking like they couldn't have cared less, but I was hoping maybe they had a shred of concern.

"Hey, guys," I said, calling over to them. "Come over and go through the closet. Maybe you'll find some inspiration." I was trying to sound decent and it must've worked, because three or four of them broke loose and joined the others in the wardrobe. Maybe they weren't all bad.

C.B. was busy pawing through her gear bag and dragging her suitcase over to a deserted corner. I knew for a fact that there was nothing in the wardrobe that would fit her. But I didn't need to worry. C.B. pulled out a red sequined tear-away gown and a black flapper headband. The tears still stood out on her cheeks, but now she had a task to do and her emotions were back in check.

"Guys," I called to the cluster at the wardrobe, "look for something red, or red and black."

Tonya poked her head out and looked in C.B.'s direction. "Oh," she said, nodding at C.B., "I see." She ducked back inside the closet and could be heard directing the others. It fell to me to find the music, so I left them and wandered back to the deejay's booth.

"I need something red," I said.

The deejay pushed the headphones back off her ears and looked puzzled. "Did you say dead?"

I shook my head. "No, red. Red."

Tina the deejay smiled. "Got just the thing," she said. "It's old and it's slow, but it's sexy. How about 'Lady in Red'? I've got a dance version where they speed it up in the middle. Would that get it?"

It would have to do. I nodded and headed backstage. The girls were beginning to file out and stand at the edge of the stairs. Tonya had managed to find them all red-and-black matching outfits, courtesy of Vincent, who'd scored the costumes, used, from a local theater group. The outfits looked like red satin corsets with black piping down the stays that framed the girls' torsos. They wore black fishnet thigh-high stockings with shiny red garters and spiky black stilettos. It was a class act, all right.

C.B. brought up the rear of the line in her red sequined gown and black headdress. By the time you took into account the feather rising from her headband and the six-inch heels, she was almost eight feet tall—all woman and all ready to go.

"You ready, C.B.?" I asked. She nodded, tears filling her eyes. "Don't do that, Candy," I said. "You don't wanna wreck your makeup for your big salute."

C.B. shook her head and fought back the tears. I walked up the steps, grabbed the microphone from Rusty's hand, and walked out onstage.

"Gentlemen," I said, and waited as the crowd fell silent. "It is the Tiffany custom to honor those who have gone on before us to that palace of good times and compassion in the sky." The men shifted in their seats, as pairing religion with exotic dancing was a foreign concept and they needed to mull it over. You could practically see the wheels turning in their pedestrian minds. Did nude dancers go to heaven? And what about those who watched them? Weren't they just as guilty? It made the customers a little uncomfortable. I let them stew in their conservative guilt for a second or two, figuring it would be good for the tip jar.

"We have lost two of our dancers this week," I said, "and the killer is still at large. A lesser group of women might cower in fear, waiting for the killer to strike again, but not us. We're the Tiffany Girls and we don't run from trouble."

There was a chorus of cheers behind me as the girls started to believe the spiel I was spinning. I leaned down and took a shot glass of Wild Turkey from Colleen the waitress.

"And don't think that we believe for a moment that Marla the Bomber did it. We know she didn't, and we know someone out there did!" I leaned forward and searched over the audience, as if letting someone know I saw him and that I knew for certain he was there.

I raised the shot glass and motioned to the crowd to raise theirs. "So here's to the girls who gave their all." The crowd stood and saluted. "And here's to the girls of the Tiffany. We're fearless and we're naked!"

The men screamed, and the dancers began filing onto the stage. The music began to thump and the girls started moving, all but Candy Barr. She stood just offstage, a frozen look on her face and sheer terror in her eyes.

The others moved in front of me and I stepped back behind the curtain. Rusty was coaxing, and finally pushing, the tall girl toward the stage. "Get out there," he urged. "They're waiting!" Indeed they were. The others had formed a phalanx and were waiting for Candy to walk out, front and center.

"I can't," she whimpered.

I wasn't about to play therapist and ask why not. The music was playing, the girls were in position, and the customers were growing impatient. I grabbed one of her arms and yanked, while Rusty applied his two hands to her ass and pushed. With a great heave, Candy Barr arrived onstage.

There was a collective gasp from the onlookers as they took in the full effect of Candy's magnificent body. Then came the hoots of approval as they waited for her to begin her routine, the only problem being that Candy had no intention of moving. She was paralyzed with stage fright.

Tonya sidled up to her and I could see her encouraging C.B. to move. Another dancer moved over to her left, and gently began bumping her with her hip. That at least got Candy to begin swaying. Whatever Tonya the Barbarian did, Candy attempted to copy, with disastrous results. It became glaringly apparent that Candy had another problem: She had no sense of rhythm. The girl just couldn't dance.

I caught a glimpse of Vincent standing by the edge of the bar, next to Little Ricky. Bruno and Gordon stood just behind them. All four men looked horrified. Vincent buried his face in his hands, and Bruno reached forward and patted him on the shoulder. What a disaster. Barry Sanduski had sent us a bombshell all right, a real dud.

The other girls sensed the trouble and began to do what they could to enact damage control. They used C.B. like a maypole, dancing around her and unwinding her clothing. Candy smiled nervously and shimmied back and forth, but not in time to the music. The customers continued to stare up at the giant woman, watching the spectacle taking place before them with mouths open and eyes wide. Only thing missing was the tips. No one reached for their wallets. They just stood there, staring.

There was no way on earth that the act could've been construed as sexy or tantalizing. Men tip because it's their way of saying, "I'd like you to do that for me and me alone." Nobody was wishing Candy Barr on themselves. They seemed, if anything, to be viewing the act as their worst sexual fantasy come true: A giant woman flops on top of you and then has no sense of rhythm. I could hardly blame them.

Rusty stood by my side, moaning until the last thirty seconds when he cranked up the smoke machine so high it covered everything but Candy's face. The customers' last vision of our ill-fated tribute was Candy Barr's head, floating seven feet above the stage floor, bouncing in an erratic pattern that had no connection whatsoever to the music.

Some days you're the windshield. Some days you're the bug. The Tiffany had just been squashed flat across the windshield of bad luck and hard times.

Twenty-eight

The night passed like one long disaster. Vincent wouldn't let Candy back out onstage, which prompted a flood of tears from her and pissed off all the other dancers, who were forced to share their dressing room with the wailing guest artist.

"At least when a kid starts caterwauling in a store, I can walk out," Tonya complained. "Now I gotta sit with it in my own dressing room. It's ruining my concentration."

When Candy started throwing things, a full-scale intervention became necessary. Bruno was sent in to deal with her while Gordon tried to cover the entire house. This led to a drunk-and-disorderly charge against an airman who scaled the runway and attempted to fondle a stripper. A fight broke out between the airman's friends and a group of regulars, Little Ricky among them, who felt protective of *their* girls. The police arrived very quickly, as half of Panama City's police force was still out in the parking lot processing Nailor's car, but they were seen as unwelcome by both the airmen and the regulars. It seems they felt they were entitled to clean up their own squabble without government interference. The police saw the situation differently and this resulted in a heavy loss of glass and furniture. Vincent screamed until his face reached a nuclear-red glow and stayed that way for the entire night. Everyone's tips were down, but all in all, as I told Vincent, it was a successful evening. The local TV news crews covered the Tiffany, giving us the lead-story slot on the eleven o'clock news.

"That's better than a one-minute commercial," I told him. "Tomorrow night we'll be jammed."

"Yeah," Vincent groused, "but with what type of clientele?"

He had a point, but I wasn't in the mood to concede. "You just wait," I said. "We'll make more money than ever."

He didn't believe me for a second, and when it came down to it, I had to admit I was blowing smoke. The Tiffany was in trouble. Clubs don't have a long shelf life once they're viewed as going downhill, or too rough for your upper-middle-class money-droppers. We were in a hell of a spot.

I left around three A.M. It felt more like I'd pulled a twenty-four-hour shift than my usual eight to ten. My body ached, my spirit was sagging, and I wanted nothing more than to crawl into bed. Nailor was nowhere in sight, and if I knew the police, he'd be downtown filling out forms in triplicate for days.

I slid behind the wheel of my Camaro and cranked the engine. Bruce Springsteen started singing about meeting someone on the strip, and I let him rasp out his tale of woe. He sang like I felt, irritated and raw.

It's been my experience that on those nights when you're really exhausted, really craving a soft pillow and a dreamless sleep, insomnia is a given. It was no different that night. I pulled up on the parking pad, saw Fluffy's eyes glowing out at me from the top step, and felt my body spring alive.

Fluffy barked softly, her way of saying, "About time you came back. I'm hungry."

"Makes two of us," I answered, and made us both a cold meatloaf sandwich.

Two lights remained on in the living room. The card table

was set up, the hands dealt, and Pa's Chianti bottle was empty. From the look of the pile of change sitting in front of Raydean's chair, Francis had gone down swinging. I heard a gentle snore and saw Pat sleeping on the futon. It had been a long night.

I assumed that Francis had gone to bed and that Raydean had returned to her trailer, but I was wrong. The scuffling sound of her bunny slippers startled me as she appeared in the living room doorway. She was wide awake.

"That brother of yours has two strikes against him," she said. "He can't play cards for shit and he can't hold his wine worth a flip. I just now got him settled in bed. Before that he was bowl-hugging the porcelain throne. Thought all you Italians could hold your alcohol."

"See, Raydean, see what happens when you stereotype a group of people?"

Raydean "humphed" and walked past me to the kitchen table, where she perched on a barstool and reached for the jar of peanut butter that sat in the middle next to the napkins.

"You got any soda crackers?" she asked. "And a knife?"

Fluffy made the leap onto her lap and the two of them waited expectantly.

"All right," I said, and sighed. "I know when I'm beat."

I pulled out the crackers and two butter knives, perched on another stool, and opened a new bottle of Pa's Chianti. Fluffy munched on crackers and Raydean dug into the peanut butter. They munched and I talked. Sometimes it's just good to put the words and events out in the open; kind of gives you a fresh perspective.

I couldn't tell if Raydean was really tracking me. She seemed more interested in spreading peanut butter on crackers and then lining them up across the table like a wall. But when I finished recounting all the events of the evening, she looked at me with her sharp birdlike eyes and sighed.

"Girl, you're always the last to know," she said.

"How's that, Raydean?"

Fluffy rearranged herself so she could watch me. Raydean pushed one lumpy peanut butter cracker forward, then looked back at me.

"It's about you this time, honey. Wake up and smell the coffee."

"What do you mean, it's about me?"

Raydean's attention had been diverted to the window. "Did you see that?" she asked.

I looked over my shoulder and saw only the glow of the streetlight. "No, what was it?" Fluffy growled low in her throat, her little body quivering.

"Probably Flemish," Raydean said. "They're nocturnal critters. Sneak up on you, paralyze your brain, and spirit you off to the mother ship. It's a certainteed fact that most alien experimentation occurs at night. That way the hapless victim don't know if it were a dream or real life."

I was about to give up when Raydean's thoughts circled back around and came in for a landing.

"What do you think all these killings and attempted killings have in common?" she asked. She sounded like Sister Boniface, my old kindergarten teacher, singsong voiced and cheery.

"I don't know, Raydean. That's what I've been sitting here trying to figure."

She shook her head, like maybe I'd never learn my alphabet, and spelled it out for me.

"Every time somebody dies, you're there. A lesser friend would think you're the one doing it, but not me." Fluffy licked her hand in approval. "Them two girls weren't killed on account of not paying up. That flat don't make sense. And then you kill the guy what came to get 'em to see the daylight? Naw." She shook her head. "And now you got your honey's car blown sky high. Figure it out, girl."

I still didn't see it. "There's a connection to you," she went on. "They were killed on account of something you were doing or not doing. What I don't understand is why they haven't come after you yet."

A cold chill ran up my spine and back down my arms.

"Maybe it has to do with the club," I said. "Maybe someone wants the club to close."

Raydean slid two more crackers across the table and molded them into her wall.

"Nope," she said. "If that were true, they'd kill Vincent and the house dancers, not your visiting team."

I mulled it over for a second, only to be interrupted by Fluffy breaking away from Raydean, running to the bay window, and barking up a storm.

"Damn," said Raydean. "Where's Marlena when I need her?"

This time I saw it. Someone moved across the front of the trailer and was heading for the back door. Fluffy didn't hesitate, she hurled herself through the doggie-door and out into the night.

"Fluffy!" I cried, jumping off my stool and running after her. "Fluffy, come back!"

I flung open the door and raced outside, not thinking of anything but my baby.

Nailor stood at the foot of the steps, Fluffy in his arms and a confused look on his face. "What's all the fuss about?"

"You snuck up on us!" I said.

"Of course I did. I didn't know if you were sleeping or not, and I didn't want to wake up that brother of yours." He smiled and I knew what he was thinking. He'd hoped to sneak in.

"What were you going to do if I was sleeping? Throw a rock against my window?"

He started up the steps. "Exactly," he said. Then he saw Raydean and the sexy smile faded.

She waved him in, still seated at the table, still spreading peanut butter crackers in a pile that threatened to spill off the tabletop.

"You need to get in on this," she said.

"I'm not hungry," he answered.

"Didn't ask if you was. I'm talking about Sierra's situation." Nailor proceeded cautiously, pulling out a barstool and perching at the table's edge. "She don't realize the danger she's in. That psycho you're after is killing everyone around our Sierra."

"With all due respect . . ." he began.

"Horsepatooty!" Raydean said. "That's cop speak for we're not gonna listen to a word you say. I heard enough people asking for due respect in my lifetime to know what's coming." She hopped down from her stool and took two steps toward him. She was going to give him a piece of her mind, maybe the very last piece of her mind. "Mark my words, alien, it ain't over till it's over, and you'd better stand by her, 'cause she's in danger."

She didn't wait for a response. She was out the door and across the street before either of us could say a word. Fluffy walked her to the door of her trailer and stood waiting until the door closed. Fluffy waited a minute, crossed back across the street, and walked into the house, past the two of us, and into the living room, where she plopped down on the futon next to snoring Pat. Obviously, she agreed with Raydean.

Nailor reached for my empty glass, poured it full of Pa's Chianti and took a long swallow. His face wrinkled, his eyes squinted almost shut, and he shook his head quickly, as if trying to knock something loose.

"Damn, Sierra! How do you drink this stuff?"

I ran my hands up over his back and across the tops of his shoulders. "Quickly," I answered. "I drink it quickly." I waited for him to drink more before saying anything else. When half his glass was gone, I continued. "Raydean says that every time someone has died, I've been there, the only common denominator. She thinks this has something to do with me."

Nailor relaxed his body against my hands, letting me knead his shoulders. This was another conversation that he didn't want to have.

"So why would someone want to kill off people in front of you or near you?" he asked. He reached for my hand and pulled me around to face him, bringing me inside his legs as he sat on his stool drinking his wine. "If Marla wanted to kill off those girls and Barboni to send you a message, I fail to see what it was. What was she doing, killing off the competition? And why kill Barboni?"

Killing off the competition? Then what was Barboni?

"Come on, babe, let's go to bed. I'm exhausted," he said.

Nailor didn't stand on ceremony. "Exhausted?" I said softly, running my fingers in between his thighs. "I don't think someone's very exhausted."

Nailor sighed as I traced an outline with my fingertip. "Now that you mention it," he said, gripping my wrist and standing, "I don't feel quite so tired. Maybe I should take you back here and show you what I mean."

He was walking across the living room, switching off lights as he went, pulling me along by the hand, and heading for the bedroom. I was in danger, all right, immediate, wonderful danger.

We tiptoed past the guest room. Francis lay tucked under the covers. He wouldn't be moving for hours.

I yawned when we reached my room. "Maybe you're right," I said. "Maybe we should get some sleep."

Nailor laughed softly and pulled me to him. His fingers started unbuttoning my blouse, but his eyes never left my face. There was no mistaking what the man wanted, and no doubt at all that he would get it.

Twenty-nine

I woke up wrapped in my sheets, the room filled with bright sunlight. Nailor was gone. For a moment I lay there, my eyes closed, my head on the pillow where he'd slept, remembering. I had to admit that Nailor had a great deal of potential. A shiver ran through my body and I felt him once again, everywhere and nowhere. I was developing a serious appetite for that man.

I lay there for a few more moments, then forced myself to think. Marla the Bomber was sitting in a jail cell, Vincent Gambuzzo was in danger of losing his club, and I was in danger of losing my life if Raydean was right about the killer. My eyes flew open and focused on the alarm clock. Ten o'clock. That's why Nailor was gone. Marla's arraignment was this morning. I had to get there.

I flew out of bed. The chances were that I'd missed it, but I needed to see for myself. I pulled on a pair of black rayon pants and a champagne-colored shell, struggled into a pair of black slingbacks, and ran out the door. I was figuring I could do my makeup in the car and pull my hair back into a bun when I arrived at the courthouse.

Francis was still sleeping as I passed his room. Pat was gone, Fluffy probably with her. I ran out the back door, down the steps, and hopped into my car. An arrangement of yellow roses sat in the front passenger seat, the now familiar white card attached. My throat went dry and my heart started pounding. I knew they weren't from Nailor.

I looked around, saw no one, and touched the roses. They were still cool from the delivery car's air-conditioning, or perhaps the florist's cooler. I stretched out a hand and gingerly plucked the card from the greenery.

Roses are red
Violets are blue,
There isn't a flame
Holds a candle to you.

"Damn!" I swore, and started up the car. What in the hell did that mean? I pulled out of the driveway, the yellow roses filling the car with their scent. *There isn't a flame holds a candle to you.* The phrase ran around in my head, distracting me as I drove, confusing me. I finally had to stop the car at a convenience mart and buy a large coffee, just so I could gather my thoughts before I got downtown. I reached the courthouse and was walking up the steps and into the building by ten-thirty, but Marla was gone.

Ernie Schwartz, the Tiffany's legal counsel, came rushing toward me, his briefcase bulging, not noticing me on account of his hurry. He would've passed me by had I not reached out and grabbed his beefy little arm. He stopped, looked up at me through thick Coke-bottle lenses, and smiled.

"Sierra, what a pleasure!"

"Good to see you too, Ernie, but I don't have time for small talk. Where's Marla?"

Ernie smiled, puffed out his pinstriped chest, and looked back over his shoulder. "Out breathing her first taste of unconfined air, I reckon. I got bail!"

"How in the world did you do that?"

Ernie looked disappointed in me, like I should've known he did it with his customary legal brilliance, but an accused triple murderer never got out on bail.

"I got them to acknowledge that they could only charge her with the Barboni murder, and even that was circumstantial. She didn't have any priors. She's clean. They didn't have enough to tie her to whacking those girls, anyway." Ernie liked to use tough words like *whacking*, but in reality he'd grown up in Boston, graduated from Harvard Law, and never known a tough guy. He lived in a Victorian overlooking the bay with his new wife, Cheryl. His biggest fear in life right now was probably that I'd somehow get to Miss Junior League and tell her about the time me and Ernie got drunk and he sang the Oscar Meyer Wiener song in his birthday suit.

"So where'd they set her bail?"

Ernie's clear blue eyes twinkled. "Five hundred thousand," he breathed.

"That's it?"

Ernie nodded. "Gambuzzo put up the club. I told him he was being an idiot and he popped off on me. Said he wasn't paying me to have an opinion." Ernie sniffed. "I understand loyalty," he said, "but to a bimbo with a fifty-two-double-D cup? Hell, that boy's thinking with the little head."

I figured Ernie was really feeling like big stuff.

"How's Cheryl?" I asked. "You never bring her around. I'd love to meet her."

Ernie pulled back and looked over his shoulder again. "Aw, you know how it is with women," he said. "They're so insecure."

"Tell me about it," I said. "Better yet, tell me about Marla. What are our chances?"

Ernie cleared his throat. "It would help if she'd be more co-operative. That jackass of a boyfriend keeps giving her bad advice.

Told her not to trust anyone. Said I'm just Vincent's mouthpiece and that he didn't know for certain that Vincent wasn't involved. Like Gambuzzo would sabotage his own club and kill off his own dancers!" He shrugged. "Well, I gotta get going. I'm speaking to the Rotary Club in Panacea."

"Do you know if she was headed home?" I asked.

We turned and started walking through the hallway out into the warm mid-morning sunlight. Ernie was fishing in his pockets for his keys, frowning like maybe they'd moved on their own.

"That stupid boyfriend of hers took her off to celebrate. God knows what his definition of a celebration is. He probably took her off to his trailer for an afternoon of beer drinking and passion." Ernie coughed like the very idea was making him sick.

"Little Ricky lives in a trailer?"

"That's his name?" Ernie asked. "Little Ricky? No wonder." Ernie shook his head and looked over at me, then around the parking lot. "She told me she's got information that can help clear her. Of course, I can't tell you all the times some potential convict's told me that very same thing and it's turned out to be nothing, but you never know."

Ernie stopped by his Jaguar and fumbled in his briefcase for his keys. "I got her to promise she'd be in my office by three. You can see her there then, if you really need to talk to her."

"I do really need to talk to her, Ern. Thanks." I kissed him on the cheek and walked off to my Camaro. The roses were beginning to wilt in the steamy heat of the enclosed car. The odor was stronger than ever.

I started the car and sat there thinking. What could Marla have that would help her? Stupid bimbo, couldn't she see this was no time for a celebration? We had work to do. Something was wrong with the way I was looking at things, I knew this. *There isn't a flame holds a candle to you.* Someone wanted me away from the investigation. Raydean's angle was that it was all somehow about me in the first place. I sat there, twisting the facts as I knew them over and over. It just made no sense.

I looked at the clock on the dash. It was only eleven. The club wouldn't open for another hour. Somehow the club was involved. *Flame.* Maybe something was going to happen involving more fire. After all, John's car had been torched in the parking lot. Maybe the next step was to torch the club. Or maybe Vincent hadn't given me all the facts. Maybe Vincent didn't owe the IRS; maybe he owed someone else and didn't want me to know. I put the car in gear and pulled out of the lot, heading down Fifteenth Street, toward the Panama City Police Department. Maybe it would help to hash it over with Nailor. Maybe it would just help to see Nailor.

I turned down the sandy side road that ran alongside the police department and turned into the parking lot. The Panama City P.D. blended in with its surroundings. It was a low, tan building that sprawled across its lot on the main drag into town. Many people drove right past it, missing it because of the dog pound that sat just next door. The pound was shaped like a giant igloo dog kennel. Most people were so busy staring at the misshapen building that they missed the police municipal building.

I drove up to the front of the building, parked, and walked through the double glass doors and into the lobby. Paula, the chief records clerk, looked up and waved through her bullet-proof shield. "I'll page him," she called through the speaker.

"Make that a large fries," I said back, and sat down across from a crew of Mexican construction workers. The men were so intent on their conversation that they barely looked up. They surrounded another worker who sat clasping his bandaged head in his hands and crying.

Nailor kept me waiting long enough to figure that the crying man had been pistol-whipped and robbed. There was much gesturing and apparently a lot of blaming going on, as the men tried to sort out their buddy's trauma. When Nailor did finally make an appearance, I was reluctant to leave. It was like watching part of a soap opera and not knowing the outcome.

"Don't you have anyone that speaks Spanish here?" I asked Nailor.

He looked over at the men and shrugged. "We've got one, but he's off today. There's a lady who works in the chief's office, but she's at lunch. She'll help out when she gets back."

I looked up at him and saw that the lines around his eyes were thickened with fatigue. Oh, well, that's what happens when you stay up half the night with Sierra Lavotini. I chuckled and saw, too late, that he had his cop face on.

"What's wrong?" I asked.

He was leading me through the warren of corridors, heading for his minuscule office. He didn't answer.

"Are you pissed 'cause Marla made bail?"

He said nothing until he had me in his office with the door closed.

"No," he said, "I'm pissed because, as usual, something's going on and I'm the last to know." He sat down across from me and folded his arms across his chest. "What do you know about a guy named Cozzone being transported to the state hospital in Tallahassee, involuntarily, because of a false commitment order?"

I returned his stare. "Not a damn thing," I answered.

"All right, let's try this on," he said. "One of my officers positively identified you as being at Ernie's when they went to pick him up. She says you were seated at a table with him."

There was no getting out of this one. "Okay," I said, "but you can't say I didn't try and get your cooperation."

Nailor's face reddened. "I sure as hell can, because I don't know what in the hell is going on, Sierra."

I stood up and leaned across his desk. "I told you that Marla the Bomber didn't kill those girls or Barboni, but you didn't want to hear it. I had to find out what I could on my own. And now you're mad."

"You're damn right I'm mad," he thundered. "You used my people."

"I did not. I didn't know Packy Cozzone was wanted."

Nailor threw up his hands. "What is it with you? Sierra, this isn't a game. You can't manipulate the system to meet your needs."

"Why not? I didn't see you or anyone else listening to me. What? I should just sit back and let Marla go to the chair for murders she didn't do? I should let a killer run around loose and maybe kill you or me next? You think I like getting death threats?"

"What death threats? What are you talking about?"

I told him about the roses. I reminded him of the other two "messages." But I don't think that's what turned the tide and got Nailor's attention. Somehow, as I spoke, I had the feeling he'd been sitting on something all along.

"Just suppose Marla didn't kill those people," he said suddenly. "Suppose Raydean's right and this is somehow about you or the club. Maybe this killer's working to kill off the other head-liners. Maybe he wants you to be the only dancer there, or maybe he wants to kill off all of you. Maybe Barboni knew something and that's why he was killed. I don't know, Sierra, but if this is about you, then don't you think it's time you let me handle it?"

"Maybe," I said. "You're telling me you believe me now?"

His eyes softened and he was about to answer, but the door flew open and his lieutenant stood there. The lieutenant did not look happy.

"Hey," he said. "We got a report of a possible abduction. Lewis is out. I need you to catch it. Call came in from an attendant at the Chevron station." The lieutenant stopped and glanced at me. "Am I interrupting something?"

Nailor stood up and gave me a look. "No, Miss Lavotini was

just leaving." His look said that our business would wait, that I should go and wait to hear from him. Well, Sierra Lavotini might wait, but then again, she might not.

I stood up, cool as a cucumber, and turned to leave, brushing past the lieutenant.

"Just remember what I told you," Nailor called after me.

I didn't say a word. I had come to an unpleasant conclusion of my own and Nailor wasn't going to like the way I handled it. I followed the winding corridors to the exit, my brain working double-time on a nasty theory.

What if Nailor and Raydean were both right? What if the killer was systematically killing off the competition? What if Frosty Licks and Venus Lovemotion died because they were headliners, visiting headliners who had been thinking of staying at the Tiffany? What if Marla'd been set up to look like their killer? What better way to get rid of her? But now she was out and telling people she could prove her innocence. If John Nailor and Raydean were right, then Marla would be the killer's next victim.

Thirty

$\mathcal{N}$ailor had been a thirty-minute waste of my time. Marla was in trouble and stupid Little Ricky would offer her about as much protection as a newspaper in a hurricane. I had to find her, that much was clear. I couldn't wait until three. I needed to track her down at Little Ricky's trailer palace of burning love.

Someone at the Tiffany had to know where Ricky lived. I slipped out of the police lot and onto Fifteenth Street, heading for the beach and the Gentleman's Club. I reached over and punched in a cassette. I felt like something loud and wild. In short, Stevie Ray Vaughan. Music helps me think, and I had to think hard if I was going to figure this mess out.

I sped up over the Hathaway Bridge, waiting for inspiration and finding nothing. The sun was almost straight up overhead, the sky a brilliant blue. It was perfect beach weather. Tourists would be flocking to the sugary sands, but I shivered. Panama City suddenly felt cold and unfriendly. Stevie Ray wasn't scared. He sang out, urging me to come closer. I stopped at a red light and sat waiting to go. I didn't hear anyone coming up behind me; Stevie took care of that. When the passenger side door swung open I was completely unprepared.

"What the fuck is this?" Packy Cozzone said, eyeing the roses and tossing them out into the intersection. He slid into the front seat, an ugly gun poking out of his windbreaker sleeve.

"Get out of my car!" I yelled, my voice certainly carrying out of the open T-tops.

"Shut up, bitch," Packy snarled. "If you wanna see that cousin of yours again, you'll drive like I say, where I say."

"My cousin?"

Packy gestured to the white sedan that idled behind us. A hand emerged from the moon roof, waving the tie Francis had worn to the meeting with Cozzone.

"I got him in the backseat. Satisfied?" Packy looked smug. He knew he had us.

"What do you want, Packy?"

"Pull over to that motel lot over there. We're gonna leave your car and take mine. I don't like your taste in music and I got air-conditioning."

There was nothing else to do but follow his instructions. I parked under a small crepe myrtle and locked the car, all under Packy's watchful supervision. I left my purse in the car, hoping that if it eventually got found by the police they'd figure I hadn't left willingly.

We walked to the sedan, the windows tinted too darkly to see what waited inside for me. Packy was practically dancing with glee at having the tables turned on the Lavotinis. I really didn't have time for this.

The back door opened as I approached the car and one of Packy's men stepped out. He did not look friendly. Francis sat hunched in the backseat, leaning against the far window. When he looked up at me, I gasped. His eyes were blackened and his nose was horribly swollen, obviously broken.

I whirled around toward Packy. "You son of a bitch!"

The muscle grabbed me and shoved me into the car, propelling me into Francis, who groaned with the pain of another sudden impact. Packy's hand shot out and smacked the back of my head, just so we could all see that he was in the driver's seat now. I bit down hard on the inside of my lip and resisted the urge to cry.

"Francis, are you all right?" I said. His hands were tied behind his back and his feet were bound together.

"Francis?" Packy said.

"That's her pet name for me," Francis replied evenly. "The people closest to me call me Francis." I remembered and took the cue. If Packy Cozzone found out that we weren't related to Big Moose, we'd be dead. As it stood now, we might be dead anyway, but at least the Lavotini name was slowing him up.

"Do you know what you're doing, Packy?" I said. "Do you know who you're fucking with? Because if his father sees him like this . . ."

"Shut up!" Packy yelled. His face was red and his foot tapped a rapid staccato burst against the car door. "Give me the stuff."

One of Packy's men reached inside his jacket pocket and started to pull out a small plastic bag.

"Boss," the other said, "that might not be such a hot idea. Don't you think—"

"Shut up," Packy said, the gun suddenly aimed at the man's chest. He took the envelope from his other goon and grabbed a magazine from the floor of the car. From the looks of it, Packy was setting up to fill his nose with cocaine. He spilled a small amount of powder out onto the magazine and began tapping it into a thick line. He reached behind him and pulled a short straw off of the ledge behind the backseat. With a quick, practiced move, he snorted the cocaine. He leaned back against the seat and sniffed deeply, pulling the rest of the powder up into his nose. For a minute no one said a word. Packy sat with his eyes closed.

I looked over at Francis. He sat there, staring at Packy, his eyes filled with hatred. I knew if he could reach Cozzone, he'd kill him. Packy's eyes sprang open and he smiled at Francis, as if he'd heard him thinking.

"You don't fuck with a Cozzone," Packy said softly. "I don't care who you are."

The car was heading away from the Strip, I could see that much. We were moving out toward the flat farmland that rimmed the rest of the Panhandle, spreading its way back into South Georgia. There were miles and miles of deserted roads and small towns, sinkholes and briny marshes that could swallow bodies without any trace. My stomach turned and flipped as we bounced over potholes. Packy Cozzone didn't seem to care that we could see outside the car window and knew where he was taking us.

"Do you know what it's like to be led off in handcuffs to the nuthouse?" he said softly.

I stared back at him, tossing my head and trying to look at him with disdain. "I imagine it was just terrible," I said. "But of course, you can understand our position and see why it was necessary."

Packy's eyebrows rose into a shocked peak. "Understand? The fuck I do."

Francis nodded. "What else could we do? You had us in a bind. In New York, we might've handled this differently, in a more, shall we say, civilized manner. But here in the boonies, we gotta improvise."

Packy looked dumbfounded, as if he couldn't believe what he was hearing.

"After all," I said, "we don't know your organization that well. We didn't know you weren't going to try and hit us right there on the deck of Ernie's. You show up with a couple of armed morons. Maybe you were thinking that the best defense would be a good offense. I mean"—here I lied outright—"you guys aren't stupid, are you?"

Packy was in a bind. To deny that he'd thought about killing us would make him look like a fool; to admit to it made anything we did to protect ourselves fair game. He said nothing.

"I didn't think you were dumb," I said. "That's why I called in a favor. See, Little Moose here, he said if you tried anything, he wanted to kill you. But I knew our two families wouldn't want a war on their hands, not at a time like this." I leaned back and tried to look like Packy should get what I was talking about. I looked like we all knew the true story. Packy couldn't stand that. He definitely didn't want to look like he didn't know what was going on between our two syndicates.

"Well, despite that," he said, "you handled it all wrong. You didn't need to disgrace me in front of my compatriots." The two goons stifled smiles.

"Better that than dead," Francis added.

Packy shrugged, possibly thinking that dead would've saved his reputation, maybe even enlarged it.

I played the trump card again. "Big Moose sure isn't gonna like this," I said. "You hurt us, and there goes the truce." I shook my head and looked over at Francis. "In light of what Big Moose was planning, I'd say you haven't talked this over with the higher-ups in your organization. Maybe they don't trust you with all the details, or maybe they thought you knew. That's why we didn't say too much at Ernie's. That's why we had to deal with you as we did."

Packy sniffed and looked from one goon to the other. "Hand me the phone," he commanded. He laid his gun down on the seat next to him and took the cell phone. I was figuring my odds if I made a grab for it, while Packy dialed.

"I'm checking you out," he said. "You'd better not be shitting me, 'cause if you are . . ." His voice trailed off and he waited for someone to answer on the other end.

"Hey!" he called out. "That you?" He waited a second then banged the phone against his open palm. He brought it up to his ear again and yelled, "It's Packy! Who's this?" There was a brief pause as Packy listened, a frustrated look on his face. "Dickie, I'm getting every third word you say. I'm in the middle of fucking nowhere. I'm losing my freakin' battery. Just tell me one thing, here. Have we got something going on with the Lavotini syndicate pertaining to Florida? Don't be specific, just yes or no." Packy listened, smacked the phone again, and looked at it in disgust. "Did you say yes, Dickie?"

He pressed the phone up against his ear, then pulled it back quickly as it began to emit a high-pitched squeal. "Shit!" he swore. He looked at his two muscleheads. "We can't take no chances. Turn off on that dirt road and stop the car."

He waited until the car stopped; then he leaned forward, picking up his gun as he did so.

"Maybe our families got something going on, maybe they don't. Whatever." He shrugged and brought the gun up level with my chest. "I can't let you two off scot-free for getting me locked up in the nuthouse." There was an ominous silence as the two men on either side of Packy slowly reached inside their jacket pockets and brought out their weapons.

"This is the end of the road," Packy said. "Open the door and step outside."

I knew I was going to be sick. The bile rose up inside my throat and I felt my stomach heave. We were going to die on a dusty back road in rural Florida. The way things were going, no one would find us. Years from now they'd find our skeletal remains. We'd be identified by our dental records, our bodies eaten away by maggots and buzzards. The image terrified me.

Francis hobbled out of the car, pitched forward, and fell against me. Packy watched the entire scene from the cool darkness of the backseat, his gun still level with my heart.

"Here's how it's gonna go," he said calmly. "I'm gonna leave you two here, out in the hot sun, your skin cooking in the heat."

I was surveying the flat terrain and deciding we didn't have a hope in hell of running, especially not Francis. We were dead meat. I wanted to cry with the sheer frustration and fear of it all.

"You're gonna feel what I felt," he said. "And then you're gonna remember that you don't disrespect a Cozzone. If our two families are going to work together, then you gotta not get carried away with the size of your syndicate. Show a little respect. Hopefully, we can both learn from this. Have a nice day."

I braced myself, squeezing my eyes shut, and reaching out to grab Francis's arm. It was coming. I waited. The engine revved, the door slammed shut, and to my immense surprise, Packy Cozzone and his idiots drove away.

"Jesus, Mother Mary, and all the saints," I said. "He didn't kill us."

Francis took a deep, slow breath. "Get me out of these ropes," he said. "And let's get the hell out of here."

My hands shook as I untied him. I kept thinking over and over, "I could be dead. He could've killed us." Francis must've been thinking the same thing, because his entire body shook with a fine tremor as I worked to undo him.

"All right," he said when I'd finished. "Let's get going." The sun beat down on our heads, and sweat was rolling down the sides of our faces. We were in the middle of nowhere and I had no idea how to get home.

Francis didn't seem to care. He put one foot in front of the other and started off at a brisk pace, cresting the edge of the dirt road and turning left out on to the macadam two-lane.

"Francis, how do you know this is the right way?"

He didn't hesitate. "We're walking East; eventually we'll turn South. If we were to keep on walking, we'd hit the ocean."

My brother the Boy Scout. Of course he was right. I glanced up at the sun and saw it had drifted slightly past dead center and was now marking our course. I looked over at Francis, taking a reading of his emotions. His face was an expressionless blank of bruises and tiny cuts. He'd gone somewhere deep inside himself and was now on survival mode. This was just the way he always reacted when things went wrong. He sealed his feelings off and kept on going, doing the next logical step to bring the situation to a resolution. He'd done it when his wife left and he was doing it now, with me, moments after we'd both thought we were about to die.

I reached out and touched his arm, making him look over at me. "I'm sorry about all this, Francis," I said. "I really am sorry."

Francis laughed, an unamused chuckle that bounced off the road's surface and echoed into the still summer heat.

"Sierra, shit happens. He caught me sleeping, literally. I was asleep on the sofa and hung over. Life's lessons learned." He sighed and continued to plod relentlessly forward. The heat made the road shimmer. I couldn't tell how far we'd have to walk before we found a phone and could call someone.

"I know shit happens, Francis," I said, "but it's all right to have feelings about it."

Francis laughed again, louder. "You damn women are all alike. Feelings! God damn, Sierra, when are you going to grow up? Feelings don't get you shit. It doesn't change anything. Feelings don't undo what's happened or take it all back. Feelings just get in the way of moving on."

I sighed. He wasn't just talking about now. He was back then, thinking about the day Lois left and took every stick of furniture in their tiny row house, leaving Francis with nothing but a smashed wedding picture in a shiny brass frame.

"Maybe not, Francis. Maybe feelings don't do anything but keep you from falling over dead of a heart attack. But all's I know is, if you walk around trying to stuff them, you'll explode. You won't make good decisions and you'll wind up bitter and alone."

"And that would be a problem for who, Sierra?"

"You, Francis, and all the people who love you and have to watch you live like that."

The conversation was veering into uncharted territory. Francis had never responded well to this kind of thing and there wasn't much of a chance that he'd hear me now.

"I didn't realize you and Ma were having such a hard time, watching me waste my life in bitter solitude. See, I was figuring you'd know that being alone beats the hell out of the alternative. What? I could be back with Lois? And walk around knowing she's flat on her back for any of my acquaintances low enough to take her up on her offers? Then I suppose you think I should walk around feeling all that? Right? Yeah, that's a real heart-attack preventative."

It was hopeless. "No, Francis, what I'm saying is, it's okay to admit that you hurt, or that you're scared. You share that with another human being and it lightens your load."

Francis stopped and turned to look at me. "Sierra, we nearly got our asses blown away back there. You want me to sit here and tell you how scared I was? You want me to tell you I nearly shit my pants knowing my little sister was going to get her brains blown out and there wasn't a thing I could do about it? All right, there! That's how I feel! Does that make you feel better? 'Cause it don't do jack shit for me."

His face was scarlet with the heat and pain. He still trembled, his hands shaking as he waved them in the air, uncontrollably angry. I reached out and grabbed his arms, holding them tightly as I stepped into him.

"Francis, all's I'm saying is that I love you and I'm on your team, even when the shit hits the fan. It's hard to love a stone statue, Francis. Perfection is even harder to deal with. I like you human. You're one of my biggest heroes, you idiot, can't you see that? Can't you see that all I want is to be okay in your eyes?

Can't you see I'd like to be there for you sometimes, instead of you always cleaning up my messes?"

His eyes softened a very little bit. "What are you talking about, okay in my eyes? Sierra, why do you think I gotta take such good care of you? You think I'd get my ass beat for someone I didn't care about?"

"No, I think you got your ass beat 'cause you were asleep on the job." I smirked at him and he shoved me with his elbow, forcing me off of the road and into the drainage ditch.

"I'm telling Ma," I yelled.

Francis reached in his pocket and flipped me a quarter. "Call her, sissy," he said. "And while you're at it, order me a pizza and a large pitcher of beer."

He pulled me back onto the road and we walked on, our energy spent and the tension between us gone. We walked on for what must've been an hour before coming to a tiny service station and convenience store. I called my backup supporters and Francis bought us both Moon Pies and Cheerwine. Around three-thirty, Pat and Raydean finally pulled into the parking lot to pick us up.

Pat took one look at Francis and whistled softly under her breath. "Who'd you run into?" she asked.

"A door," Francis said. "I wasn't watching where I was going."

"Happens to me all the time," Raydean said, but continued to stare at him as if perhaps he were Flemish.

The four of us squeezed into the broad front seat of Pat's pickup truck. Francis sat next to Pat and I sat between him and Raydean. Fluffy took turns bouncing from one lap to another.

"We've got to get out to Ernie Schwartz's office," I said. "Marla had an appointment at three and I've gotta talk to her."

"Is his office still over there near the courthouse?" Pat asked.

"They got razor wire up over that jail," Raydean said, apparently attaching the jail to the courthouse. "A boy tried to break out of there once and fell in that black bayou. Remember that,

Pat?" she said. "It was February and them po-lice liked to let him drown. I don't like it over there."

"That makes two of us," I said, patting her wrinkled hand. "But Marla might be in trouble."

"She's too big-chested to be pregnant," Raydean said. "I had a cat like her once. Litter nearly smothered."

"What kind of trouble?" Pat asked.

"I'm not sure. But I got another bunch of flowers this morning and I got to thinking about what Raydean said. I think the killer might try and hurt Marla if he thinks she's about to go free."

Francis winced and held a sweating soda can up against his bruised face. "Sierra," he said, "I'm having a feeling, here. You want me to share it with you?"

I almost went for it, but the look on his face stopped me. "No, Francis, this would not be one of those opportunities for sharing."

" 'Cause I was gonna tell you I'm having a bad feeling. I'm having one of those call-the-police-and-let-them-handle-it feelings. I think we should go home and call your friend Nailor. I think he should know about our little sojourn into the heart of freakin' Florida. I think we should share with him."

Raydean leaned over and stared at Francis. "You must've had the same therapist I did," she muttered. "Young chick named Mavis, all the time trying to get us to share our feelings with the group." Raydean rolled down the window and spat, then looked back at Francis. "Didn't nobody ever tell you that sharing your feelings is nothing but a bunch of hooey?"

Francis leaned back against the seat and shut his eyes. "Raydean," he said, "I'm beginning to think you're the sanest one of the bunch."

"Thank you," Raydean said, a smug smile on her face. "Up at the big house they call that an affirmation."

Thirty-one

A huge pin oak leaned over the brick walkway leading up to Ernie Schwartz's office. The office itself was a two-story brick colonial, with white trim and black shutters. The entire scene had been arranged by professional designers, from the landscape on into the interior of the building. It looked like a movie set of an attorney's office and nothing at all like the Ernie I knew. It lacked charm and personality. Worst of all, it lacked Marla the Bomber.

"I don't know what to think," Ernie said, looking out of place behind a mammoth mahogany desk. He glanced at the Regulator pendulum clock, silently swinging away, and shrugged. "Maybe she and that idiot boyfriend of hers got carried away. Whatever, she never showed."

Little prickles of anxiety traveled up and down my skin, stinging me with intuition. Somewhere inside myself I'd known she wouldn't keep her appointment. Something was horribly wrong and I knew it.

Fluffy, always overjoyed to see her godfather, sat in Ernie's lap and frowned. She understood the tone. She knew things didn't look good.

"I don't suppose she left you Little Ricky's phone number?"

Ernie shook his head, riffled through some papers, and looked up at me again. "You know," he said, "I like to think I'm a good judge of character. I really didn't think she'd run off. If anything, that boyfriend convinced her to run off, but only after he'd filled her with enough alcohol to cloud her thinking."

I could just see Little Ricky sweet-talking Marla, and I knew she was totally gone on him, but I couldn't quite see her leaving town, not when she thought she could prove her innocence. And not when she thought she still had a shot at being the top headliner at the Tiffany Gentleman's Club. Marla the Bomber wanted the top billing at the Tiffany almost more than she wanted Little Ricky. She had to be in trouble.

"Ernie, I'm going to find her for you. I'll find Little Ricky and then I'll find Marla and then we'll get this mess taken care of. I don't think she ran off." Fluffy, sensing an impending departure, jumped off Ernie's lap and ran to the door. "Call me if you hear from her. I'll check my machine from the road."

Ernie shook his head again. "Sierra, I'd stay out of this one if I were you."

Fluffy moaned. Apparently she echoed Ernie's sentiments.

My crew of misfits sat under the pin oak, leaning against its broad base. Pat looked worn-out and Francis looked worse.

"How about you guys drop me at my car and go on home?" I said. "I can call you if I need you. You look beat. No pun intended, Francis."

Pat struggled up to her feet and limped a few steps toward the pickup. "Well, if there's nothing for us to do, and if you don't need help, I might just take you up on that. I could use a nap and your brother could use a trip to the hospital to get his nose set. I could drop him off."

Francis stood up. "Where's your friend?"

"Ernie thinks she took off with Little Ricky."

Francis raised an eyebrow. "Yeah, but what do you think?"

I looked around the parking lot, hesitating, then turned back to him. "I think she's in trouble and I need to find her."

He nodded and started walking toward the truck. "I think I'll come with you."

He opened the door and swung up into the front seat.

"I think you should see a doctor," I said. "Pat can drop you at the medical center and I can come get you after I run out to Little Ricky's house."

Francis stared back at me, stony and determined. "No," he said. "I *feel* like going with you." Then he smiled a little and winced when it hurt.

Raydean and Fluffy filed back into the truck and Pat cranked the engine. "You coming?" Raydean asked. She patted Francis's knee. "He's a big boy, Sierra. Let him go with his feelings."

There was no point in trying to get anybody to do anything. They were going to do exactly as they pleased and I could like it or lump it. It made no never mind to them.

"My car's in the Days Inn parking lot off Middle Beach Road," I said. Pat nodded and took off. The clock was ticking. I was due at the Tiffany in two hours and a killer was out there somewhere, looking for Marla—that is, if he hadn't already found her.

Raydean was humming to herself, a mindless tune that ceased abruptly when we pulled into the Days Inn parking lot and saw my car.

"Sierra, when did you get a valet service?" she breathed.

Packy Cozzone's white oversized sedan sat next to the Camaro. The back door was open and Packy's legs protruded from the backseat, tapping their familiar rapid staccato on the asphalt. His two hoods were leaning over the hood of my car, polishing it.

Pat drew her breath in sharply and veered toward the left, but Packy had spotted us. He jumped up, his head appearing over the door, his arms waving wildly as he tried to get our attention.

"I'll kill the little punk bastard now," Francis growled.

"With what, Francis, your looks? We don't carry. They've got three guns and probably two of them are trained on the truck right now." I looked over at the three crazy men and saw that they seemed to show no intention of reaching for their weapons. "I think we should go over there," I said. "If we don't, we come off looking scared. Do you think Big Moose would want to hear that his son ran scared?"

Francis shook his head and looked over at me. "Sierra, I'm not Big Moose Lavotini's son, remember? You made that up."

"Well, it's too late to go back on that now. We gotta play it out. Pat, you guys wait here. If they shoot us or something, take off and call the police. That's Packy Cozzone, out of New York City."

Fluffy started to growl and bark, and Raydean held her back when Francis and I jumped out of the car. Packy came out from behind the car door, both hands held out in front of him, like he was trying to show us he meant no harm. The goons kept right on polishing my car. One of them held a squirt bottle and was cleaning the wheel rims on each of my tires. All in all, it made a very strange picture.

"Mr. Moose," Packy said, when Francis got within earshot, "I owe you the very deepest of apologies."

"You're damn right you do," Francis said, "and that may not be enough to save your sorry ass."

Packy looked very contrite. "I would hope that you wouldn't do that," he said. "I'm in enough trouble already." He lifted his head and looked at me. "You see, I got the full story. I am very sorry. I had no way of knowing. I just thought you guys were fucking with me."

I shrugged. "Well, sometimes you can't be too careful," I said.

"Dickie called me back. Someone in our organization spoke to someone in your family, and well, it eventually got to Big

Moose." Packy looked at the ground again. "I am so sorry," he said. "I didn't know Big Moose was looking to make an investment down here, totally unrelated to our piece of the pie. It was a case of poor communications. Big Moose sent the word out directly that we were to cooperate fully with you and to help in any way possible."

"He did?" Francis and I said. What was going on?

Packy nodded. "He in particular said to send his regards to you, Miss Lavotini. He said he always loves to hear news of his relative in Florida. But he said he don't always know himself what Little Moose is up to." Packy cut a sly look in Francis's direction. "So what are you up to?" he asked.

Francis shook his head and waved Packy off. "I'm not discussing it with anyone, not until it's a done deal. It's a present for my father. I just want it to go smoothly." That Francis, he had balls the size of Boston. Didn't he get that Big Moose Lavotini was on to us?

Packy shook his head, like maybe he'd been an idiot. "I am truly sorry. My men and I are at your disposal."

"Don't worry about it," Francis said. "You guys go on about your business and if I need you, I'll call you."

This brought an unexpected response from Packy and his men. They straightened up, closed ranks, and took a step forward.

"You don't understand," Packy said, the smile still in place, but his face hardening to stone. "Big Moose, he said to stick by you like glue. He said he wants to make sure his family in Panama City is protected. Each and every day I am to report back to his office directly what I have done to ensure your safety. He wants to know every move you make, and in what way I made things go smoothly. If we don't take care of you," Packy said, twitching nervously, "he'll take care of us. Now, we wouldn't want that, would you?"

This was all we needed. It was too much to believe that Little

Moose Lavotini was actually in Panama City. No, we'd been brought to the attention of the real Lavotini Syndicate, and now Big Moose was curious and watching our every move. We were dead.

I felt Francis sigh softly. "All right," he said. "You follow us. You stay back, out of the way, unless I signal you."

"What's the signal?" Packy said.

"Oh, you'll know," Francis said. "If I give you a signal, you'll definitely know."

"Good enough for me, boss," Packy said. "We'll follow you."

Francis looked over at me, then back at Pat. "Well, let's go," he said. I dug my keys out of my pants pocket and walked over to the gleaming Camaro. I looked back at Pat and saw her jaw stiffen. She wasn't about to go anywhere, either. When I pulled out into traffic it would be with an entourage.

"You wanna tell me how you feel," Francis asked, as I settled into the driver's seat and cranked the engine.

"Hey, Francis," I said, not even looking at him, "fuck you and your feelings."

He laughed and we tore off out of the lot, chirping the tires and jumping the curb. I heard Packy scream out a war whoop and saw the sedan jump the curb. Pat chose to drive in a more restrained manner, bringing up the rear, with Fluffy's little head hanging out the passenger-side window.

Francis rooted through my cassettes and chose Bruce Springsteen. I had to put Big Moose out of my mind. We had larger fish to fry. Moose could wait. We were on our way to the Tiffany. Little Ricky and Marla had disappeared. Little Ricky. Why hadn't I thought about him before? Why hadn't I picked up on the signals? Why didn't I get it? He'd been with each of those dancers before they'd died. He'd made countless passes at me. He'd supplied me with all the information on Marla, information that was supposed to help her and only implicated her further. Little Ricky, the same guy who'd seen me snub him in order to talk to Barboni. The same guy who'd had access to Marla's gun.

I punched the accelerator and started weaving in and out of the five-thirty traffic. What if he'd killed her? What if I'd been too slow in figuring the whole deal out?

"Sierra, do you want to get us all killed?" Francis cried.

I kept on driving, the others following behind me as best they could. Packy was flashing his headlights off and on and honking his horn. I paid no attention and kept on speeding toward the club. An image came to me of Marla, zooming out over the club runway, hooked up to guy wires and pullies, dressed in her now infamous B-52 bomber costume, all silver sequins and glitter. She was smiling, her lips painted a brilliant red, her eyes thick with navy-blue mascara. Despite her petty manner and simpering ways, there was a lonely little girl inside Marla. She just had no awareness of her real potential, and now maybe she never would.

I ran the red light out onto the main beach drag and made a ninety-degree turn into the Tiffany parking lot. The after-work crowd was skimpy, with only a few of the regular cars in the lot. I stopped right in front of the door and charged inside. Behind me I could hear the opening and closing of car doors as my entourage arrived.

Vincent was behind the bar, an apron around his ample waist and a cocktail shaker in his pudgy hands. He was not a happy camper.

"Have you seen Marla?" I asked.

He looked surprised. "No, why? She ain't due in here for another two hours."

"Where does Little Ricky live?"

Vincent put the cocktail shaker down and leaned on the bar. "Sierra, what the hell is going on? Why're you looking for that scumbag? Why don't you know where Marla is?" Worry etched its way across his face.

"He's gonna hurt her, Vincent. Little Ricky, he took Marla."

Vincent frowned. "No, he didn't." He looked behind me, over my shoulder. "Who are those guys?" he asked, nodding toward Packy Cozzone and his colleagues.

"My associates," I said, "from New York." Francis shook his head.

"Do you know where Little Ricky lives?" I asked Vincent again. "Does anybody here know where Little Ricky lives?" I called out to the bar in general.

Panic gripped me when no one answered. Did they not get the seriousness of the situation?

"Come on! Think! One of you has to know where Little Ricky lives!"

The men's room door banged open and a familiar voice rang out: "Hell, I can answer that question. Do I get a prize?"

The entire bar turned around and stared. "I live at 1604-A Twenty-ninth Street. Now what do I win, darlin'? You?" Little Ricky started walking toward me, still zipping his pants. He was drunk, snot-nosed, drooling drunk.

"Don't worry," Vincent said softly. "I took his car keys."

"Where is Marla, Ricky?"

At the mention of her name, Little Ricky's face fell. "I don't know," he moaned. "She left me."

"I don't believe you," I said. "I think you killed her and the others. Now where is she?"

Packy Cozzone didn't like the sound of things and lifted his chin ever so slightly to the goons. All three of them dipped their hands into their pockets and came out with weapons, the same nasty guns that had been pointed at my heart only hours before.

"Jesus!" Vincent swore. "Sierra, we don't allow guns in here."

"Those aren't guns, Vincent," I said. "Those are reminders, reminders of who is in charge, and right now," I said, turning back to stare at Little Ricky, "that would be me. Where is Marla?"

"I don't know, I tell you! I haven't seen her since they took her off to jail! I was planning on going to the arraignment, but my agent called with a job."

"What agent, Ricky? Cut the crap. You don't have an agent!"

Ricky squared his big shoulders and glared at me. "I do, too!" he insisted, his voice slurring slightly with the effort it cost him to think and talk. "Got him day before yesterday. He called me, as a matter of fact. Said he'd seen me fight one time and wanted to represent me. He's the one sent me on the job."

I had a sinking feeling and looked over at my brother. He was looking at Ricky like he couldn't believe what he was hearing.

"But you got to the job and no one was there, right? And nobody had ever heard of your agent, right?"

Little Ricky's eyes widened. "Damn, you're clairvoyant, too?"

"No, Ricky, it's just common sense."

Packy Cozzone stepped closer. "Sierra, you want we should slam him? We do that real good."

"No, I do not want you should slam him, Packy. I'll slam him if I need to."

Packy shrugged. "All right," he said, "but he's a little big for you to be slamming."

That's when I began to think I knew who killed the girls and Alonzo Barboni.

"Packy, you got your phone on you?" He reached inside his jacket pocket, pulled out the little black phone, and passed it over. "Don't worry about how long you stay on," he said. "I got unlimited minutes."

"Shut up!" Francis barked.

I dialed Ernie's office and waited for him to pick up.

"Ernie Schwartz," he said. He sounded beat.

"Ernie, the guy who picked up Marla, what did he look like?"

"Scrawny kid. You know, little, as in Little Ricky, just like you said. Had a goatee."

I snapped the phone shut without saying good-bye and turned to Vincent. "All right, I know you know this: Where does Gordon live?"

"Out off of Ponce De Leon on Deco Street," he said. "You won't miss it. I took him home the other week when his car wasn't working. It's nothing more than a shack, white peeling paint and a blue-gray railing around the roof. It's about six blocks back off Front Beach Road."

I whirled around, heading for the door. It was starting to make sense. Snippets of Gordon approaching me, telling me he'd take care of me, telling me no one would ever take my place, ran through my head. "Don't you believe I can take care of you?" he'd asked. I remembered the disappointed look on his face when I'd turned him down and blown him off. But I was missing something. I didn't know why Gordon felt the need to take such "good" care of me.

"Do you want me to call the cops?" Vincent called after us.

I stopped at the door and looked back at him. "No, Vincent. Do not call the cops. If Marla's still alive and Gordon hears sirens, he might kill her. No, let us take care of it. Wait thirty minutes and then call the cops."

Vincent nodded and began pulling off his apron strings. "You hear that?" he said to the poor frightened bar back. "You wanted to be a bartender? Here's your shot. The guys will help you out. The substitute's due in at six-thirty. Call the cops at six. Ask to talk to a Detective Nailor."

Nothing would've kept Vincent from Marla. I couldn't have stopped him if I'd tried. The eight of us stepped out into the late-afternoon sunlight.

"All right," I said, "here's the plan. Gordon wants me, so I'm going in. We'll play the rest by ear."

"Damn," Raydean said and spat across the parking lot. "I

knew I should've brought Marlena!" Fluffy growled low in her throat.

"I don't like the 'by ear' part," Francis said.

"We'll talk about the rest of it in the car," I said. "We've gotta move."

I didn't give anyone a chance to argue with me. I was not about to make a decision by committee. Someone told me once that if you act like you're in charge, then others will follow you. It seemed to be working, because when I started the engine and pulled out onto Front Beach Road, the others were right behind me.

"I don't like this," Francis said. He pulled Bruce out of the tape player and sat frowning at me.

"Yeah, he hasn't been as good since the late eighties."

"Not Springsteen, Sierra. You know what I mean."

I was driving fast, letting my unconscious hone itself in on the battle. I didn't need to do too much thinking on the surface, better my inner child should get ready for this fight.

"Look, we got seven people on backup," I said. "I'm going to get inside Gordon's house, get him indecently occupied, and let you guys come in the best way you can. If Marla's still alive, you take her out. If she's not, kill Gordon."

I meant what I said. I wasn't going to entertain the idea of saving him for the police. If he'd killed Marla, I wanted him dead. Not politically correct for a liberal like myself, but nonetheless true.

We turned off Front Beach Road and began the countdown to Ponce. Vincent, squeezed like an overly ripe tomato into my backseat, leaned forward. "There it is, up there. That's his street. It's about six houses in."

I pulled over onto the sandy roadside and got out of the car. "Vincent, you and Francis get in with Packy. I need to drive in alone." Francis wanted to object but knew it was the best way to tackle the situation. I walked back to Packy's car and ran down the directions. "Francis is in charge, Packy, so don't go getting any smart ideas about hotdogging it."

"Me?" Packy squeaked. "Why would I do a thing like that?"

I looked at Vincent. "Don't go trying to be a hero," I said. "This is a situation best handled with finesse, not bravado, okay?" He nodded, not like I had to worry about him suddenly becoming a macho man, but you never knew. Love does funny things to people.

"When I want you to approach," I said, turning to the assembled others, "I'll somehow get to that window on the side of the house and flick the curtains back and forth. If I'm in trouble, I'll just jerk them open."

"And what if you're in trouble and you can't reach the window?" Pat asked quietly.

"If I'm gone more than ten minutes, and you don't get a signal, one of you call nine-one-one and the rest of you come get me. Except for you, Raydean. I want you and Pat to watch Fluffy."

Raydean nodded. "You never know what them aliens will chow down on. He's already come after her once."

"Right," I said. I looked at Francis. "So let's go kick some ass, right?"

He stood looking at me, concern written all over his face. He didn't want me to go and he knew I had to. It was the only way to save Marla, if it wasn't already too late.

I walked the few feet back to my car, hopped in, and pushed the Bruce Springsteen tape back into the cassette player. "Summer's here and the time is right . . ." he sang. "Damn straight, Bruce," I said, and turned onto Gordon's street.

The little white house stood in the middle of a lot overgrown with sparse grass and weeds. Pieces of bleached gray wood lay around the yard, some with rusted nails poking out, others splintered and tossed aside. No one had cared for the structure in a very long time.

I parked the car right out front and carefully followed the rutted pathway to the front door. A battered black Escort stood by the side door. I figured Gordon was home, but there was no sign of life from the tiny cottage.

When I reached the front stoop, I stopped and banged on the front door, the sound echoing off inside the tiny house.

"Gordon!" I yelled. "It's me, Sierra. Open up! I need your help!"

For a minute there was no sound whatsoever. I surveyed the houses that lined either side, pinched together like irritable siblings, and saw few with cars in the driveways. It wasn't a tourist neighborhood. The people who lived here worked, probably blue-collar or service jobs.

I heard something rustle off to the side of the house. I looked back down the street toward Ponce, where my teammates waited out of sight, and then took off around the side of the building.

"Sierra." A husky whisper seemed to emanate from the battered Escort. "Over here."

My heart rose up in my throat and I stepped closer to the car. Weeds scratched at my legs as I slowly stepped closer to the rusting vehicle. Gordon was crouched down on the far side of the car.

"Gordon, what're you doing there?" I said, my voice a shade louder than normal.

"Quiet," he hissed. "Come with me. Everything's going to be all right."

I reached his side and crouched down beside him, hoping to soothe him by going along with him.

"What are we hiding from?" I whispered.

Gordon's hair stood up in wiry tufts. His shirt was partially unbuttoned, ripped and bloodstained, but he didn't seem to notice. Instead he peered out from behind the car, darting his head back below the car's fender.

"All right," he whispered. "Follow me. Keep your head down and run low."

I assumed he was taking me inside, but instead ran in a straight line toward the house next door. I hesitated, then followed him. I had to follow him. He was our only link to Marla. Unfortunately, my backup would now be useless.

Gordon ran up onto the screened-in side porch of the tiny bungalow and quickly opened the door into the house. I let the porch door slam behind me, but its echo sounded like a small, hollow slap. No one a block away would've heard that sound.

Gordon locked the door behind us and turned to face me. His demeanor had changed with the closing of the door, from wild man to genial host.

"I'm so glad you came," he said. "What's wrong?"

"Wrong? Nothing's wrong." But my voice cracked, breaking into a high-pitched squeak.

Gordon stared at me. "You were knocking on the door and saying you needed my help. Something must be wrong."

I looked around the tiny cottage, staring past him into the living room. It was furnished with a shabby-looking plaid couch and a matching recliner. The coffee table was a thick, rustic wooden piece. Sitting on top of the table was a small vase full of yellow roses.

"Well, yes, actually something is very wrong. Marla's missing and no one seems to know where she is. I guess I just didn't know who else I could turn to."

Gordon seemed to relax even further. "Oh," he said, "is that all?" He moved toward the tiny galley kitchen that stood beside the living area. "Let me get you something to drink," he said. "You want some tea?"

Tea? Now? I bit my tongue. "Sure."

I wandered closer to the flowers, my shoes sounding like echoing slaps as I walked across the scuffed wooden floor. Gordon reappeared with the tea and set the glasses down on the coffee table, right next to the flowers.

"You like roses, I hope," he whispered. "They're the only flower as regal in their bearing as you."

He sat down on the sofa, pulling me beside him. I looked into his eyes and saw the madness stare back out at me. I don't know what he saw when he looked at me, or how long it would take before he realized I knew.

Gordon stuck out a hand and brushed a curl back behind my ear. "You are so lovely," he said softly. "No one can hold a candle to you."

I tried to think of something to say. I willed my mouth to open, but nothing came out. I felt frozen. *No one can hold a candle to you.*

"Didn't you get the messages I sent you, the ones with the flowers? I told you not to worry. I told you I'd take care of you. I want to take you away, Sierra," Gordon said.

"I can't," I said. It sounded desperate, but I covered it. "I have a job, Gordon." I smiled like I meant no offense, but he just stared, regarding me solemnly.

"They don't appreciate you. They keep trying to replace you. I can't keep them away forever. They'll keep coming and coming, trying to knock you down off the throne. And the men, Sierra, their hands are dirty. They all want to get you, Sierra. I only want to protect you." He looked sad, staring at his shoes for a moment. "I couldn't help Lori, so I have to help you."

"Who's Lori?"

Gordon's attention shifted back to me. "My sister."

I made myself stretch out a hand and touch his knee. "The sister with the flowers?" I asked.

Gordon nodded. "She worked with them, up in Atlanta. She

wanted to be an actress. My parents and me, we thought she was making it. Lori told us she was dancing and acting and selling her flowers."

Gordon looked over at me, anguish etching its way across his features. "You look so much like her, Sierra. That's why I started working at the Tiffany. I came here to get away, just like we used to when I was a kid. And then I'm driving down the main strip, and I looked up and saw your picture up there on that billboard by Sharkey's. That's when I knew what God wanted. Don't you see? It's my second chance."

I felt sick. Gordon was talking, all the while patting my knee like an uncle.

"I got here just in time, didn't I? Gambuzzo invited those evil Syndicate people right into your club, Sierra. It would have been only a matter of time before they put you in the movies. They control everything in Georgia and North Florida. You would've had to work for them."

"Gordon, I wasn't in any danger. No one was going to hurt me."

"They said they'd protect Lori, but they didn't, did they?" Gordon smiled softly. "Those girls would've seen your beauty. The other dancers didn't like Lori because she was beautiful. Barboni didn't protect her. Nobody did. They got her high, they made her work for drugs, and then they let some pervert kill her." Tears welled up in his eyes. "But now I have you. I'm your guardian angel, Sierra."

I couldn't help it. "If you're my guardian angel, then why did you try and hurt Fluffy? For that matter, why'd you blow up Detective Nailor's car?"

Gordon's eyes clouded. He looked as if I'd physically hit him. "I wouldn't have hurt your dog. I just wanted to scare you a little. Make you more careful ... keep you from getting hurt." He scowled. "And that cop ain't your friend. All he wants is to own you. Besides, if he's such a good cop, then why can't he catch me?" Gordon's features relaxed into a smile of satisfaction.

I stood up. "Where's your bathroom, Gordon?" I was going out the window. Maybe. First I was going to see if Marla was in the house.

It took him a moment to process my request, then he stood and took me by the hand. "Use this one," he said, and led me to a tiny bathroom in the hallway. There was no window. No way out. Gordon stood there as I started to close the door, obviously intent on guarding me.

"Gordon," I said, "I'm starving do you have anything to eat?"

He smiled. I wasn't going anywhere. "Sure," he said. "I'll make you a sandwich."

I closed the door and leaned back against it. He loved me, enough to kill for me, enough to protect me from any perceived threat. I knew without a doubt, he'd never let me leave, not willingly. I crossed to the toilet and flushed it, then pulled open the medicine cabinet. It was crammed with tiny bottles, all of them partially full of pills and capsules. Zyprexa, Prozac, Trazodone, Wellbutrin, Remeron, Clozaril. The same medications I'd seen on Raydean's countertops before the docs realized she wasn't taking them. I read the dates on the bottles and realized that Gordon hadn't taken his medication in quite some time.

"Sierra?" Gordon's voice echoed down the hallway.

"Coming," I answered. "I'm washing my hands. Hey, do you have any pickles to go with that sandwich?"

"I'll go look," he called. He sounded so normal.

I slid my hand into my bra, removed my Spiderco knife, and slipped it into the palm of my hand. Then I carefully opened the door and slipped across the hallway to Gordon's bedroom. It was a shamble of disorganization. Clothes lay in wrinkled heaps on the floor, sprawled across chairs, piled up with the quilts on his filthy bed. The room smelled faintly of blood and decay.

I tiptoed across the room to the closet and began to turn the doorknob. It wouldn't budge. It was locked. I looked at my watch. I had ten minutes to find her and get her out of the house before the cops came screaming down the street and all hell broke loose.

"Marla," I whispered, "are you in there?"

I paused, listening with my ear against the door. I couldn't tell. I thought I heard a slight scrabbling sound.

"Honey, it's Sierra," I whispered again. "I'm going to get you out of here. Just hang on."

I turned around and found Gordon standing in the doorway, a plate with a sandwich in one hand and a gun in the other.

"Oh, Sierra," he whispered, "I wish you hadn't done that." The plate slipped from his hand and fell to the floor, shattering into pieces. "You know I can't let you leave. You're all mine now. We'll never go back."

"Gordon, no." My throat went dry and my heart was beating so loudly I was sure he could hear it.

He walked toward me, a heavy, slow step that seemed to drag him forward, almost against his will. He reached me, grabbed my arm, and pulled me to the bed.

"We'll always have each other," he said softly, and raised the gun to my head.

"Gordon, wait!" I said, trying to keep my voice down, trying to hide the panic. "We're not finished."

Gordon was listening.

"There are things we can do here on Earth that we can't do in eternity."

I shifted my body toward him, turning my head so I could look at him, ignoring the barrel of the gun.

"Gordon, you can't shoot me. You wouldn't shoot Lori." I was grasping for something, anything, to help me stay alive long enough to get help. "Talk to me, Gordon," I whispered.

His eyes flickered and I began to unbutton my blouse with one hand.

"Help me, Gordon." I moved closer, offering myself to him. The knife hidden in my other hand comforted me, offering me the only hope I had.

Gordon's hands shook. The gun trembled but barely moved. He slowly raised his free hand and stretched out his fingers to touch my breast.

"I want you, Gordon," I said softly, and began to move toward him. "Put down the gun, baby."

"Not yet."

I pulled off my shirt and unfastened my bra. While he sat there watching, I stood up before him, moving in between his knees. "Touch me, Gordon. Put your face right here."

As I pulled his face toward my breasts, I slipped the Spiderco open, its razor-sharp blade cold against my palm. As I began to push him backward onto the bed, straddle his thighs, and climb on top of him, I heard the dim wail of sirens turning onto his street.

Gordon snapped back up, shoving me to one side as he listened.

"See?" he said. "Just like Lori. You didn't listen to me. You called them."

He didn't wait for me to answer. He pushed me off of him onto the bed and sprang on top of me, his face suffused with rage. With a trembling hand he raised the gun, pinning me down with one hand as he pointed it first at his head, and then at mine.

I moved, reflexively, swinging my arm up and into the pressure point inside his arm. He fell heavily on top of me and the gun exploded with a deafening roar as we began to fight.

I couldn't move him, and I couldn't let him kill me. I lashed out, kicking and screaming, hoping someone would hear me but knowing they wouldn't.

Gordon brought his hands up, free of the gun, and began to choke me. He rose up, bringing the full force of his upper body into his effort to kill me. I hurt. I couldn't breathe and I was terrified.

Get your money's worth. I heard Nailor's voice ringing inside my head.

With one last burst of energy, I forced my hands up, inside his arms and lashed out, but this time I used the knife, slashing deep into his arm as I pushed him over. I screamed and ran, ignoring the howl of rage and pain that followed me.

I got as far as the door, fumbling with the lock, before he reached me.

"No!" he screamed. He slammed into me, pushing me into the hard wooden door. I bucked backward, lashing out with the knife at any portion of his body I could reach. He shrieked and jumped backward, and I ran, picking up the vase of roses and hurling them out through the living room window.

Gordon ran back into the bedroom and returned an instant later. He'd found the gun, but I'd found the window and was jumping out as he ran after me, trying to aim, trying to make his bleeding arm cooperate.

I fell out the window, not at all gracefully, and began to run. Behind me a gun exploded. In front of me another gun exploded, but I couldn't see. I was running for my life, sprinting the short distance toward the other house and the swirling lights of the patrol cars.

"How about that, eh?" someone said.

Someone grabbed me, pulling me to the ground behind a squad car. "Jesus, Sierra," Nailor said, his body shielding mine.

There was total silence for a brief second, and then Packy Cozzone's voice rang out. "Hey, you Ninjas," he called. "I shot the little fucker, you can quit pointing them rifles like you are actually serving a purpose. He's dead. I saved your miserable little butts."

Nailor, sensing an impending second death, raised his head. "All right," he said, "hold your fire." He looked back at me. "We found the kid that Gordon paid to deliver the flowers, caught him in a drug raid. I've been trying to reach you all afternoon to tell you. We would've had Gordon in a matter of hours. Is there anyone else in the house?" he asked.

I shook my head. "He was by himself, but his bedroom closet door's locked. I thought I heard something in there, but—"

He didn't let me answer. "Search the house," he said. "There may be a hostage in the bedroom closet."

Panama City's finest, with weapons drawn and fierce, fierce looks on their young faces, strode past us into the tiny bungalow. Nailor followed and so, unbeknownst to Nailor, did Vincent Gambuzzo and I. For a brief moment everyone was silent. That's when we heard the thumping in the bedroom closet. That's when Vincent lost his head and pushed right past a young kid with the Colt M-16 fully automatic rifle, and pulled open the door with a force that ripped the fragile lock right out of its frame, oblivious to the police commands to "stand back!"

Vincent knelt down and pulled a bruised and bleeding Marla out into his arms. She smiled up at him softly and then began to cry. Vincent Gambuzzo took her up onto his lap and sat on the floor cradling her, his big puppy-dog eyes filling up with tears, even while he tried to smile his reassurances. Marla looked at him as if she'd never really seen him before, and stretched out her hand to wipe away the lone tear that escaped down his cheek.

"It's going to be all right, baby," she said. "The Bomber's back in business."

Thirty-two

The thing I like about the South is this: It's not really any different from Philly, except it's cleaner. Back when I was a kid, we lived in a brick-and-siding row house. The front yard was concrete and the backyard was a postage stamp of green grass, flowers, and a huge old walnut tree.

In the summertime, the old people, my parents and their parents, would drag out green metal chairs and position them under the tree. On Saturday nights Ma would set up a card table with a worn white tablecloth on it, and the next thing you knew, it was a party. She'd stick candles in old Chianti bottles and the party would break up as the last nubs burned down and out. I remember lying up in bed, hearing the grown-ups talking and laughing outside under the walnut tree, and feeling safe and loved. I just knew the whole world was a happy place.

My trailer has a tree out back, a scrawny old pin oak, with branches that reach out into the little square of burnt grass they call the common area. I put my own chairs out there. In the summer, me, Raydean, and Pat will sit out for hours on an off night, listening to the whine of bug zappers, and sniffing the scent of citronella oil that wafts out of the tiki torches I stuck into the hardened ground.

The Saturday after Gordon died, three days after it all came to a head, my friends began to gather in the backyard. It was a way to bring closure to the horrible events that had taken place, a way for us to begin healing. The table was bigger than Pa's, but his Chianti bottle had its customary place of honor in the center. Everybody cooked, even Francis, who tried and failed to re-create Ma's cannoli. Pat brought a seven-layer salad and fish for the grill. Raydean pulled a few of her famous consolation casseroles out of the freezer and heated them up just before we served.

Marla and Vincent came. Marla was still limping, walking like she hurt and nursing her broken arm. Vincent practically carried her out back and put her in a soft chair that he'd bought especially for her for the evening. He went back to his car and returned with big containers of pasta salad and his famous lasagna.

Packy Cozzone even showed up, accompanied by Guido and Hamm, his sidekicks. Packy, good New York family boy that he was, didn't want to come empty-handed. He had hoagies flown in from New York, thick with Capocola ham and Provolone cheese, bursting with fresh tomatoes and shredded lettuce. Guido and Hamm tugged a keg of beer out under the tree and packed it in ice. Clearly they expected to stay for a while.

Ernie Schwartz arrived a little after eight, walking up the driveway in a Hawaiian shirt with his ukulele tucked under his arm. His wife trotted along quietly by his side, sniffing disapproval, and carrying a box of Godiva chocolates.

"So pleased to meet you at last," she said, sticking the candy in my hands so we wouldn't have any physical contact. "I've heard so much about you."

"I'll bet," I said, and turned to watch a familiar car nose its way slowly down the street, a light blue Lincoln Town Car.

"Francis," I yelled back over my shoulder, "tell me you didn't!"

He walked up, looking all innocent, a beer in his hand and a smile on his face. "What can I say?" he said. "I messed up the cannoli. You can't have a party without cannoli."

Pa and Ma rushed out of the car, the trunk sprang open, and I just knew what was inside. Ma had brought cannoli all right, and every other commodity not found south of the Mason-Dixon line.

"Sierra!" she screamed, making a beeline straight for me. "You look hungry! My poor baby!"

Francis smirked and danced around her, heading down the driveway, prepared to tote groceries for hours until the bottomless pit of a trunk was finally emptied.

What none of us counted on, and certainly no one expected, was the reaction Packy Cozzone had to meeting Pa.

He and his men raced down the driveway, terrified looks on their faces. They stopped by the trunk of Pa's car and stared. When Pa turned around and smiled, Packy dropped to his knees, seized Pa's hand, and kissed his wedding ring. Guido and Hamm followed suit before Pa could react.

"What the hell kind of—" Pa started to ask, but Francis cut in.

"Pa, these are friends of the family, Packy Cozzone out of New York, and his colleagues Hamm and Guido."

Pa stared hard at them for a moment and then said, "Pleased to meet youse guys, but no more kissing, all right? We're not in the old country."

Packy backed away, his arms now loaded with brown paper sacks. "Gesture of respect, Mr. Lavotini, that's all."

"Oh, Pa," Ma shrieked, "they was raised right. That is so beautiful."

The music got louder, flooding the street and capturing the attention of my parents, who stopped under the streetlight, frozen with memories and smiling.

"Come here, you," Pa said, grinning at Ma. "When's the last time you heard this one, eh?"

Ma smiled, like the whole world had suddenly shifted, dumping her back into another time and place. "Oh, Pa," she cried. "Remember? It was the night before Sierra was born and I couldn't sleep. You took me out into the kitchen and . . ."

Ma stopped talking and began to cry. Pa pulled her to him and slowly they began to dance. Pa was humming to her and smiling as they whirled around the empty street.

Nailor picked this moment to arrive, cutting the lights on his brand-new black Crown Victoria, and coasting to a stop behind Ma and Pa's car. He sat there for a second, watching my parents dance, and then quietly slipped from his car without them even noticing his arrival. He walked up and stood behind me, his arm resting across my shoulders, a smile on his face, watching. Then slowly he pulled me around to face him, moving me gently into his arms as we began to sway with the music. I closed my eyes and listened very carefully as Nailor started to hum. In the distance Packy said something and Raydean cackled. Fluffy yipped and Francis spoke to her. I settled in and nestled my head against Nailor's shoulder.

"You know," he said softly, "this could be going somewhere."

"You think so, do you?" I murmured.

"Yeah," he answered, whirling me around in an imitation of Pa's fancy turns.

I pushed back and looked him straight in the eye. "Well, then, you'd better hang on tight, 'cause it's going to be a wild ride."

Nailor's laugh echoed down the length of the street as his arms tightened around me.

"I wouldn't want it any other way," he said.

We stayed like that for what seemed like hours, but must have only been minutes. He smelled so good and I felt so safe in his arms. When Francis touched my shoulder, his face tight with some unnamed tension, I jumped, startled and reluctant to leave Nailor's arms.

"Francis, can't you see I'm busy here?"

Francis was holding the cordless phone and he wasn't smiling.

"Call for you," he said, his eyebrows going up like I should catch on to something.

"So tell 'em I'm busy," I said, and turned back to nestle my head on John's chest.

"Sierra! No can do. Take the call." He spoke slowly, each word a bullet. What was with him?

"All right, all right! Damn, Francis, lighten up! You're on freakin' vacation."

I snatched the phone from his hand. "Hello?"

"Miss Lavotini," a deep rasping voice said. "This here is your uncle Moose."

If it were possible to be temporarily dead, I was. My heart stopped, my blood ceased to flow, and I was frozen.

"Hey," I said weakly, "how you doin'?"

Big Moose chuckled softly. "We should talk," he whispered.

"Sure," I said. "Whatever you say. When?"

Nailor and Francis were watching me. Francis looked like a 911 call, sheer emergency, total concern.

"Soon," he murmured. "I'll be in touch. In the meantime, I'll be keeping an eye on you."

The line went dead and I looked up at Francis.

"Who was that, babe?" Nailor was smelling trouble.

I smiled up at him just like I used to smile at Sister Mary Ignatious right before I told her a big, fat lie.

"Oh, nothing. Just my uncle wishing me well. You know how family is."

Nailor smiled, but it was a cop smile, a look-out-'cause-I'm-getting-to-the-bottom-of-this-one smile.

"No, babe," he said, pulling me back into his arms and starting to dance. "I don't know how families are. Why don't you tell me?

I figure I've got all night to hear more about your family. Why don't we start with that famous uncle of yours?"

The music switched to Dean Martin crooning some old tune about love. Nailor's grip on me tightened as I sighed and settled into his arms. It was going to be a very long night.